Sheffrou Betrayed

The Color of Treason

Cami Michaels

The Sheffrou Trilogy

I Am Sheffrou

Sheffrou Betrayed

The Sheffrou's Gambit

Contents

Author's Note	VII
Chapter 1	1
Chapter 2	16
Chapter 3	25
Chapter 4	33
Chapter 5	47
Chapter 6	54
Chapter 7	64
Chapter 8	72
Chapter 9	82
Chapter 10	97
Chapter 11	109
Chapter 12	117
Chapter 13	123
Chapter 14	128
Chapter 15	138

Chapter 16   144

Chapter 17   157

Chapter 18   165

Chapter 19   175

Chapter 20   181

Chapter 21   183

Chapter 22   190

Chapter 23   197

Chapter 24   207

Chapter 25   216

Chapter 26   222

Chapter 27   230

Chapter 28   242

Chapter 29   245

Chapter 30   254

Chapter 31   272

Chapter 32   276

Chapter 33   284

Glossary   289

Acknowledgements   292

Meet the Author   293

Author's Note

Welcome to the sci-fi fantasy world of The Sheffrou Trilogy. To enjoy this novel to the fullest, please refer to the glossary in the back.

Thank you,

Cami Michaels

Chapter 1

Tamara contemplated a future spent with Maashi, her alien friend and lover, as her hopes of returning home to Earth had almost vanished until, a few weeks ago....

She paced the length of her small receiving room and pondered the recent events. Over six months had passed since she fell into a wormhole and landed on this desolate planet called Chitina. Aliens called Chamranlinas, or Chamis as she liked to call them, rescued her, and brought her to their underground realm of caves and tunnels embellished by holograms to create a new reality indistinguishable from the real one.

She played with the gold bracelet on her left wrist, a gift from Maashi, a symbol of his everlasting affection, and stared at her reflection on the granite wall of her room. Slim and fit, she appeared younger than her forty-four years. Wearing her khaki shirt and pants, she pulled both ends of her turquoise sash with its cobalt blue wave, showing her status as a young Sheffrou, and secured its knot. In an alien world so thoroughly linked with colors, only the sash confirmed someone's occupation or rank.

Tamara shook her head in disbelief as she thought about Maashi and their first official 'meeting'. She had been conflicted about the 'meeting' because she thought it was some type of alien intercourse but was pleasantly surprised when she found out it consisted of exploring each other's body and a joining of minds only. The powerful Maashi proceeded with respect and kindness and seduced her with his unique charm. Tamara became infatuated with the Sheffrou. She shook her head in disbelief. She had never imagined becoming physically and emotionally involved with an alien such as him, a most unlikely partner.

A chime rang.

The two-paneled door slid open, revealing Chopa, Maashi's close companion, or Chowli, right on time as usual. The tall and wiry Chopa, over seven-foot and a half, wore Sheffrou Maashi's standard colors: a chocolate-brown shirt with a salmon tear-drop pattern and gray pants.

With thumbs hooked in his sash, milk chocolate with a thin pink wave, indicating a character defined by precision and accuracy accompanied a gentle disposition, he executed a slight bow and staring at her with his warm oval eyes, said in perfect English, "Chimitanga, good day to you. Are you ready to see the Sheffrou?"

"Yes. Is Maashi in a good mood today?"

"Sheffrou Maashi is calmer," said Chopa in a low voice, "however, he has not ingested food for two days."

Tamara pursed her lips. Maashi's depression wasn't improving.

Twenty-five days ago, on the night of the Great Eclipse Celebration, a time of joyful reunion to celebrate the orange sun's eclipse by its two moons, Ara and Kori, and the beginning of the season of renewal, the Krakoran had attacked the Chamis. They suffered a horrendous loss of life. The enemy targeted four Sheffrous, all close friends of Maashi, two were kidnapped, one seriously injured, and one killed. The news had overwhelmed Maashi, and he had sat for hours in a daze without saying a word. Losing Sheffrou Shoban, his mentor for over fifty sequences, had been especially difficult to bear.

Day after day, Maashi silently mourned his friends. He escaped in his private encounter room where he could hide and express his grief away from the ever-present monitors. Since the attacks, the population was on edge and reacted swiftly to any sign of disturbance. Any public expression of distress by a high-ranking Sheffrou such as him elicited an intense response from his entourage; his Chowlis Rahma and Chopa, the guards, and even other Chamis in the vicinity would converge at his side to protect him and offer support. In the Chami world, Sheffrous were precious, and everything was done to ensure their comfort and wellbeing.

Because of this situation, Maashi stayed in his quarters like a recluse and didn't associate with anyone except his Chowlis and Tamara. He didn't engage in swimming, his favorite activity, and often refused to eat, which exasperated everyone.

Tamara glanced at Chopa and saw his wide brow darken, a sign of grave concern. He harbored a strong affection for Maashi, and she knew he was worried.

"Chopa, don't you think it's odd that all these Sheffrous were attacked the same night at the same time? I can't imagine something like this happening."

"It was a sorrowful night."

Tamara frowned, hands on her hips. "Perhaps someone betrayed them? I can see that. A high-ranking Chami who loathes the fact that only Sheffrous can mate develops an intense hatred against them. In a fit of rage, he gives crucial information to the enemy." Pacing the room, she added, "After all, Maashi confirmed the Purples, the Blacks, and the Reds were furious at the last Council gathering when the Elders refused to hear their requests to change the mating law." She looked up at Chopa. "That law has been in effect for over fifty sequences. Hasn't it?"

Chopa snapped his head sideways. "Tamara," he said in a sharp tone, "although the Multis and the Pure Colors often clash over the mating decisions by the Elders, the notion that someone could act in a disloyal manner against the Sheffrous, or their entourage cannot be entertained. As you know, Sheffrous fulfill a crucial role in our society." His eyes narrowed. "And the word you are using, 'betrayal' does not exist in the Chamranlina language because that type of behavior does not occur." He headed for the door and said, "Let's not keep Sheffrou Maashi waiting."

Miffed by his response, Tamara huffed in frustration. She understood his reluctance to accept such a foreign concept, but the facts pointed in that direction. She trusted her instincts. They were usually right.

She followed Chopa down the hallway wide enough for two Chamis to walk shoulder to shoulder. The ceiling was twelve feet high, and the mocha brown granite walls veined with gold lit by oval sconces, glowed with a soft, soothing light. A small engraving like a coat of arms located beside each double-paneled door down the hall identified the Pure Color in charge. Tamara's quarters were near Maashi's in the Central Compound, the largest among the fourteen compounds of the colony. Maashi, First Lord and proud member of the elite third gender, the Sheffrous, governed the Central Compound. His people loved and cherished him and his unique skills and exclusive capacity to father female offspring.

Tamara couldn't stop replaying the details of the attacks on the night of the Great Eclipse Celebration in her mind. The three attacks happened right as the Celebration was winding down and the departing guests were at their most vulnerable, intoxicated by the intense and pervasive holoma, the mind-altering fragrance radiated by the Sheffrous. Drunk with pleasure from close contacts with various Pure Colors, Sawishas and Sheffrous, and Multicolors, the guests left the Rashandomora cave in high spirits unaware they were headed straight into an ambush.

The enemy struck in narrow tunnels, in groups which included at least one Sheffrou but few guards. The Chamis were aghast when they discovered the carnage: one Sheffrou and eight guards killed, another Sheffrou severely injured, three guards and two Sheffrous kidnapped.

She shuddered at the thought of all those lives lost or altered forever. She had witnessed many a time the grief and distress inflicted upon the ones left behind. As an Emergency Room physician, she knew how death could destroy families and loved ones.

Chopa stopped and nodded to the guard standing in front of the ten-foot large metal door. The guard turned, pressed on his wristband, and the door chime rang. The two panels slid apart, and they entered Maashi's receiving room.

Tamara's heart leaped with joy as soon as she saw him. Sitting on a couch, dressed in a plain outfit, khaki shirt, and pants with a short cobalt blue sash, Maashi still looked stunning. She loved his golden skin, wavy chestnut hair, broad shoulders, and wide chest. His warm amber eyes held a dignified sadness and though burdened with grief, showed pride and grace. As they entered, he raised his hand and with one swift wrist signal made the multi-colored virtual screen hanging in mid-air in front of him disappear. He nodded to Chopa who greeted him with a hug and kissed his left shoulder. Chopa then sat on a couch opposite Maashi.

The two wide couches with reclinable backs sized to accommodate eight-foot-tall individuals overflowed with large, royal blue cushions with gold trim. Apart from the couches, the sparsely furnished room contained only three small, c-shaped black granite tables. The slate gray encounter room, an egg-shaped room within a room, was set at the far end, and contrasted with the bright granite walls, which were the color of warm sunsets.

Maashi called in a low voice, "Come, Tamara."

"How are you Maashi?" she asked in a concerned tone. She strolled over and sat beside him. Her heart thumped hard in her chest. Maashi wouldn't easily accept her betrayal theory. She needed to wait for the right moment to tell him, but she couldn't wait too long. He was Sheffrou therefore, his life was also at stake.

"I am as well as I can be under the circumstances." Maashi said, looking straight ahead. "And you? I sense you're disturbed. Is it because we found that spaceship with the two humanoids on board?"

Two weeks ago, the aliens intercepted a distress call from a ship in a decaying orbit around a planet in a nearby solar system. They retrieved the ship, which contained two human males. Tamara had accepted the fact she might never see her children again and she refused to get her hopes up and think these humanoids were from Earth. The probability of finding humans so far from her world was infinitesimal.

"Yes, that and something else." Her mouth went dry.

Before Tamara could react, Maashi extended his long arms and picked her up.

"Maashi, please put me down. I don't want you to kiss me."

Ignoring her protest, Maashi enveloped her with his arms. "I won't kiss you, Tamara. I just want to hold you." He gently slipped his fingers into her silky hair and caressed her scalp. "I've noticed that talking about your feelings helps to release tension and makes you feel better."

Tears welled up in her eyes. The stress of the last few weeks and the fear his life could be in danger troubled her. She couldn't utter a word.

Maashi bent down and with his long, slender middle finger tilted her chin upward. "I can hold you close, but I can't kiss you, Tamara. My kisses would transfer the sadness and grief I feel."

"I'm worried... about so many things."

"Why are you so worried? It would seem finding Humans is a most fortunate event."

Tamara turned away from his searching gaze. "I've been pondering different scenarios." She cleared her throat. "At first, I was confident we would locate the wormhole which brought me here. Then, I lost hope and accepted the idea that I could live here, happy and content with you, but it seems neither will happen."

Maashi said, his voice soft, "All isn't lost, Tamara."

She shook her head. "Your people found two humanoids. Are they actual humans like me or some other type of alien? Are they from Earth? My head throbs just trying to understand what this implies. I must see them. I have so many questions. My whole life may change because of them." Her voice faltered.

"I don't know if I'll ever see my children again. If these humans came through a wormhole like me, I might return to my family, but I fear they are from the future. In the twenty-first century, humans travel only to the space station and back. If they are from the future, my family is already dead." She couldn't say another word. Her eyes brimmed with tears. She turned her head away.

Maashi hugged her. He held her gaze with gentleness. "Tamara, we will greet them together. This is a complex situation and requires careful consideration. I will accompany you and nothing will be decided without your consent. You will always be welcome here." He paused, waited till she settled. "Come, I want to show you something."

Maashi rose. A few inches shorter than Chopa with a leaner frame and more elegant features, he clicked something to his Chowli who left. He exited in the hallway, and she followed. The guard posted at the door stayed one step behind.

"Where are we going?" said Tamara. She swiped a lone tear rolling down her face.

"Something on the surface will happen shortly. If leave now, we will be there just in time."

Tamara raised her head with questioning eyes, but he added nothing.

They soon reached an underground tunnel. About six feet wide, lit by sconces high on the walls that turned on and off automatically after they went through, the tunnel was much darker than the hallways and not recommended for travel without adequate protection because the enemy was often spotted here. Accompanied by the guard, after a quick trip of only ten minutes, they arrived at their destination, a large empty room with several wide doors.

A Silver Guard in charge of internal security opened one door, scanned the inside with a hand-held device, and stepped aside to let the Sheffrou and Tamara in the elevator. Maashi clicked orders to the other guard who had accompanied them in the tunnels. He nodded and quickly left.

"Maashi, where are you taking me? Why all the secrecy?"

"Patience, little one. You'll soon find out."

The elevator, powered by anti-gravity, swiftly brought them to the surface. They stepped out into the thin, cool morning air. Tamara shivered in the light breeze. Little puffs of dry soil disturbed by their steps floated about, then dispersed behind them. A small moon shone high in the indigo sky amidst the stars and spread its pale glow on the barren landscape. The other moon, the bigger one, was barely visible above the horizon.

Tamara took in the view. She shuddered at the memory of her first few days in Chitina. This surface was the same as the one where she had arrived months ago. The land was bare, with no signs of life, a palette of browns and rusts with a few hills and boulders the size of big vehicles. The ground, covered with fine dust, smelled like burned toast. Without water or shelter, after days under an unforgiving sun, she had lost all hope and was close to death when the Chamranlinas found her.

A loud snort a few feet behind startled her. A musky odor spread through the air. Tamara turned her head and wrinkled her nose at the potent smell. The guard from Maashi's quarters stood holding the bridle of a tall creature that towered two feet above him.

Tamara had seen those creatures before, but only from a distance. The long-legged shoshan appeared to be as tall as a giraffe with a graceful neck. It snorted and pranced around when it saw Maashi. He clicked, extended his arm, and caressed its cheek. The creature settled under his calming touch.

"Let her smell you, Tamara, so she will know you," said Maashi.

Tamara brought her hand close to the shoshan's nostrils, and it delicately sniffed her hand and her arm. With a long, thin head and a soft muzzle, it kept its eyes locked on her but didn't make any aggressive move.

"Can I touch her?"

"Yes, she is gentle."

Tamara stood on her toes and touched the side of the creature's head. The hair felt coarse and dry. "She's got a fine head like a horse," she grinned. "But long straight legs like a giraffe." Her color, blonde mane and golden fur, reminded her of a palomino horse.

"She is a beauty among her kind," Maashi said, his voice soft. He stepped close to the shoshan's flank and in one swift bound, sprang atop the animal's wide back with the agility of a feline.

Tamara shook her head in disbelief as she watched him sitting bareback on the beast. Maashi removed his shirt to allow his skin to soak up the energy of the early morning light and set it on his right thigh. Tamara gasped as the guard grabbed her, lifted her high, and handed her to the Sheffrou. She sat on the shoshan's wide back in front of Maashi. He immediately put his arm around her waist to steady her.

She clung to his arm. "Oh. This is much higher than on horseback."

"Stay calm, little one," said Maashi in the musical voice Tamara loved. "I'm holding you securely."

She relaxed her shoulders and reclined against his bare chest.

Maashi clicked, and the shoshan advanced in long, easy strides.

"No racing, right?" Tamara said. The shoshan was only walking, but it already felt like it was gathering speed.

Maashi chuckled. "No Tamara, just a stroll. This female is quite old and can't run even if I try to coax her."

She looked back and saw the guard was following a short distance away to avoid the cloud of dust billowing behind the beast. Once she got used to the shoshan's swaying pace, she relaxed, forgot the pungent smell, and concentrated on admiring the view. The area was hilly with fewer boulders as they progressed, a desert landscape like she had often seen on documentaries on Earth. All the way to the left lay the tall peaks of the Chizoo Mountains. A few were covered with white caps.

"Is that snow on the mountains?"

"Yes. In the coldest months, it snows for weeks at a time."

"Where does the water go when it melts? There's no water on the surface."

"The water will flow above ground for a few hours every sequence, then it evaporates quickly under the blazing sun. Closer to the mountains, it gushes down deep gorges to produce fast-flowing underground rivers, lakes, and streams. We harvest this water for irrigation for the plants and trees we grow under the four domes spread out on the surface of the colony."

They arrived at the top of a hill and stopped. From that viewpoint, they could marvel at the first rays of the orange sun on the horizon. The sky, dark blue moments before, turned to a light purple while the remaining gray clouds thinned, then dissipated altogether. The light quickly spread over the valley below, chased away the shadows, and bathed the barren landscape in a remarkable rust color.

A sudden popping sound on the ground close to them made Tamara jump. "What was that?"

"Look." Maashi pointed downward to an area on the right where the first orange light hit the ground.

An eggplant-colored stem had sprung out of the reddish soil. Tamara watched wide-eyed as the foot-tall stems popped all around them, and within seconds, the movement spread all over and covered the valley below. One by one, each plant opened a single bud and revealed delicate lavender petals with a lemon-yellow center, just in time to catch the first warm rays of the rising sun. The pale carpet covered the ground as far as one could see where there was only dry soil moments before.

"Wow," she said. "This is incredible. I never thought there would be anything growing here."

"Nature can surprise us. We must always hope for a better future."

"Are they from Chamtali, your home world?"

"No. They are indigenous to this planet. We call them tell-isha."

"They're lovely." She turned and dropped a kiss on Maashi's smooth bare chest. His body glowed a warm golden color under the orange sun's rays, which provided life-giving energy for him. His amber eyes grew bigger. For the first time in a long while, Tamara saw a timid smile. His holoma, his fragrant, alluring body odor, hung around them like a veil, a sign he was pleased.

Tamara took a long breath and said, "Maashi, I'm worried all the crazy things that occurred on the night of the Celebration might happen again."

"You mean the attacks?"

"Yes."

Maashi raised his head and stared at the horizon.

"Don't you think what happened that night was odd? I've thought about this over and over and these attacks were not a coincidence."

Maashi's brow darkened. "Explain what you're saying."

"All the attacks happened at the same time. They all involved groups which included a Sheffrou. The enemy could've targeted other groups like the Sawishas or the Fanellas. Even the young Sheffrous, who didn't possess the same security coverage as the older ones, weren't attacked."

"The enemy usually targets the more mature Sheffrous because they serve their purposes."

"What purposes?"

"The amoeban-like Krakoran live in a parallel dimension and have followed us even after we left Chamtali, our home world. We've been hunted without mercy for centuries by these horrible creatures. They target Sheffrous because we can share our sensations with others, especially pleasure while they cannot experience this sensation on their own."

"Can't you fight back? You must have weapons against those creatures?"

"We have developed ways to track their ships and retrieve the ones kidnapped, but the attacks are unpredictable, and we have few effective weapons against them."

Tamara shook her head. "You told me before the Chami population is declining. If these attacks persist, your population will soon reach critical numbers."

Maashi lowered his head, spread his hands on his knees, and stared at his fingers.

"I think these attacks were planned."

"Of course, Tamara. The Krakoran planned the attacks."

"What I'm trying to say is: this was an inside job."

"What do you mean?"

"Someone worked with the enemy to get rid of Sheffrous," Tamara said in a firm voice. "You have a traitor among you."

Maashi's face and neck paled. "That's not possible. We are Chamranlinas. We are not disloyal to each other. Each individual has a role to play in the colony. An act such as this would bring unforgivable shame and dishonor to the perpetrator. A Chamranlina who dared to attempt such a deed would be banned forever from the colony."

"Someone informed the enemy about the locations of those Sheffrous."

Maashi froze. His face paled. Tamara saw doubt creeping in his mind.

She glared at him. "It happened," she insisted. "Don't you see? Denying it is precisely the type of thinking that lets the traitor get away with it."

"I cannot believe..."

"Maashi, any other explanation wouldn't make as much sense. I'm convinced it's the most probable scenario."

Maashi signaled the guard and as soon as he was close, handed her back down to him, and jumped off his mount. The shoshan lowered its head, snatched a mouthful of flowers, and munched happily.

Maashi paced, stomped the ground, producing clouds of dust, and hissed his displeasure. After a few minutes, he scrutinized the horizon and said, "It's not possible. I could never believe it." He hissed again. "And yet..."

Strengthened with newfound determination, Tamara seized the moment. "Which Chamis would gain the most from eliminating Sheffrous?"

Maashi's eyes were now black slits, his chest and face pale as alabaster.

"Think about it. It's important."

"The Sawishas." He crossed his arms on his chest as his to protect himself. "The green and purple Sawishas, also the Reds who have been clamoring for changes in the mating laws for many sequences. The Elders would allow them to mate if there were no Sheffrous." He shook his head to one side. "But to think they would betray their own people is preposterous." He produced a loud and prolonged hiss.

The guard moved closer and clicked to the Sheffrou. Maashi didn't respond.

"What about the Outcasts? You said yourself those Chamis were enemies of your society, and they were banished from the compounds."

"They rebelled before but swore to the Council of Elders they would never attempt that again."

Tamara followed right behind him; hands fisted, rigid, relentless. "Maashi, you'd better start believing someone betrayed you before it's too late. There are only a few Sheffrous left. At this rate, your people won't survive."

Maashi gazed at her without seeing her. With an icy voice, he said, "We should leave now. The sun is getting higher, and your skin will burn." He hopped back on the shoshan. The guard picked Tamara up and put her on the shoshan. They went back in silence to the elevator as the orange sun grew bigger and glared over the landscape.

Chapter 2

Dejected, Maashi sat in his quarters and stared at the walls. His Chowlis had embellished them with silky ribbons in Maashi's favorite colors, light shades of cerulean blue and chartreuse green, to lift his spirits. The lighting originating from the base of the walls created a soft soothing mood, but under his calm demeanor, his anger simmered. He held in his left hand the gold chain his close friend Tomisho had given him. He rolled it between his long fingers for a moment then put it in a concealed pocket inside his shirt.

Tomisho was one of two Sheffrous kidnapped on the night of the Great Eclipse. The Black Guards picked up his trail and with their swift interstellar ships, intercepted the enemy and rescued him. However, there wasn't any current report on his condition or the location of the ship transporting him back on Chitina. Overwrought with anguish, Maashi recalled his tall friend's confident persona and booming laugh. Would Tomisho be the same after suffering this ordeal? Would his spirit, his charissa or joie de vivre, still be amazing, or will it be crushed by the enemy's torture?

The other Sheffrou kidnapped was his pupil, Ashani, a promising young Sheffrou. The Black Guards had tried in vain to find a trace of his whereabouts. Who knows what horrible torment the Krakoran had planned for him? These awful creatures could decide to keep him for their own pleasure or sell him to the Rodenegad as a sex slave. Maashi closed his eyes. His chest tightened with dread. Over a sequence ago, he had been captured by the Krakoran. He survived five months before his rescue. The trauma had been so great that to this day, he couldn't recall much of the time spent in captivity. His mind had buried all memories of the ordeal.

He reviewed once again on his virtual screen the details of the attacks on that fateful night. He juggled and weighed the facts over and over. After a meticulous analysis, he had to agree with Tamara's suspicions. There were strong indications insiders had communicated with the enemy. They gave the co-ordinates of the Sheffrous' positions as they traveled back to their compounds after an intense night of celebrating. One or more Chamranlinas had cooperated with the enemy.

Maashi's long, slender frame heaved with pain and sadness. The mere thought of betrayal by his own people was inconceivable. There were so few Sheffrous and with each sequence their numbers declined. Every attack by the Krakoran cost more lives. Who among the Chamranlinas could plan and execute such a despicable act?

Minutes later, the chime rang and Chopa joined him. He had accompanied Tamara back to her quarters. He kissed Maashi's shoulder and sat beside him.

"Are you all right, Shonava, my lord? Your chest is as pale as choun. Wasn't the sunrise pleasant this morning? Did something upset you?" Hearing no response, he asked again. "Would you like a glass of water, sir?"

Maashi asked in a low voice, "Besides my kidnapping by the Krakoran over one sequence ago, when was the last successful attack by the enemy?"

Chopa enjoyed staying up to date on a multitude of subjects and beamed with pride when the Sheffrou relied on him as a source of information. He carefully answered the question. "There have been several attacks in the last twenty sequences, including yours last sequence, but the deadliest was sixty and a half sequences ago. That's when Shonava Shanadou's party was ambushed by two Krakoran entities. That was the first time a guard survived and confirmed there were two Krakoran involved."

"Tell me more. I recall there was a scandal related to that attack. Being a young Sheffrou younger than you are now, and a Pure Color, my mentor shielded me from the details of the scandal."

"Yes, sir. Of course," said Chopa. "The attack was eerily similar to the recent one. The enemy struck during the night of the Great Eclipse as the festivities were winding down and the Sheffrous and Sawishas were returning to their compounds. That's when they ambushed Sheffrou Shanadou's group. The scandal was related to the fact that his first Chowli wasn't with the group when the attack occurred. He had lingered for a while longer at the celebration. When he rejoined his party, all the guards except one had been killed and Sheffrou Shanadou had suffered life-threatening injuries.

"That Chowli, a Ghouli Ghouli called Chari Varian, couldn't provide the investigators a satisfactory explanation of why he wasn't with his group when the attack occurred. His excuse for not being in the tunnels alongside his Sheffrou was deemed insufficient and was refused by the Council of Elders. He claimed he meant to leave with them, but as he was exiting, he ran into a long-lost friend and engaged in a conversation with that individual. Many Sawishas suspected foul play."

"I see," said Maashi.

"No wrongdoing on his part was ever proven. After that incident, however, he was shunned by all."

"Where is he now?" Maashi asked. "Is this the one who is the leader of the Outcasts?"

"Yes, sir. After the investigation, Chari Varian was recruited by an extremist faction of Ghouli Ghouli. As you know, sir, Ghouli Ghoulis are the exception among Multicolors because they are fertile. Chari Varian became the leader of the extremists who demanded changes to the mating laws. They wanted to be allowed to mate when only the Pure Colors and the Sheffrous could. The Council of Elders refused. Negotiations broke down. Two sequences later, Chari Varian instigated and led the infamous Ghouli Ghouli Rebellion."

"Yes, I remember the Rebellion." Maashi lowered his head. "A deplorable time for our people."

"After months of unrest, intimidation and destruction of property, Chari Varian and his followers were caught, found guilty, and exiled to the Burned Zone, an area subject to extreme weather in the equatorial region of the Southwest. Today, their group is still referred to as the Outcasts."

Maashi waived his hand to stop Chopa who often got carried away with lengthy explanations. "Yes, Chopa. I know about the Burned Zone and the Outcasts." Maashi nodded his head sideways. "I find it sad that the Elders couldn't negotiate a mating agreement with the Ghouli Ghouli. This represents a loss for Chamranlinas in terms of diversity of the gene pool. Ghouli Ghouli are more resistant to disease than the main population and I disagree with those who say their copper skin color is unappealing." Maashi spread his hands over his knees and stared at his long middle finger. "You said nothing about Sheffrou Shanadou. What happened to him? Did he survive?"

"It is rumored he is still alive, but mentally and physically compromised. I have been told he lives under close surveillance in a secret location."

Maashi raised his head and shook it. "Such a sad ending for a most promising Sheffrou. A life cut short by a ruthless enemy. Too many died that night and since. Did the investigators find why there were two Krakoran entities during the attack?"

"No, sir. The attack that occurred a few weeks ago is the only other attack where we are sure that more than one Krakoran was involved."

Maashi folded his arms against his chest and nodded.

"Another important detail to note is that Sheffrou Shanadou had mated with seven Fanellas two sequences in a row and produced fourteen offspring like you did, sir. Both you and Sheffrou Shanadou are the only Sheffrous since the beginning of record keeping who have accomplished this feat."

Maashi stretched back on his lounge chair and crossed his long legs. He grabbed a large rectangular cushion, held it tight against him, and traced its intricate gold embroidery with his middle finger. His mind escaped to the last time he mated and dwelled on lovely memories. He didn't hear the chime announcing his other Chowli, Rahma. In three rapid strides, the young and muscular Chowli bounded in the room and stood in front of him.

"Good morning to you, sir," he said and bent low to kiss Maashi's shoulder. "I bring some important news."

"Yes, Rahma." Maashi said, reconnecting with reality. "What is it?"

"I've been in contact with the Black Guards who are keeping track of the rescue ship bringing home Sheffrou Tomisho. The ship has been chased mercilessly by the Rodenegad." He stopped to hiss loudly, as was the custom when mentioning the ruthless slave traders. Normally, Rahma would also spit to show his disgust, but he refrained because it wasn't appropriate to do so in the Sheffrou's quarters. "There were some tense moments. The ship fled and hid in the Korkarian Nebula. We suspect they will hide there for some time, perhaps weeks."

The cushion Maashi held flew across the room as he leaped off the couch. "Weeks?" He hissed his displeasure and, with hands fisted, paced in front of Rahma. That meant he wouldn't see Tomisho for much longer than he had expected. His friend would have to wait for the necessary treatment after his capture by the Krakoran. Maashi knew the torture the Krakoran inflicted on Sheffrous broke the charissa of the strongest. He had suffered the same fate last sequence. To this day, he suffered the consequences: the inability to engage in deep connections with Sawishas, frequent debilitating nightmares, and failing to regain his normal weight because he developed an aversion to feeding.

Maashi glared at Rahma. "Can I at least contact him?"

"No, sir," said Rahma. "Communications are restricted to reduce the risk of detection by the Rodenegad."

Maashi closed his eyes and pursed his lips. He hated that he couldn't reach his friend and provide emotional support, if nothing else.

"Sir," Rahma said in a soothing voice, "I know you're not pleased, but I heard the Rodenegad are actively harassing all our transporters and scanning every ship for Sheffrous. It would be most unwise to establish any contact with Sheffrou Tomisho."

Maashi ceased his pacing and faced Rahma. "Don't you think I know that?"

"Yes, sir." Rahma shot a quick look at Chopa who blinked at him and discreetly waved his hand.

A chime rang. Insistent.

"Who can this be?" asked Rahma.

The wide door slid open. A Silver Guard wearing the official uniform of the internal security, silver shirt and sash with black pants entered. He bowed. "An urgent message for Sheffrou Maashi."

"I'll take care of it, sir," said Rahma.

"The message is for the Sheffrou's eyes only," said the guard.

Maashi asked the guard, "Who sent this?"

"The message was sent by the Elders, Shonava." The guard walked over to Maashi and handed him a small communication device. "I must wait for your answer. I'll be outside in the hall."

The only messages Maashi had received from the Elders were requests for mating. At the thought of mating, a surge of desire gushed through his flesh and his mouth filled with saliva. His quatay, the markings of a Pure Color on his upper chest, swelled and tingled. Caught by surprise and annoyed by his quick mating response, Maashi swallowed hard. He strolled to the door and inserted the device into a control panel beside the doorframe. The text lit up. He read the note then read it again. He emitted a low hissing sound.

"Sir," asked Rahma, "is everything all right?"

Maashi raised his head and turned to face Rahma. "I've been summoned by the Elders for mating. There are two Fanellas who haven't mated yet. They should be ready in two to four weeks."

Both Chowlis emitted excited clicks. Rahma's face glowed. He approached Maashi, hugged him, and kissed his left shoulder and neck. "It's a great honor, sir. We rejoice with you. You'll mate this sequence after all."

Chopa rose and kissed Maashi's shoulder. "Congratulations, sir." His voice was warm with affection.

Maashi stepped a few feet away and didn't comment. He shuddered, inhaled a long breath, and held it to control his consternation.

Fate could be so cruel. He was offered a chance to mate, his only chance at mating this sequence, at the same time as Tomisho's projected arrival. Maashi had planned to be with his friend to help him at the beginning of a hard recovery. Disgruntled, he clamped the device in his hands. He had to choose between his sacred duty to mate and his friend.

Closing his eyes, he straightened his shoulders. He knew the rules. Refusing the Elders' offer was unacceptable. There was only one likely choice. He entered his answer into the device and gave it to Rahma with a nod. Rahma stepped out into the hall and handed it to the Silver Guard.

"There is one more thing, sir," said Rahma who was back at Maashi's side. He pulled at his chocolate-colored sash and shot a quick look at Chopa.

Maashi glowered at him and said, "What?"

Rahma spoke in a slow even tone. "As you know, sir, I've kept in touch with security concerning the two Humans. They have landed safely, and the pods have been brought to a secure area close to the Chizoo Mountains. The Humans won't be allowed to come here because of the Fanella compounds close by."

Chopa rose. "The Chizoo Mountains," he said, "require at least one week of travel and there is a high likelihood of heavy snowfall this early in the season."

"You are the official representative, sir," said Rahma. "You are scheduled to accompany Tamara to the first official greeting with the Humans. They are expecting you. What will you do?"

"I promised Tamara I would go with her." Maashi's amber eyes darkened. "I could appoint another representative or postpone the greeting." He shook his head and clicked in annoyance. "She will not be pleased." He hated the fact he wouldn't be available to meet the humanoids with her. Tamara was concerned about facing them without him at her side. He had to tell her he couldn't go because his mating responsibilities wouldn't permit him to do so. Would she understand? He hissed under his breath. "I will go talk to her."

As he exited the room, his mind struggled to make sense of the disturbing news. Why did fate play with their lives this way? So many obstacles appeared to arise between him and the little human female. He had found such joy and pleasure with her at his side. Was there a hidden meaning behind the fact her path and his were going in different directions?

Chapter 3

T amara followed the pattern of white waves coursing along the beige and blue walls of her receiving room. The luxurious, wide couch and the plush feel of the floor under her feet brought no comfort. Since her first day on Chitina, the Chamis had been kind to her, treating her arrival as a good omen for their people. They called her Ishkibu Sheffrou, which literally meant a traveler, a Sheffrou who brought hope and promise. Now everything was changing.

Tamara shuddered. She tried to reason away her apprehension and fear about meeting the humans, but there remained a stubborn sense of unease. She was grateful Maashi had been chosen to be the Chamranlinas representative. He would attend the first official meeting. She toyed with the gold bracelet Maashi had given her weeks ago. The delicate filigree design shone like a jewel. Her unease relented at the memory of his commitment to always protect and cherish her.

She paced the length of her receiving room. How would she and those humans communicate? What language did they speak? How long had it been since they gained the capability of traveling through space? Was it measured in hundreds or even thousands of years? What sort of people were they? Did her species evolve and become more peaceful or more warrior-like? On Earth, history had proven multiple times that first contact had been disastrous for one side. The Huns led to the fall of the Roman Empire. Spaniards decimated the Incas. Europeans brought war and pestilence to the American Indians. Would these humans bring positive or disastrous changes to the Chamranlinas? Would the Chamranlinas prove to be a threat to them?

Tamara chewed her nails. She never got rid of the nasty habit. In the last few days, she had been feeling jittery and overwhelmed. She plopped back down on her couch, grabbed a small apple-green cushion with a gold design, and toyed with the corners. Bright lights twinkled before her eyes, a sure sign of an oncoming migraine.

The door chime went off and Pini, her assistant, strolled in. She shook her head in disapproval. The notion of privacy was foreign to these aliens. She needed to explain to him he couldn't just walk in her quarters at all hours.

Maashi was the one who had decided she needed an assistant. He told her Pini would teach her more about them: provide her with details about their customs and habits, remind her of their basic language rules, and answer her incessant questions.

Pini's face beamed, and he smiled when he saw her. He looked so young and handsome with his longish, wavy chestnut hair and turquoise eyes. Tamara couldn't believe it when Maashi explained Pini was a pink of thirty-four sequences, a mere teenager in his eyes but more like seventy in Earth years. He wore his signature cream shirt and loose chocolate-colored pants held at the waist by a thin unicolor pink sash to signal his status as a Pure Color member of the fertile elite.

"Good afternoon, Tamara," he said in his mellow voice. "How are you feeling?"

"I'm fine," she said. Her migraine was progressing, but she wasn't in the mood to explain this to Pini. Stress and anger issues often brought on migraines. The last few days were filled with both.

"Can I get you some food?"

"Not right now."

"A glass of water then?"

"No, thanks."

"Are you warm enough?" The Chamis tolerated extreme temperatures with no untoward effects, but they understood she couldn't.

Before he said anything else, Tamara shot him a stern look. "I don't need anything, and I don't want anything right now."

He sat down beside her. "Chopa told me you are worried about the meeting between the Chamranlinas and the Humans."

Tamara nodded. "You could say that."

He glanced at her sideways. "Chamranlinas are intelligent and not without resources. We have been in contact with other sentient species before. You should not worry so much."

"I just hope everything goes well." She wasn't in the mood for small talk. "I want to take a nap now. I'll see you later."

"Do you want me to stay while you nap?"

"No, thanks." She rose and turned to go towards her sleeping area.

Pini stood. "Perhaps I can come back after your nap?"

"Okay." She waited for him to leave, went to her bedroom, then she lay down on the couch she used as a bed. She closed her eyes. Perhaps a little sleep would decrease the heavy weight settling on her head. The chime rang, and the door opened.

In an irritated tone, she said, "What do you want, Pini?"

No one answered. Instead, she was swept off the couch and lifted high up. She knew right away who it was. His fragrant aroma was unmistakable.

"Maashi." Her lips stretched into a tight smile as she fought to ignore the pain tightening around her head like a vise.

He held her tenderly, like a baby and kissed her neck just below her ear. She exhaled a long-held breath.

"How are you, Shapinka?" His fingers caressed her scalp and lingered in her hair. He set a gentle hand over her forehead and her headache dissipated like it had never existed. He carried her to the receiving room, sat down on the reclining couch, and hugged her close for the longest time. His eyes changed to an intense amber color. "It's such a pleasure to hold you and touch your smooth hair." He tilted her chin up with one finger and pressed his cheek against hers.

"I feel much better. Thank you." The tightness wrapping her head had disappeared. Tamara sighed with relief. "How do you do that?"

"It's a Sheffrou trait. I can share pleasure, but I can also heal and remove pain."

"Wonderful qualities. No wonder so many Sheffrous are also physicians."

"We're all trained in the art of healing. Some of us possess remarkable skills."

Tamara examined his oval face and high cheekbones with a wide brow. She caressed his face. She loved the silky feel of his golden skin. Then she noticed his pale sunken eyes. "What's wrong? Are you upset about what I said about the attacks?"

He held her hand and pressed his lips on her palm. "I have something to tell you." Maashi hesitated. "I am deeply troubled by our earlier conversation, but I am concerned about something else." His jaw tightened. "I am not pleased."

"About what?"

"You wanted me to accompany you to the greeting of the Human males, but it will be impossible."

"Why? You know this is important to me. What changed?"

"The spaceship containing the two Humans has successfully established orbit around Chitina. The suspension pods have been transferred safely to the surface of the planet. They are in the northernmost Chizoo Mountains."

"And we'll have to travel there." Tamara recalled the last time she had traveled a long distance with Maashi. The ride had been anything but pleasant. Was he upset because of that?

"I guess I'll just have to go with it." She looked up, but his head was turned away. She touched his arm. "Maashi? What else is there?"

"We can't leave together."

"Why not?"

"You're my Chimitanga. You have an official title. It's forbidden for the two of us to travel together. I have made arrangements to ensure your safe travel."

Tamara sighed. She stared at her too short fingernails.

"You will leave in the morning. Three guards will accompany you. I have instructed them, and you'll be able to communicate with them in English. You must stay close to them and do everything they tell you to do."

"Will Pini come with me?"

"No." Maashi blurted out the answer. In a softer tone, he said, "He didn't get permission to go."

She frowned. "When will you leave?"

"You'll have to meet the Humans by yourself. I'll join you when I can."

"What do you mean?" Tamara untangled herself from his warm, fragrant embrace. "You promised you'd be there."

"It's not possible." His voice was soft, apologetic.

Tamara glared at him. "Well, that's just peachy."

Maashi blinked. "I've been summoned by the Elders for mating."

"Really?" Tamara huffed. "Now?"

"The two other Sheffrous did not complete the mating. There are two Fanellas left. I was chosen third this year, I must go."

Tamara growled and threw a cushion across the room. "This couldn't have happened at a worse time. I so wanted you to be with me." She blocked the thought of Maashi holding one of the beautiful females in his arms. She bounced to her feet and paced the room. "This is just great."

"The Fanellas are fertile for a short time only. I must remain here and be available to respond as soon as they call me."

Tamara understood that there was no way out of the impasse. "I guess I'll have to meet the humans alone then." She thought about the trip. "You know I hated riding that flying bus. The one we took before the celebration."

"You won't be flying in a ship. The high elevation is subject to unpredictable winds at the beginning of the season of renewal."

"Are we going to travel underground in the tunnels?"

Maashi's posture changed. He appeared tense. "During daytime, you will use small surface vehicles with the guards."

"What about at night? Where will we stay?"

"You will sleep on the surface."

"And the Krakoran?"

"They won't attack in the next few weeks because the volcanic fields become unstable. There is a greater risk of explosion."

Tamara raised her arms in alarm. "The area is too dangerous for the enemy but we're going to travel there and sleep on the surface."

"All necessary precautions will be taken." Maashi kept his head down and spread his fingers on his lap. "You will be provided with appropriate garments to keep you warm and safe. The weather is much cooler and changes without warning in that sector."

"Why can't you just bring the humans here?"

"Species from other worlds are not permitted in the south near the Fanella compounds."

"Then, that's it. Isn't it? I don't have a choice." Tamara slumped down beside Maashi.

"Maybe I should stay here and not go at all."

"Tamara," Maashi said in a calm even voice, "the guards will keep you safe. This is your chance to connect with your own species. You must go."

She closed her eyes, grunted, and shook her head from side to side. "When will you join me?"

"I don't know."

The thought of meeting them by herself made her sick with apprehension. She couldn't explain it. A premonition, perhaps?

She stood and stared at Maashi with a fierce look in her eyes. "I'm going to tell you something. Listen carefully because I'll say it only once and I won't change my mind." She frowned and spoke with authority. "I will not meet these humans or whatever they are until you're present. I'll wait for you. That's my last word." She clenched her fists. "Do you understand?"

Maashi tilted his head sideways. He observed her in silence for a moment then nodded. "I understand. I will join you soon." He pulled her into his arms. "I'll let you rest now. You'll be departing tomorrow, at first light." He ran his slender fingers through her auburn hair and caressed the nape of her neck. "Stay safe, little one," he whispered.

Tamara watched him leave. A sudden wave of intense sadness overcame her. Tears filled her eyes. Maashi was not hers alone. The Elders' summons to mate was a harsh reminder of the fact. She knew she had to share him with many others but didn't expect to do so until later, after Tomisho's arrival. The loneliness she felt was more than she had felt in weeks.

She strolled over to the water room and splashed her face with cool water. Back in her receiving room, she settled on her couch among the colorful cushions. Her thoughts wandered. She concentrated on the salty smell of the ocean and the cool breeze of her hometown, the golden hue of the sand under the rising sun, the sound of gentle waves rolling to shore one by one, the lone call of a single gull echoing on the empty early morning beach. Longing for her family hit her and she wiped the tears that slowly rolled down her cheeks. How was it that Maashi's world was beyond reach by her loved ones and yet, humans had somehow traveled here, wherever here was? An icy blast of dread made her shudder.

Chapter 4

In the middle of the night, when darkness hides everything and his whereabouts would be difficult to track, Maashi set out into the tunnels alone, to seek the leader of the Outcasts. He lied to his guards, told them he wanted to swim in his pool without being disturbed. He hated to deceive the ones dedicated to his protection, but he was determined to go. The lie weighed heavily on his conscience, but to have any chance of success in what he planned to do, he had to be alone. Maashi swept aside the risk of traveling without at least one guard. It was a well-known fact that the Krakoran never attacked twice in the same sequence, and they had already done significant damages this sequence.

After his brief discussion with Chopa earlier that morning, Maashi wanted to solve the mystery of the simultaneous attacks on the Sheffrous. The first place to look for answers was the Burned Zone. The Ghouli Ghouli leader, Chari Varian, might clarify certain details and provide him with leads in his quest to find the traitor, if he existed. That the leader of the Outcasts could refuse to see him had flickered in his mind and quickly been dismissed. Part of the elite in Chamranlina society, Maashi had lived in luxury all his life and had been treated like royalty. He was a Sheffrou 8 and first Lord of the Central Compound, the most strategic of all, located close to two Fanella compounds. He couldn't imagine that anyone would refuse to see him.

The attack sixty sequences ago on Sheffrou Shanadou's group had strong similarities with the recent attacks. *Did Chari Varian play any role sixty sequences ago? Did he conceal crucial evidence from the investigators?* A meeting with Chari could provide critical information.

Several hours of a brisk pace in the well-traveled tunnels brought him to the southern edge of the Central Compound. By morning, he changed course to reach the surface. Although the air above ground was suffocatingly hot because the flow of active lava fields in the South progressed daily and covered wide expanses of desert, Maashi tolerated the heat without untoward effects. He removed his shirt and held it in one hand. His body used light in a manner similar to photosynthesis and transformed it into energy. The orange sun's rays provided him with life-sustaining energy and made his golden skin glow.

Maashi grunted with the realization that the trek was more strenuous than he had anticipated. He should've followed Rahma's advice and fed more regularly these last few weeks. Poorly nourished since the attacks and out of shape, he paused and rested several times along the way. His tortured mind gave him no respite. Over and over, the questions came and taunted him. *Why so many attacks on the same night? Why had more guards been assigned to his party than for the others, thus saving him from the claws of the enemy?*

Maashi pressed on. Instinct showed him the way. He stopped a few times, closed his eyes, and his mind found the right direction. He walked all day. When night came, he came upon the entrance to new tunnels and slowed his pace.

Early the next morning, at the same time as the sun spread its rust-colored glow on the horizon on the desolate surface of Chitina, Maashi came upon larger and brighter tunnels. Widened by the Chamranlinas with rock blasters decades ago, they allowed to travel in underground vehicles. These transported either goods, passengers, or raw ore, the result of selective mining to trade with other aliens on neighboring worlds. One tunnel with centuries old carvings on the walls led to a cavern the size of a large receiving room.

The place looked abandoned. Rocks of all sizes covered the floor. No humidity in the air here. Water had long deserted this hollow and dried up area. The walls' rough edges seemed to threaten him, a warning to stay away. Maashi advanced carefully and bent down to proceed through an opening with a six-foot ceiling, which led into a larger cave. He took one step inside and right away, four Ghouli Ghouli, recognizable by their copper skin, raven hair and black hands surrounded him. None of them wore a sash. They were dirty and disheveled.

"Stop right there," said one of them.

A fifth individual joined the group and shot Maashi a hateful stare with his characteristic black eyes shrouded by black eyelids. Old, dusty clothes hung loose on him. "What are you doing here, scum?"

Cleanliness was of the utmost importance for Chamranlinas. Maashi disregarded the feelings of disgust the Ghouli Ghouli elicited. He ignored the insult and raised his head. "Bring me to your leader."

"What makes you think you can come here and give orders?"

"Look at him," said another. "He's wearing silk pants and shirt like he's going to a celebration. His khaki sash screams outsider." The entire group choked with mocking grunts.

"We hate your kind here," said another who spat a foul-smelling blob of saliva on the ground. "Go back where you came from."

Without showing emotion, Maashi insisted. "I need answers. I need to talk to your leader."

The fifth one growled. "I'll give you answers, dirt trawler." His fist flew and slammed Maashi's jaw. The blow sent Maashi reeling. He wiped a trickle of blood which oozed down the side of his mouth. He inhaled deeply and stood his ground.

"I want to see your leader."

The fifth one signaled the others, and two of them grabbed his arms.

"Didn't you hear what I said?" He hissed and punched Maashi in the stomach.

Maashi flinched but kept his jaw locked tight.

"There is no need for violence. I only want to talk to your leader." He swallowed saliva mixed with blood.

"You still don't get it?" the Ghouli Ghouli threw a combination of punches hitting his stomach, chest, and head.

Maashi closed his eyes. The cave swam around him. Pain seared his ribs. Hot and dizzy, he forced a step back and pulled his arms as hard as he could to free himself, but it was useless. They held him fast.

Why were they so aggressive?

The notion that his request to meet the leader of the Outcasts could be construed as an insult had never entered his mind. For the first time in his life, Maashi faced a brutal realization: he was Sheffrou, and therefore a living affront to the Ghouli

Ghouli. Being a Sheffrou meant he was revered and allowed to mate, while the Ghouli Ghouli's rights to mate had been permanently rescinded after the Rebellion by an official decision of the Elders fifty-eight sequences ago.

He heard grunts from further into the cave. A few more individuals had joined them. They clicked and stomped their feet to show their approval.

His assailant doubled his attack. One uppercut to his face and the sound of bone cracking resonated above the clicks of the onlookers. Maashi held on with desperation.

A sharp voice silenced them all. "Enough."

The attacker hissed. "He's an outsider. Let me play with him a little."

The voice cut through the stale air of the cave. "Enough, Zaren. Don't you see he's just skin and bones? What are you trying to do? Kill him?"

The group parted to give way to a tall, wiry, broad-shouldered Ghouli Ghouli. Dressed in a short-sleeved fitted black shirt and tight dark pants, this one wore a purple dominant sash veined with red and pink. With a twig of the fragrant kego plant between his teeth, he approached Maashi.

He tilted his head sideways, chewed on his twig, and examined Maashi. He stretched his arms out and ripped open Maashi's shirt. Touching his chest with a long black middle finger, he traced Maashi's quatay, confirming he was a high-ranking Pure Color, and whistled. He pulled the twig out of his mouth and deposited it in a breast pocket. "You're far from the compounds, Sheffrou. Why are you here?"

With his head ringing from the blows, Maashi blinked, and his words came out slowly. "I want to see your leader. I have questions."

The black-clad Ghouli Ghouli snorted. "You're either very brave or incredibly foolish."

The people behind the Ghouli Ghouli sneered A few stomped their feet. The Ghouli-Ghouli lifted Maashi's bloodied chin with his black hand and scrutinized his face. "I would say foolish." All the ones present hissed. He took a step back and folded his arms across his chest. "I like that." Turning his back to him, he said, "Follow me."

A short skinny Multicolor in the back said, "Sir, he could be a spy."

The Ghouli Ghouli stopped in his tracks and chuckled. "Look at him." He gave Maashi a good shove, and they saw how he wobbled from side to side. "He can't even stand straight. I think I can handle him." He stared at Maashi. "Come."

Maashi straightened his lean frame, concentrated on putting one foot in front of the other to keep up with his res- cuer. The blows to his chest and abdomen had caused damage and he couldn't breathe well. He sensed he had broken ribs and telltale cold tendrils spread inside his abdomen, signs of internal bleeding. He lumbered on behind the Ghouli Ghouli in silence. They walked across the cave, followed one narrow tunnel, then another, and finally reached an ample receiving room with polished black onyx walls.

"Do you want a drink, Sheffrou?" The Ghouli Ghouli asked without offering a seat to his guest.

Maashi's legs shook, but he refused to ask to sit. "No, thank you."

"Suit yourself." The Ghouli Ghouli pressed controls on a small table and a tray appeared with a collection of glass carafes, each containing a different liquid, from ruby red to cobalt blue. He chose a bright green fluid and added two leaves from the tinqua tree, an aromatic plant from the mother world Chamtali, now growing under protective greenhouse domes on Chitina. "Tinqua leaves add flavor."

Maashi ignored the taste of blood in his mouth. He said with a voice that sounded weaker than intended, "Are you the leader?"

"What if I am?"

"I want to ask," Maashi paused. A gray cloud settled over his mind. In a last-minute decision, he dropped all diplomacy and confronted the leader. "Why did you betray the Sheffrous?"

Chari stirred his drink with his ebony middle finger. With no visible reaction, he said, "What are you talking about?"

Maashi's legs shook with the exacting effort of standing. He gathered his courage, took a deep breath, and winced with the pain. In a low contained voice, he said, "On the night of the Great Eclipse Celebration, two Sheffrous were kidnapped, one killed and one severely injured. Someone gave the coordinates of the Sheffrous' whereabouts to the Krakoran." He stopped, struggling to sort his thoughts and push away the cloud progressively obscuring his mind. With labored breathing, he blurted, "Why would you do such a thing?"

Chari Varian sipped his drink. He didn't answer. He put his twig back in his mouth and shoved it from side to side. "What coordinates?"

"The Krakoran," Maashi slurred, "attacked Sheffrous... at three different areas, at exactly the same time. I believe someone helped them."

The other shot him a look as hot as molten rock.

"Come with me," Chari ordered, and sauntered to the back of the room.

Opening his eyes wide, Maashi followed, each step harder than the last.

They went through a storage room filled with purple bins of different sizes stacked up high, a wide tunnel, and at last came upon the edge of an enormous pit.

Maashi widened his stance to keep steady. He stared with horror at the bottomless hole.

"What do you see?"

"It's gigantic, empty," was all Maashi could mutter.

The other shook his head in agreement. "Nothingness. Void."

Maashi's brow darkened in puzzlement.

Chari stepped closer to Maashi. "This is the future, Sheffrou. Nothingness." He grabbed Maashi by his shirt and forced him to look deeper into the void. "Take a good look," he growled. "For Multis including the Ghouli Ghouli," he yelled in Maashi's face, "for Pure Colors and Sheffrous, our future looks like this. Empty. Nothing matters anymore. The Multis have no offspring, no future. The Pure Colors have no future either."

"No," Maashi shouted, but his voice sounded little more than a whisper. "There are offspring. The Fanellas are pregnant. We will survive."

"Tell me, Sheffrou," Chari blasted, "how many Fanellas actually deliver a live baby? How many offspring survive the first two sequences? Did the Elders tell you? Do you really know?"

Maashi tried to raise his arms in protest, but they felt as heavy as lead. "Some survive," Maashi insisted. "A few survive." His mouth kept on moving, but no sound came out.

The leader yelled with tremendous energy. "You're wrong, Sheffrou. You've been deceived, tricked. All but one of the youngest offspring are dead."

"No." Maashi shook his head. Dizziness made him sway right and left. A wave of darkness washed over him. "No, that's not possible."

"Why," Chari screamed with rage, "why would anyone bother to give coordinates to our enemy when the future doesn't exist?" He grabbed Maashi and shook him like a rag doll. "Why?"

Maashi finally understood what the other meant. He closed his eyes and collapsed in his arms.

Chari Varian sat on a low bench in his receiving room, his back against the black granite wall. He bit hard on the twig between his teeth as he surveyed the unconscious Sheffrou on his couch. He had examined him with care and concluded he had sustained a fractured cheekbone and several fractured ribs. His abdomen was rigid and swollen, a most definite sign of internal bleeding. The Sheffrou squirmed when Chari checked him but make no sound even though he must've felt excruciating pain. Sheffrous were trained from a young age by their mentors never to cry out with pain or pleasure. Chari moved the twig between his lips. Such idiotic traditions. Raised in the more tolerant Ghouli Ghouli customs, Chari abhorred that kind of barbaric training.

Chari pulled the twig out of his mouth, took a sip from his drink, and swirled the tangy fluid in his mouth. He had to admit it took guts for a lone Sheffrou to show up in unfamiliar territory, face hostile guards, and demand to see their leader.

Chari chuckled at the title leader of the Outcasts. Over sixty sequences ago, he was the one who had questioned the Chamranlina laws and challenged the Council of Elders. He never expected his actions would start a revolt and he would become the leader.

With time, the Rebellion was crushed. All the sympathizers who had fought for a brighter future, more power in the Council, and the right to mate, became the Outcasts. They were sent to the hot and deserted Southern Hemisphere, subsequently renamed the Burned Zone. No one could travel out of the region unless they sought prior approval by the Elders, and their requests were usually denied except for his; he had the right to travel everywhere with impunity. The right had been granted because he was an advocate for peaceful change even though his tactics were reviled by the general population. He rebelled against old and new laws alike and wouldn't stop until he got answers. This led to provocative gatherings, trespassing, looting, and rioting.

With his virtual screen in front of him, Chari consulted the records from the main computer of the colony. He chortled with disdain at the Elders who, with some urging, had granted him access to the data. After encountering a few dead ends, he identified the Sheffrou lying unconscious on his couch. A Sheffrou 8, no less, captured one sequence ago by the Krakoran. He was a prisoner of the enemy for five months before the Black Guards rescued him. He whistled, plopped the twig back in his mouth, and his lips moved it up and down. The slender, foolish Sheffrou had suffered cruel conditions. He was tougher than his looks suggested....

Why did this Sheffrou travel here? What was at stake for him? Did he lose a friend during those attacks? He came alone. *Could he not trust at least one guard?* Showing up without guards or Chowlis put his life in danger. Did he not know that? Did he stumble upon information unknown by the authorities? Chari was aware the Black and Silver Guards responsible for security could be hopelessly lacking in intelligent reasoning from time to time. Perhaps the Sheffrou was misinformed, but he knew enough about Sheffrous not to underestimate their psychic abilities. Their instincts couldn't be ignored.

Chari had seen how this one collapsed when he disclosed the multiple unexplained deaths in the youngest offspring and how their species' survival, including that of the Ghouli Ghouli, was doomed. The Elders had done everything in their power to prevent the information from reaching the main population, especially the Sheffrous, even threatening reprisal to the Gray Feeders, who fed and insured the females' safety. The consequences, if this sensitive information were to be leaked, could be catastrophic, tantamount to inciting civil war among the fertile Pure Colors and the Multicolors alike.

Chari checked the records once more. He searched for names of Sheffrous who had mated one and two sequences ago. His brow darkened. He emitted a long hissing sound and banged his fist on the table. "Damn you, Sheffrou."

It was this Sheffrou 8, Maashi Torrenadanga, First Lord of the Central Compound, this one only, who had mated with seven females two sequences in a row. They were the only females in the colony who had ovulated these two sequences. The fourteen Fanellas he mated with had conceived and delivered a healthy female offspring.

The fourteen young offspring lived in the same colony, and that's where the plague hit. Four months ago, the first child died. Then the others followed. The sterile Gray Feeders in charge of the Fanella compounds tried all the remedies they knew to save them. They were so distressed by this unspeakable tragedy that, under strict orders by the Elders to keep this plague secret, they had reached for answers in all avenues without alerting Sawishas and Sheffrous. As their desperation grew, they even requested the Elders' approval to seek help from the Outcasts. Sadly, no one could find an explanation for the death of the youngest offspring.

Chari had offered his sympathy and vowed his complete cooperation in the investigation. That's how he had been kept abreast of any development on the plight of the little females.

Why did this Sheffrou, the progenitor of the stricken off-spring, come here? Perhaps he had sensed abnormal vibrations in the void and came to the Burned Zone following some inner urging. Whatever the reasons which brought him here, he had become Chari's problem. His presence here would attract radical Ghouli Ghouli Outcasts, and this would bring discord and mayhem in the compound. He had to be disposed of, i.e., brought back to his own compound, quickly and quietly. Chari called his second in command by a telepathic wave, an effective and discreet way to communicate.

Less than a minute later, the big green and red called Tanyel or Tan for short knocked on the door and stepped in. He eyed Maashi and grunted, "You think he's a Sheffrou?"

Chari nodded. "I'm sure he's one. Think you can carry him? We have to bring him back to the Central Compound."

"He looks thin enough, but it's a long way, sir." His brow darkened. "It would be a lot faster if we were two. Why is he out?"

Chari gulped down the rest of his drink. "Zaren and his friends attacked him. I'll deal with them later. Get a strong guy you can trust. We'll leave as soon as possible."

Tan nodded. "I'll be back shortly."

Chari sat on the couch beside Maashi. He checked his pulse and gently pressed on his stomach. He wasn't pleased with what he found: a weak pulse and pooling of blood in the lower abdomen. Chari growled. There was firm evidence of active bleeding. In his semi-comatose state, the Sheffrou wasn't aware of this and therefore couldn't stop it. He was in stable condition for now but would soon require emergency care.

Chari hissed in anger. The last thing he wanted was a Sheffrou, famous for surviving at the hands of the Krakoran, dying in his compound. The inquiries and questions would be endless and the Sawishas, including the Black and Silver guards, would descend on his domain like the Night Creatures from the Korr nebula.

Chari had to admit the fool had impressed him, a rare occurrence. Very few Sheffrous had succeeded in mating two sequences in a row and produce fourteen viable females. The long-repressed memory of one Sheffrou who had accomplished this feat long ago surfaced in his mind and brought deep sadness. He shook himself and chased away thoughts which threatened to overwhelm him. Whatever the current circumstances, this Sheffrou had proven his courage and fearlessness unlike most Sheffrous who in recent times were spoiled and selfish individuals.

Chari and his men were soon on their way to the Central Compound. Chari told them the Sheffrou's injuries were severe and ordered them to carry him with the utmost care; one mishap and he could die and their hard-earned rights as Outcasts would disappear like morning dew under Chitina's blazing orange sun.

The damp smell of familiar tunnels woke up Maashi. Unable to move at first, he concentrated on inhaling and exhaling deep breaths every few seconds. His chest and face throbbed, and he stretched his tongue with difficulty to lick his dry lips. Pain shot up in his abdomen like hot embers and a low moan escaped his lips when he tried to turn on his side. Maashi put all his remaining energy to contain the active bleeding in his entrails. After several minutes, it stopped, leaving Maashi exhausted.

Chari's words came to mind: 'Why would anyone bother to give coordinates to our enemy when the future doesn't exist? You've been deceived. All but one of the youngest offspring are dead.' The thought made his stomach heave. *How could this be true? Why wasn't he informed the little offspring were dying?* Although in Chamranlina society, the progenitor's role was limited to conception, as the father, he felt responsible for the safety and health of his offspring.

Chari was wrong. He had to be wrong. But what would he gain by deceiving him? Maashi took a long breath in to chase away the darkness invading his mind. He surveyed his surroundings. This tunnel was close to the main entrance of the Fanella compound just north of the Central Compound where his cherished Ileana lived with their offspring. He closed his eyes. Soon, in an hour, the two guards would leave to be replaced by another pair. He would wait and rest until that time, then he would sneak inside the Fanella compound and find out the truth.

Chapter 5

After a sleepless night, Tamara went for an early morning swim in Maashi's favorite pool, the one with the blue walls speckled with gold and turquoise mosaics. Afterwards, she went to join Maashi for a breakfast of fruit and puddings as she often did and was surprised to find his quarters were deserted. Even his guards and Chowlis were nowhere to be seen. "Maybe they all went somewhere together," she said out loud.

Puzzled, but not suspecting anything serious, she went back to her receiving room and prepared a small bag. She took her personal items (including the little writing pad Maashi had given her that never left her side) and a change of clothes even though clothing could be replicated anywhere. Pacing the room, she ate a toughi, her favorite fruit, which tasted like a blend between pear and apple. She sat down and waited. An hour passed. Unable to stand the wait any longer, she bounced off the couch and trotted back to Maashi's quarters.

Chopa was sitting on Maashi's preferred couch. "Where is everybody this morning? Maashi said I would leave at first light and it's way past that time."

Chopa twirled his fingers, and the virtual screen in front of him disappeared. His brow was thick, his oval eyes were dark. He stared at the blue and green wall. "We are not leaving today."

"We? I thought I was the one leaving. Are you supposed to accompany me?"

"The Sheffrou instructed me to go with you, but the weather has changed overnight. Strong winds are preventing any type of travel. Also, we are expecting knee-deep snow in the next two days."

"What about the two humans? Will the weather cause any problems? Will they be safe?"

Chopa nodded to one side. "They are in a safe location. We canceled the awakening process."

"You mean they're still in their suspension pods, whatever these things are called."

"Yes."

Tamara examined Chopa closely. She knew him well enough to suspect there was something else bothering him. He held his back straight as a rod, and he looked tense like he was about to snap. She stepped closer to him. "Chopa, is there something else you're not telling me?"

He adjusted his shirt, tightened his sash, and said, "We are looking for the Sheffrou. No one has seen him this morning."

Tamara's heart skipped a few beats. "What? Do you think… Do you mean he's gone missing?"

"Rahma checked the recordings and all we know is he told the guards in the mid hours of the night he was going to swim in his pool. He often does this when he's preoccupied. Earlier this morning, the guards went to the pool and couldn't find him there or anywhere else in his quarters. They sent out an official message to alert everyone in the compound to report his location, but no one has seen him since last night." Chopa paused, and his gaze settled on Tamara. "Sheffrous are notorious for their sudden urges to run away especially if they are experiencing intense stress. However, to my knowledge, Sheffrou Maashi has not attempted anything similar in the last three decades."

Tamara plopped beside him on the couch. "So, you don't suspect anything awful. You think he took off even though he hasn't done this recently. Maybe he just wanted to be alone for a while." Tamara understood that perfectly. Being under constant surveillance could rattle your nerves. Sheffrous were monitored night and day to ensure their protection, but sometimes that became unbearable.

The door opened and Rahma burst in, knocking over one of the small tables. "I have checked all the sectors and scanned the entire compound with Pini and two other friends. I tried to communicate with him telepathically without success." With long fingers, he rubbed his head and a strand of hair fell on his forehead. "No one has seen the Sheffrou." He paced back and forth in front of them. "I have contacted Khon, the head of internal security. They are going to check the other compounds and may send a team to the surface. There is no evidence of a Krakoran attack; my scanner would have picked up some residual signs. At least, that is reassuring."

"I guess we'll just have to wait then," said Tamara. "How long do these escapades last? If you think that's what it is, when should we expect his return?"

Rahma's head jerked. He stared at her. "If he ran away, only a day, 26 hours. I am concerned however because Sheffrou Maashi has never left without informing one of us."

His face paled when he made that statement. He seemed quite disturbed by the situation and with good reason, because he was the leader of the two Chowlis.

"There's not much I can do to help then," Tamara said, glancing at both Chowlis with an expectant look. Neither responded nor offered more information. She rubbed her forehead. She sensed the beginning of a new migraine. "This is just what we needed." She turned her head from side to side in disbelief. "I think I'll go back to my quarters and take a nap. I didn't sleep well last night." She rose.

"Do you want me to accompany you?" said Chopa.

Tamara looked down; her auburn locks hid her face. "I'm fine," she said. "Just find him."

Chopa was not pleased. Sheffrou Maashi had been gone for over two days. After his

disappearance, every effort was made and all available Chamranlinas were put to task to find him. Both he and Rahma searched the entire compound sector by sector twice with no success. Frustrated and worried, Chopa scanned other sectors in surrounding compounds and once more contacted Kohn, head of security, who paid him a visit.

"We're doing everything we can," Khon said, eyeing the young Chowli. "We have contacted a great number of Sawishas and there are no signs of Sheffrou Maashi." He folded his arms across his chest and leaned against the doorframe.

Chopa didn't like his attitude. Like most guards, he was cold, harsh, and never admitted any errors. "Perhaps we should widen the search," Chopa said. "Search areas where you wouldn't expect a Sheffrou to go."

Khon dropped a condescending stare on the inexperienced Chowli. "We will keep you informed of our progress. Good day."

Chopa watched Khon's black clad frame exit in the hallway. His thick-soled boots resonated with each step he took. Chopa tasted the bitter saliva of anger and indignation. *What an idiot.* He hissed between his teeth.

Tamara and Rahma joined him. Maashi's disappearance had triggered a significant change in Tamara's demeanor. Chopa noticed her pale sad expression and trembling hands. He agreed with Sheffrou Maashi's belief that she often behaved like a Sheffrou in times of stress. He was fond of the little female and made a mental note to inquire about her emotional state and to keep track of how much food she ingested.

"Any news?" she asked. The white of her eyes had changed to a pinkish color that Chopa knew came from excessive crying. Sheffrou Maashi would not be pleased.

"I just met with Khon. He has nothing to add."

"I don't understand," said Tamara. "Do you think Maashi's hiding somewhere?"

"The Sheffrou," said Rahma, scratching his scalp, "is either out of range or seriously injured since he hasn't responded to my telepathic calls. His ability to communicate by telepathy is much greater than the average Chamranlina. He may hear us but cannot respond."

"What? You think he's hurt?" Tamara said with rising alarm in her voice.

Chopa stared at Rahma who lowered his head. Rahma then turned his attention to the bracelet on his right wrist. He was receiving a transmission. He clicked and said, "It was a Silver Guard, calling from the northern part of the Central Compound. They had located the Sheffrou in a tunnel leading to the main Fanella compound, but he was gone by the time a team went to retrieve him."

He looked down again. "The guard is sending me the co-ordinates of the location. We should go there right away to see if we can find any clues they might have missed."

Tamara clasped her hands together and her voice trembled as she said, "Hurry. Send news back to me as soon as you find something."

The two Chowlis bolted out of the room. They ran all the way and arrived at the location within the hour.

"What do you think?" asked Rahma who paced the tunnel with his hands on his hips. His resounding steps echoed in the tunnel.

Chopa said, "Stay still." He closed his eyes and let the odors and residual particles in the air permeate his senses. "I feel the dust, the humidity, and coolness of the rock. I can also pick up the scent of the guards." He turned his head to face the other direction and his features softened. "There are faint traces of the Sheffrou." His fingers traced Maashi's distinct fragrance on the rough granite of the walls, but it dissipated a few feet away.

"My conclusion also," said Rahma. "I'm sure it wasn't a scanning error. He was here a short time ago."

Chopa hissed in annoyance. "Where is he now? Where did he go?"

Rahma grunted. "I don't understand. What's going on? Is he willfully trying to elude us or what? I have been on the alert since I got the communication from the Silver Guard, but I can't sense any telepathic signal." He slapped his thighs in frustration, then fisted his hands.

Chopa lowered his head. "Perhaps he's sick."

Rahma's eyes shrank to small black slits.

"If something were to happen to him…" Chopa wiped his brow. "A sick or injured Sheffrou is a terrible thing to contemplate. My heart aches just to think about it." Dejected, he stared at the ground. His eyes lost all color. He added in a sad tone, "We lost four Sheffrous already in this sequence. So much grief and misery. There are very few Sheffrous, and their presence is vital to the colony. We can't lose Sheffrou Maashi. It would be a catastrophe."

"Don't say that my friend." Rahma patted Chopa's back. "I'm sure we'll find him… in good health."

The two hugged and held each other for a long moment then made their way back to Maashi's quarters in silence. They passed through well-traveled tunnels and couldn't escape the accusatory stares of the Chamranlinas who lined the hallways leading to Maashi's quarters. They had heard the Chowlis went to investigate a lead and waited impatiently for news of the Sheffrou's whereabouts.

Chopa didn't utter a word, confirming their trip had been unsuccessful.

The onlookers kept silent. A somber cloak of shame and guilt weighed heavily on Chopa's shoulders. He knew what they were thinking. What kind of Chowlis would lose their Sheffrou?

Chapter 6

Maashi lifted his head above ground inch by inch. His face throbbed below his left eye where one blow had fractured the cheek bone. The pain in his abdomen seared like fire. He inhaled and exhaled several times to focus his mind and lessen both pains down to more tolerable levels.

He blinked, evaluated his surroundings, and leaned on the wall for support as he stood. The low lighting in the tunnel showed early dawn. He took a few tentative steps forward. The odors were faint yet vaguely familiar, a mixture of sweetness and dampness. He knew exactly where he was: in a tunnel slightly north of the Central Compound, close to a Fanella compound where the offspring less than six sequence-old lived.

Chari Varian, leader of the Outcasts, had sounded so utterly sure when he had declared the little ones, less than two sequences old, were all dead, except one. The statement was so weird, so improbable that Maashi refused to believe any of it. He had to verify the facts for himself. Find out the truth. Everything would be altered if the little females were dying. He straightened his back, clenched his jaw, ignoring the pain gnawing at his insides, and headed for the closest entrance to the compound. Healing his wounds would have to wait.

The Fanella compound was well guarded. Patrols crisscrossed the paths leading to the entrances every few minutes, but the guards weren't expecting an intruder so late at night when all the Chamis were sound asleep. Maashi proceeded with utmost caution. The guards would have to be on high alert to catch him. Maashi's saweya, his life energy, was the lowest it had ever been. This would render him impossible to detect on the scans and at this hour, at the end of their shift, the guards weren't as vigilant. They could easily miss a slow moving and low energy target.

Maashi progressed along the tunnel without a sound and avoided touching the walls and leaving his scent. After only ten minutes, he spotted the entrance. He stood completely still behind a pillar and waited. Two guards walked back and forth in front of the great door but slowed their pace when the relief team approached. The others were still far down the tunnel when one of them stopped in his tracks and growled with pain. "My shoulder! My shoulder is burning!"

The two standing at the entrance ran into the tunnel and rushed to his side.

"What happened?" said one of them.

"My shoulder is burning, as if it's on fire."

"Did you see anything? How about your scans? What do they show?" said the night shift guard.

The one with the injured companion said, "Our scans show nothing."

"Are you sure?" said the other as he rubbed his sore shoulder.

"There are no signs of any disturbance. Are you still hurting?" the night shift guard said.

"I don't understand it. The pain is easing off."

His companion grunted. "Maybe you overdid your workout today. That wouldn't be the first time."

"You've been pushing yourself too much," said the fourth guard who had remained silent so far. "Your mind is playing tricks on you."

The two teams slapped each other's shoulders and clicked good-humoredly. They strolled together to the entrance.

The fourth guard part of the relief team said, "You can leave now. We'll re-scan the tunnel carefully."

"Don't worry," said the first one, "we never find a thing."

While the teams congregated further down the tunnel, Maashi slipped inside the compound and slid unseen behind a series of columns flanked by an overgrowth of large bushes. He was relieved his subterfuge had worked even though he disliked the use of mind control to inflict pain.

Faced with the tremendous challenge of remaining undetected while trying to contact Ileana, the one his heart favored, he planned his next move with care. He knew the risks. Anyone found inside the secluded compounds without proper authorization faced serious consequences.

The multicolor Gray Feeders were ever present in the compounds, but he could not see any at this early hour. Maashi moved quickly without making a sound. He lowered his head, ignored the pain churning in his stomach, and increased the pace. The sun would rise in a few hours and the light inside the dome would expand. Hiding would become impossible. The Fanellas had been confined in underground caves since the recent attacks by the enemy. Fortunately, he was within reach of the entrance of the deeper caves, where each female had her private quarters.

Maashi surveyed the area carefully. The vegetation above ground differed from what he remembered. In his haste, he stepped too close to a cookra plant, and a thorn scratched his side and broke off. A heavy, musky scent filled the surrounding air. Maashi held his breath and froze. Three Gray Feeders were approaching.

The Grays had shaved their heads and wore steel gray clothing in mourning. Maashi's brow darkened at their sight, and his heart thumped hard in his abdomen.

"What an awful smell!" said the short, fat Gray Feeder to the others. "Maintenance needs to remove all these ugly plants."

The tall one snickered, "You should send a note about it to the one in charge."

The third one lamented in a sad, deliberate tone, "We have more pressing problems to worry about."

With a side nod, the trio agreed. They turned their heads away and covered their noses just as they walked past Maashi, rigid as a stalk amidst the offending plants. He breathed a sigh of relief after they left but couldn't help but wonder why so many of those foul-smelling plants had grown unattended and like offensive weeds, had invaded most of the areas usually reserved for cultivating edible vegetation.

As soon as they were out of earshot, Maashi scampered into a large cave. Once in, he advanced slowly in the wide tunnel in search of Ileana's crest. He had successfully mated with her two sequences ago and the last sequence. The memory of her lovely body and her delicate fragrance lingered in his mind to this day. His mating with her had been perfect. If he never met another female and could mate with her once every sequence, he would gladly relinquish all others. She was the one closest to his heart and his soul. He expected a warm welcome. He needed to see and confirm his little offspring were healthy.

Maashi glimpsed Ileana's crest about ten yards away to the left. He hugged the wall and remained unseen. He stood close to the entrance to her quarters. She stepped out and saw him.

"You." She rushed the distance between them in one stride and slapped his face. "How dare you come in here?" her icy voice cut the air. With eyes black with fury, she spat at his feet.

Taken aback by an outburst so out of character, he took a deep breath and blinked. Then he noticed she wore the steel gray color of death. He bowed, put a hand on his chest to show he meant no harm, and whispered, "Ileana, Shapinka, tell me. Tell me about the little ones. Is it true? Are they sick?"

She hissed between her teeth to contain her anger. "Don't you know? Don't you know about the terrible sickness?"

Maashi gasped. Were Chari's words true? He inhaled sharply. "I learned of it only two days ago. I need to see the little ones. Maybe I can help."

"Do you think I'm a fool?" Her eyes glowed with fury. "Do you think I would let you see Shalina, the last one still alive?"

Maashi stared at her with wide eyes. He put a hand on the wall to steady himself and suppress the growing darkness around him. A sick feeling crept in his chest. He took a deep breath and stepped closer to Ileana, ignoring her outburst. "The last one! Ileana, I beg of you, tell me this isn't true."

"How did you not know about the sickness which has struck all the one and two sequence-old Fanellas? There is only one clinging to life, and each day brings her closer to death." Ileana's voice broke.

Maashi's face and chest paled, and his eyes lost all color. "How can this be?" he said in a low, strained voice. He wobbled as if he had lost all strength. His breathing became erratic, and he rested his lean frame against the wall of the cave. He gaped at Ileana with such intensity she looked away. "I swear on the bones of my ancestors that I didn't know. None of the Sheffrous or Sawishas know about this."

He extended his arm and touched Ileana's hand with the tip of his fingers. "Please," he whispered, "I beg you. Let me see her."

Ileana didn't say a word. She searched his eyes. "I have always trusted you, Maashi," she said in a voice filled with sadness. "Don't betray me at this dark hour. She is my heart and soul." She then turned and led him to her quarters in a connecting chamber in the back. Two young Fanellas dressed in steel gray were at the bedside of a small child. As soon as they saw the Sheffrou, they covered their mouths and fled the room, leaving Maashi alone with Ileana.

Maashi hurried to the child's bed and kneeled beside it. The little one was lying on her back, still as a corpse, her wide eyes staring into nothingness.

He took her hand in his. Her icy fingers lay inert. He brought them to his lips and kissed them one by one. The little female closed her eyes but otherwise didn't move at all. Maashi slipped his arms under her frail body and brought her against his own. He unfastened his shirt and held her close to his warm chest. He whispered softly and kissed her forehead.

Ileana kneeled beside him. Tears rolled down her cheeks, but she remained silent.

The child whimpered and snuggled closer to the Sheffrou. Maashi sat unmoving. He concentrated on transferring as much as possible of his saweya to the child. The little one's color improved, and her breathing became regular. She slid into a peaceful sleep.

At last, Ileana spoke. "The sickness started four months ago. We did everything to save them." Her voice choked with emotion. "She is the only one left." She tilted her head and noticed his swollen and battered face. "What happened to you?"

Maashi shook his head and said, "It's not important. I must put all my energy and my resources to find out what is ailing the child. I won't abandon you, Shapinka. This entire ordeal... what you went through... the pain and grief must have been terrible. I wish I had known about the illness." He took her hand in his and held it. His eyes brimmed with tears.

A moment later, they heard a commotion and the venerable Lady Shanaka, the eldest among the Fanellas, stormed into the room, her wrinkled face pale with anger. A gray veil of mourning covered her head, and she wore a black robe embroidered with her crest in gold on the collar and shoulders.

"Shonava Maashi," she hissed, "how dare you come here and put your hands on the last offspring? You are the source of this calamity. This is an insult I will not tolerate."

"Lady Shanaka," Ileana clasped her hands and said, "Sheffrou Maashi didn't know about the illness."

Maashi said, "Forgive my intrusion but ---"

"Silence!" The lady's voice resonated in the small room, "Of course, he didn't know. The Council has forbidden us to inform the Sawishas and especially the Sheffrous of the illness." She turned and faced Maashi. "I refuse to hear anything from you. Your poisonous seed has contaminated this haven and now there is only death and sorrow."

"What?" Maashi said, his voice choking with emotion.

"Spare me your lies, Sheffrou. Shame on you. All your offspring are dead except for this last one." Overcome by anger, she put a hand against her chest. "The Gray Feeders are on their way.

They will apprehend you and you will pay for daring to invade this sacred place and for your malevolent deeds." She spat on the floor, pivoted, and left the room in a flurry of black and gray.

Maashi had no choice. He had to leave. The penalties for intruding the Fanellas compounds included incarceration and flogging. He whispered to Ileana. "Ileana, you must believe me when I say I would never hurt the little females."

He put the child in her mother's arms. He removed his shirt and said, "Wrap her in my shirt. Burn her couch and destroy all the linens in this room. Have someone bring clothing and linens from my quarters that I have worn. Hold her in your arms only and as much as possible. Do not give any kind of food besides choun. Let only one trusted feeder breastfeed her."

Maashi rose with difficulty, weary beyond words. He held on to the wall and stood. The room danced before his eyes. "I will be relentless in my efforts to find what is causing her to wither away." He bent his head and kissed Ileana's cheek.

Footsteps resonated from outside the room. Maashi froze, uncertain.

Ileana sprang into action. She handed the sleeping child to a young Fanella who had appeared at the door. "Come this way," she whispered, "quickly." She led him to another room. A small doorway connected to a narrow corridor. "Go all the way down. You will find a hallway leading upward to an ancient tunnel with a steep incline. The end of that tunnel connects to the surface."

"Ileana, I..." Maashi's eyes filled with tears.

"Go... before they come for you." She raised her head and the look in her eyes told him he could trust her.

He took off at a brisk pace to escape his followers and stumbled several times. Each time, he got up with increasing difficulty. He frantically checked behind. The corridor was so black he couldn't see anything. He listened intently but a slow steady ringing in his ears covered all other sounds.

Maashi pushed on and held his abdomen. The pain had reawakened and gnawed at his insides. He reached a narrow tunnel and crouched low to enter. Crawling upward on his stomach, the irony of the situation hit him. Only a slender Fanella or an emaciated Sheffrou could hope to escape through this tunnel. Maashi concentrated hard to stay focused and avoid passing out with exhaustion. His saweya had dropped to a dangerous level, and sheer willpower alone made his progress possible.

The last few yards were the hardest. He fought for every inch and finally reached the surface. The orange sun's glare filled the sky, and its warm glow covered the desolate land. Maashi's third transparent eyelid automatically shielded his eyes from the blinding rays. He rested on his back for a few minutes so his body could absorb the life-giving energy from the sun. Reestablishing normal energy levels was a long process and quite impossible at this moment, but even a few minutes of exposure would be beneficial.

Maashi sat up and scanned the horizon. Hills and boulders lay scattered to the northwest. He grunted as he realized that his current position was much too vulnerable. It would be easy to spot him from afar. Rising on his knees, he pushed on the ground and stood. Taking a few deep breaths, he steadied himself and started walking towards the hills. After several yards, he increased his pace and advanced without faltering. He made good progress and was a mile away from the first boulder when he turned around. To his horror, he saw three Gray Feeders on the horizon.

Maashi took off at a much faster pace, trotted and ran, and sprawled on the hard ground a few times. The unmistakable smell of methane gas filled the air. Maashi hesitated and slowed down. Methane was dangerous and possibly deadly. He looked back. The Feeders were closing in. The vision of the little female with wide eyes staring into nothingness compelled him into action. He had to escape at any cost.

Maashi entered the Goolalong Fields, notorious for their concentrated methane pockets right under the surface. He zigzagged between the boulders, retracing his steps until they were all jumbled and then progressed further towards the hills. He hoped the methane concentration was lower over there. Perhaps he could even find a cave to hide in. He had to become invisible to the scans.

He picked up handfuls of dirt and spread it over his skin and clothing. It would block off his energy source but would decrease the absorption of methane through his skin, warding off the most serious side effects. He spotted an opening that led to a cave and crawled in. Digging in the soft dirt, he prepared a place to rest and lay down, exhausted. He closed his eyes and to avoid detection by the Feeders, sent only one weak telepathic distress signal to Rahma. Then his world went black.

Chapter 7

Tamara sat in the lounge-chair in Maashi's receiving room, now operating as general headquarters. Everyone who thought they had heard something or had a lead on Maashi's whereabouts came there. Close friends and Sawishas from distant compounds who wanted fresh news on the search stopped by and offered support to Rahma and Chopa.

Shonava Benshimu joined the two Chowlis. The big green's experience and expert advice were invaluable. Benshimu wasn't easily intimidated, slow to anger, and ready to reevaluate the course of action if results weren't satisfactory. Although troubled by the news of Maashi's disappearance, he was an optimist at heart and raised the morale of the young crew. He appointed himself official negotiator with the chief of security who remained as cold and impassive as ever.

Confused and disturbed by the turn of events, Tamara hadn't bothered to shower that morning or the two days before. For the Chamis, this was odd and an insufferable lack of good manners. She couldn't conceive of a life without Maashi, and any negative comment about his disappearance sent her running for a modicum of privacy in the water room where she cried in silence.

Rahma sent her assistant Pini back to his original compound to serve as a communication link. Tamara's mood changed from bad to worse. She picked at her food, snapped at everyone, and didn't listen to any urging to get some sleep by the overburdened Chopa.

What Tamara feared the most was to find out Maashi had been kidnapped. She clung to the thought that the Chamis couldn't detect any residual evidence of the enemies, so, at least for the moment, that possibility was discarded. The next most plausible explanation for his disappearance was that he voluntarily left the compound but suffered a serious injury or lay trapped in a place where he couldn't contact them for help. Neither scenario was reassuring.

Chopa joined Tamara on Maashi's favorite couch. He reviewed the plans of the tunnels around the compound for the hundredth time.

"As you can see, Tamara," he said, "two of the tunnels in the northern section connect to the largest Fanella compound. That area is guarded night and day by guards and yet, no one has seen anything." He fidgeted with his sash. "Sheffrou Maashi wouldn't have gone to the Fanella compound. It is absolutely forbidden to enter without proper authorization, and he had no reason to go there."

Tamara chewed her lower lip as she considered his comment. "Is there any way to find out for sure? Perhaps Maashi went in without being noticed by the guards?" As an Emergency Room physician, she often faced uncommon problems and had learned to keep in mind all diagnoses even those who seemed implausible.

Chopa looked at her. "There might be a way to communicate with someone inside, but since the attacks the Council of Elders has ordered a complete shutdown of communications with the Fanella compounds." He paused, as if considering some new idea. "I'll see what I can do." The door chime rang. With a hand signal, he made the virtual screen disappear. "Another well-wisher, I suppose."

Chopa pressed a control on the side table and the door opened.

A tall lean Ghouli Ghouli entered, dressed in a tight-fitting black shirt, and wearing a faded sash with purple as its dominant color. One corner of his mouth curled upward in a cold greeting. Tamara averted her gaze to avoid staring at his strange copper skin. She had heard about this type of Chami, but this was the first time she had seen one.

"I want to speak to Sheffrou Maashi," the Ghouli Ghouli said in the Chami language of clicks and "sh," sounds. "I saw him a few days ago. Is he well?"

Chopa jumped to his feet, bolted towards the door, and delivered a powerful punch to the stranger's jaw. The Ghouli Ghouli raised his fist, but the blow missed the young and agile Chopa.

Tamara stood and screamed. "Rahma, Rahma, come here quick."

Chopa rushed the stranger and caught him in a chokehold. The other fought to shake him off and punched him hard in the stomach. He attempted to topple Chopa over, but Chopa held on and choked him even tighter. The Ghouli Ghouli tried to reach and grab his genitals, but Chopa compressed the other's neck with surprising strength. His copper face paled, changed to dark red, then gray. His arms fell limp at his side. Only then did he lower his eyes in submission.

Rahma burst into the room accompanied by two guards.

Chopa blurted out in English. "This Ghouli Ghouli knows something."

Without hesitation, the two guards held the stranger and fitted him with restraining wrist bands. Chopa released him, and the stranger inhaled a long breath of air. He cleared his throat and emitted raspy clicks. "Your choking technique is quite effective for someone so young," he said in their language.

Rahma glared at the stranger. He responded with a voice as cold as ice water rushing out of the Gorganna gorge, "Who are you? What do you want?"

"My name is Chari Varian. You are probably not familiar with ---"

"Leader of the Outcasts," blurted out Chopa. "Led the mass rebellion against the Council of Elders fifty-eight sequences ago. Lives with his followers in the Burned Zone."

"Congratulations," said Chari whose face was regaining some color. "Well trained for combat and well informed."

"Enough." Rahma cut him short, his eyes wild with fury. "We want answers. Start now."

Tamara stared in amazement at the Ghouli Ghouli's shiny skin, black hands, black eyes and eyelids, as he slowly recuperated from Chopa's hold. She could make out only a few words of their conversation. The Burned Zone was an expression she remembered from a discussion between Chopa and Rahma. "Chopa," she said, "you told me Maashi asked a lot of questions about the Leader of the Burned Zone. He probably went to see him."

"I want to speak with Sheffrou Maashi," said the Ghouli Ghouli. He eyed Tamara. "Who is this creature? What does he or she have to do with the Sheffrou?"

"First, tell us what happened when you last saw the Sheffrou." Rahma raised his arms, fisted his hands.

Chari took a deep breath, exhaled, then said, "All right, I will comply."

Chari kept his comments to a minimum to avoid giving out too much information that could inculpate him or his men. He explained the sudden arrival of the Sheffrou in the Burned Zone and his rapid intervention to minimize his injuries when his men attacked him. He told them he informed the Sheffrou that the Outcasts weren't responsible for the coordinated attacks by the Krakoran on the night of the Great Eclipse.

He left out the part about the offspring and the plague since this information was privileged and hidden from the main population. He said he and his men accompanied the Sheffrou at the northern edge of the Central Compound and made sure the recording system picked his signal up. Afterwards, their group left, and he came here today to inquire about the Sheffrou's health and to discuss the details of the Krakoran attack.

Rahma, Chopa, and the alien appeared to argue about the Sheffrou, the only word Tamara could make out clearly. She stood, arms crossed over her chest, fuming. It took all her self-control not to yell at the copper alien and demand what happened to Maashi.

She tapped her foot to get their attention. "Chopa, what is he saying?"

Chopa gave her a quick summary of Chari's remarks. Tamara eyed the copper alien with suspicion.

Rahma circled the Ghouli Ghouli. "Give me the precise co-ordinates of the area where you abandoned Sheffrou Maashi."

Chari's eyes shrunk into small slits. "Don't insult me, Chowli."

"Give us the coordinates," ordered Chopa, taking a threatening step forward.

"I agree on one condition," said Chari. "You must let me speak with him."

"What does he want?" Tamara hissed.

Chopa explained in English. "He wants to see Sheffrou Maashi. But we need to know the coordinates of the area where he saw him last."

With his confrontational airs and aggressive stance, the stranger reminded her of a bully. Tamara had dealt with bullies before. She addressed the alien in a clear, strong, assertive tone. "You can speak to Sheffrou Maashi after you give us answers, not before."

Chari stared at Tamara and tilted his head. He moved his lips from side to side as if chewing on something.

Rahma took a few steps and stood within inches of Chari's face. "Give us the coordinates."

Chari shot a sarcastic stare at the two Chowlis. "Give me access to a computer."

Chopa pointed to a series of controls. "The access is on the wall over there."

Chari offered his wrists to the guards. "No reason to keep these anymore." The guards clicked at Rahma who nodded, and they removed the restraints. Chari punched on the controls and entered the data, and it corresponded exactly to the coordinates of Maashi's most recent position in the tunnel. Only a few Chamis knew his last coordinates. His story matched their findings, at least for the moment.

As soon as he was done, Chari rushed out of the room through a door which led to Maashi's pool. The others ran behind with Chopa hissing his anger.

Chari stood at the edge of the clear blue water and turned towards them. "Smart trick," he said. "The door leads to an empty pool." He crossed his arms over his chest. "Now tell me where your Sheffrou is."

The group stood on the edge of the pool. No one said anything. Chari hissed. "This is not amusing."

Rahma clicked an order. The guards left.

"The Sheffrou isn't here," said Chopa. "We haven't found him... yet."

The two Chowlis glanced at each other.

"What's going on?" asked Tamara.

Chopa explained what Chari told them, and that the coordinates were a match.

Tamara eyed Chari. "Ask him what was Maashi's condition when they left him? Why didn't he contact us?"

Chopa clicked at Chari who stared at Tamara.

Tamara frowned when they moved closer and kissed each other. Then she remembered. It was their way of transferring a great deal of information all at once. Chopa, in one long kiss, taught him how to understand, speak, and think in English.

Chari made his first attempt to speak English. "We brought him into the tunnel almost two days ago." His whole face darkened.

Tamara was furious. "Are you telling us you brought him, and he was so weak, perhaps even injured to the point he couldn't call for help, and you just left him there?"

Chari looked down. He didn't answer.

Tamara raged on. "Why didn't you call for help yourself if he couldn't?" She could feel her face burn with anger. "If something bad happened to him, you're in serious trouble."

Chari's black eyes zoomed on Tamara. He ran his fingers through his coarse raven hair. "I don't understand. He should have contacted you," he said under his breath, as if he was speaking to himself. "His life may be in danger." He shook his head as if he came to his senses. "We must act quickly and find him."

"We?" Rahma growled. "You're not included in the search. You're the one who abandoned him in the tunnel."

Chari shot them a contemptuous stare. "If I had done something wrong, I wouldn't be here."

"Nonetheless," Rahma responded with his icy voice, "your story smells rotten and I'm sure you aren't telling us everything."

"I agree with Rahma," said Tamara.

Chari clicked with a condescending tone, "And who might you be?"

Chopa answered. "Tamara is a Human. She is Sheffrou Maashi's Chimitanga and is an Ishkibu Sheffrou. I suggest you treat her accordingly."

Chari tilted his head back. "An Ishkibu Sheffrou. A traveler. Where are you from?" He appeared to be dumbfounded.

Rahma said, "We don't have time for questions. If Sheffrou Maashi is hurt, we need to retrieve him as soon as possible."

"You're right," said Chari. He turned to Chopa and said, "I suggest you send a general alert with the information about the coordinates and an additional note to insist upon the fact the Sheffrou's life is in danger. In the meantime, I'll go back to the tunnel where we left him. I think I know where he went."

"I'm going with you," said Chopa in a decisive tone.

Chari's mouth stretched in a half-smile. He tilted his head sideways to better observe Chopa. "Yes. Come. I'll need a smart Chowli when I find your Sheffrou."

Chapter 8

Chari and Chopa reached the tunnel where they found the last signs of Maashi. At fifteen feet wide, it was wider than most tunnels and led directly to the main Fanella compound.

For their safety, the Fanellas lived in four well-guarded areas segregated from the other compounds of the colony. The Chamranlina population had changed drastically over the last two hundred sequences. The males now outnumbered the females by a thousand to one. To avoid fights between the fertile Pure Colors, Sawishas and Sheffrous alike, at the time of renewal when Rue Kish, the instinct to mate, reached its peak, the Fanellas had agreed to live in compounds separate from the males. There, protected by the Gray Feeders, infertile multicolor males, they lived a peaceful life raising the offspring.

The young remained with the females until they reached adolescence, which was around twenty sequences old. After that, the young males or Shoulans, as the Chamis called them, were transferred to the standard compounds, and completed their education under the supervision of Multicolors. The young Fanellas however continued their lives in the protected areas under the mentorship of older females. All reached adulthood at forty sequences.

The four Fanella compounds, covered by gigantic domes, recreated the same environment they had known on Chamtali, their home world, destroyed centuries ago by volcanic eruptions. Two domes also served as greenhouses and enabled the Chamis to grow many of the original flora and fauna brought with them from Chamtali.

Chari and Chopa searched for thirty minutes in the dim light of the tunnel to find the scent of the Sheffrou. Both smelled the air in the hope of pinpointing his characteristic holoma and palpated with their sensitive fingers the reddish and ochre veins in the cocoa granite walls in case Maashi left a sign of his presence. At last, they found a faint aroma which disappeared abruptly, near the entrance to the Fanella compound.

Chari pulled out from the inside pocket of his black shirt a small twig. He poked at the rock with it, then slipped the twig between his teeth and chewed on it.

"Touch this," he said, "there's a long break in the stone and I feel a slight draft."

"I feel it," said Chopa, his fingertips running over the granite. "It goes upward way above my head, about twelve feet high. Most likely an old tunnel leading to the surface."

"I agree," said Chari, "and that's where we lose the Sheffrou's scent."

"Yes," said Chopa, "although quite faint, his holoma is still perceptible. And this must be the door."

Chari tapped the other's shoulder. "Let's push against the wall and see if we can open it."

The granite door moved just a little at first, but with the continued combined efforts of the two Chamis, it gave way just enough to let them slip in.

Chopa took the lead in the dry, dusty, and dark tunnel, abandoned for a long time. He covered a hundred steps before he picked up the scent again.

"The Sheffrou's holoma starts here," he said. "He must've entered the tunnel through another opening."

They traced the holoma to a secondary tunnel, which continued for a mile, then made a sharp turn to the right. The pair followed a narrow winding path that climbed upward at a steep angle for two miles until it reached the surface.

The two hastened their pace, hoping to catch up with the Sheffrou. Every couple of hundred feet, they paused and ascertained his faint holoma was still present and that they were still on the right tract.

"Shonava Maashi was rushing to the surface, concealing any sign of his passing," said Chopa. "He left no clear footprints, no evidence he had stopped to rest, no fingerprints on the walls. There is little trace of his trip through the tunnel."

"You're an excellent tracker," said Chari. "I like the way you think. I'd say your Sheffrou was running for his life, trying to reach the surface through this secret passageway."

Chopa grabbed Chari and pinned him against the wall. "I suspect he was fleeing from your followers," he growled. "You came to us to confirm he was done with. Maybe he knows something you want to cover up, and you want him eliminated."

"Back away, Chowli," Chari said. He shoved back Chopa. "The Sheffrou wasn't running from my people. I came out of concern for him, to insure he was out of danger."

"I don't believe you're telling us the whole truth," Chopa snarled. "Beware, I'm watching you."

They emerged on the arid surface. The intense heat assaulted them. The orange sun sat in Chitina's purple sky, glaring at the land like an emperor surveying his domain. Its intense rays flooded every inch of the barren soil and chased away every shadow. Both Chamis blinked and closed their transparent second eyelids to protect their eyes. Chari's copper skin shone under the powerful light.

Chari carried a handheld device on his belt. He pulled it out and scanned the horizon. Out in the distance, the purple sky morphed to a deep magenta which clashed with the soil's rusty color. No vegetation softened the sharp, angry landscape teeming with rocks and boulders. He muttered between his teeth. His lips moved his twig, and it flapped up and down.

"I've been in this area before," he said. "We are entering the Goolalong Fields. This area hides pockets of methane under the surface especially behind the boulders on your left." His eyes narrowed as he stared at Chopa. "If the Sheffrou has been exposed to the methane, he may already be dead."

Chopa shook his head in disapproval and stared at the Ghouli Ghouli with contempt. "Shonava Maashi would never have come close to the methane. It's too dangerous." With his fingers, he flicked the dust from the tunnel off his clothes. "Why do you insist on saying he traveled here?"

Chari squatted down and grabbed a handful of the dry soil and let it slide through his fingers. He looked up and said, "You told me you checked the underground tunnels and security has been to all the pools and fast-moving currents. The only logical option is the surface and the tunnel he took leads us this way."

Unconvinced, Chopa maintained his assertion. "The Sheffrou would never put his life in danger by exposing himself to an unsafe environment. Methane can cause disorientation, weakness, and death can occur after four hours of exposure. He would've gone in the opposite direction." He pointed south-east with a slender middle finger.

"Don't lecture me, Chowli. I know all about methane. The Goolalong Fields would be the logical choice if someone were pursuing him."

The young Chopa stared due north. "If he felt he was in danger and ran close to those boulders," he paused, "we must find him quickly."

"I'll go check the boulders," said Chari. "You go east."

Chopa hissed. "If you think I'll let you go by yourself ---"

"Too dangerous to expose both of us to the gas. When I find your Sheffrou, I'll need someone with a clear head to call for help."

Chopa hesitated. "What if you're here to get rid of him?"

Chari's black eyes glared at the young Chowli. "It would've been easy to finish him in the tunnel where I left him." In fact, he thought to himself, it would have been so easy he had been tempted, but he admired the Sheffrou's guts. "He came to see me alone to find answers, without Chowlis or guards to protect him. I don't know the truth about the attacks on the night of the Great Eclipse Celebration, but I suspect foul play same as he does." He spat on the ground. "Among the things I hate the most are conspiracies and dishonorable deeds. I came to see the Sheffrou to offer my help in solving the mystery of the attacks."

"I still don't trust you, Outcast," Chopa said, "but I'll follow your plan for now."

Chari bristled when he heard the word Outcast, but he let it be. "Let's go then. Time is short. The sun is moving fast."

Chopa took a few steps towards the east, stopped, turned, and shouted. "Contact me every twenty minutes. Don't think you can leave without me." He added as an afterthought. "And don't get yourself killed."

With a sarcastic laugh, Chari said, "And this from the same spotted brown Chowli who almost choked me to death two hours ago."

Chopa didn't answer. He shot him a hard, cold stare.

Cautious and double-checking his position every two hundred feet, Chari progressed at a slow pace. He was familiar with this kind of terrain, frequently found in the Burned Zone where he and his followers, the Outcasts, had been exiled. His light clothing let the sun's rays pass through to his skin to provide him with energy but still offered protection against burns when the sun reached its zenith.

He skirted around the most concentrated pockets of methane and covered a wide area in the first twenty minutes, using his scanning device to sweep the horizon for signs of the Sheffrou. A light breeze lifted the dust in little puffs behind him and his footsteps left no trace. Boulders of all sizes, from small to huge ones hundreds of feet across lay over the ground, and in the distance even larger rock formations were visible as he got closer to the Chizoo mountain range.

He called Chopa. "No signs of him."

"Nothing here either."

During the next twenty minutes, Chari made quick incursions into the danger zone and then retreated to a safe distance. He signaled back to Chopa. "I have to go farther in. My scans don't penetrate through the larger pockets. The Sheffrou could be there but undetectable by my scans."

"Do what you must. I haven't found anything. I'm going to push further. Next contact in twenty."

"As long as you don't forget me," Chari answered. He set his methane scanner to high. He advanced with caution around the larger boulders, so big he had to circle them, and avoided the big pockets of gas trapped just below the surface.

"By the night creatures of the Korr Nebula," he hissed. A dark premonition invaded his mind. "Where are you, Sheffrou?"

He paused, made a complete turn, scanning all the while. The twig moved from side to side between his lips, then he clenched it hard with his teeth.

"I'm going at this the wrong way," he thought aloud. "Instinct would drive the Sheffrou to find refuge in the rare oxygen areas." He adjusted his scanner to find oxygen and tried again. There was one good pocket half a mile away behind a boulder about six hundred feet wide and a hundred feet high.

Surrounded by high concentrations of methane, the boulder was covered with fine sand and quite steep. "Why did I get involved in this?" he hissed, "I didn't even have a proper meeting with this Sheffrou." He knew why. Sixty sequences ago, he could not save his own Sheffrou, and the pain and guilt weighed on his soul to this day. Anger and frustration made his blood boil. "I can't get around this huge mound. I'll have to climb the annoying thing."

Still agile as a young Chamranlina at one hundred and seventy-two sequence old, he ascended the boulder. Halfway up, he got a signal from Chopa. He continued his climb until he found a flat rock and sat down to transmit his position.

"Are you out of your mind? The Sheffrou wouldn't have climbed there," said Chopa. "Get down and come join me in this section."

"Do what you want," Chari answered. "I'm surveying this area because I have a strong feeling he is behind this boulder. I'll check it out whether you agree or not."

Anger flared in Chopa's response. "Don't call me if you get in trouble."

"I know how to take care of myself, Chowli. I'll call you when I find him."

Chari turned his transmitter off. He climbed a little more, then he stood at the top of the boulder. The view was spectacular. The bleak rust and gray Chizoo mountains with their sharp white peaks were visible to the north-west while the desolated flatlands stretched as far south as the Burned zone where the Outcasts lived.

He surveyed the horizon with eyesight sharpened by the dim lighting of the tunnels. All he saw in front of him was an empty land, seared by the sun's merciless rays, splattered with five to ten feet wide boulders.

"Nothing. Still nothing," he hissed. He calculated the time; more than two hours had elapsed since the search started. The minutes were slipping away. Time always did that when you needed it the most. "Damn you, Chitina," he cursed the valley and the planet. "I was convinced I would find him here."

With his scanner set at its most sensitive, he scanned the region below with care to make certain he didn't miss any oxygen pockets. He double-checked the data. He sent a widespread buzzing call with his device, something security advised against because of the risk of the signal being picked up by the Krakoran. Still no response.

He checked how much time had elapsed, and his vision blurred a few seconds. He pulled out his micro-oxygenator from his service belt and applied it to his chest to increase his own concentration of oxygen. It wouldn't do any good to get himself sick with the high doses of methane. He sat down on the parched soil, ran long rough fingers through his unruly black hair, and waited.

There was a small area, only twenty square feet, where the scanner couldn't pick up any signal at the foot of the boulder. "Fine," he thought aloud, "I'll go down and verify it. I'm not leaving until I've looked everywhere."

He made his way down with sure, deliberate steps. Way below, the valley was littered with sharp pebbles. Chari treaded on the surface, careful to stay on the perimeter of the more concentrated methane areas. He rechecked his oxygen level and glanced at the time: two hours and thirty minutes since they had left. There was no signal from Chopa. Chari assumed he hadn't located the Sheffrou either, so this meant he had to be here.

Chari came upon a small cave with enough oxygen to keep a Chamranlina alive for a few hours. He couldn't find any signs of life. Furious, he spat out a thick glob of saliva and kicked up a cloud of dust. Even with a stronger scanner, he wouldn't be able to locate anyone on the lifeless surface of this wretched planet.

"You win, Chitina," he muttered, disgusted.

He stepped back outside the cave.

The life-scanner flashed.

Chari froze. He scanned again, checking all the perimeter in a slow sweep. Yes. The Sheffrou was in there somewhere. Chari stormed back into the cave. He looked in every crevasse and behind every rock.

At last, he found him, hidden by an irregular granite formation. He was rolled up in a ball and covered with fine dust.

"By the mighty and powerful orange sun of Chitina," he hissed. "You couldn't have found a smaller, more secluded place."

Chari went to the Sheffrou and took him in his arms like a child. Conscious but with eyes closed and his breathing slow and irregular, his sunken face was as white as Choun. Chari took his oxygenator and pressed it on the Sheffrou's quatay.

The Sheffrou's breathing stabilized. He regained some color, opened his eyes and, for a brief instant, they shone with recognition. With a faint voice, he said, "You were... right." He grabbed Chari's sleeve. "You must... You must help the Fanellaaa...." Color drained from his eyes, and he collapsed in Chari's arms.

Chari's heart sank. "Damn you, Sheffrou," he hissed, his twig held on one side of his mouth. "You had to see the little Fanella for yourself. And the truth almost killed you."

He held him, pressing his chest on the other's chest to ensure his own life energy would flow with ease in the Sheffrou's body.

"Hang on, Sheffrou," he said between his teeth. "You can't die. The Chamranlinas need you." Chari tightened his embrace and sent three emergency calls to Chopa.

Chapter 9

Maashi was brought back to the safety of the caves by Chari Varian and Chopa, his Chowli. The methane gas had poisoned Maashi's body and attacked his brain. It scattered his thoughts, erased crucial memories, and left him lost, vulnerable, in critical condition.

After Chari found Maashi, he appealed to the Council of Elders for help.

The Council was as he remembered: Fourteen Sawishas representing the fourteen compounds of the colony. They were old, stubborn, and averse to change. They agreed by unanimous vote that Sheffrou Maashi needed treatment after Chari convinced them that no one in his right mind would run away to the surface and get lost in the Goolalong Fields. The Elders decided the best way to help the Sheffrou was to send him to a safe place under the care of a Tousanou, a healer specialized in the care of injured Sheffrous and Sawishas, called Chendor Aramashan.

A faraway baritone voice pierced the black veil that shrouded Maashi's mind. "Where are you?" It called.

Maashi didn't respond.

The voice asked again, "Where are you? Talk to me."

Maashi's mind answered, "I am nowhere."

"I will help you," the deep voice said.

Oblivious to its call, Maashi's thoughts retreated further.

The voice insisted. "Shapinka, precious one, come to me."

The familiar term stirred Maashi. His mind floated back to a conscious mode, to reality. The world around him focused. He opened his eyes, keeping the clear protective second eyelid closed.

Large, muscular arms circled his waist. A faint light shone in the small receiving room and etched the outline of a huge Chamranlina sitting by his side. His fragrant holoma floated in the air, stirring Maashi's senses. He pulled back to free himself from the binding embrace. He called for help, but no sound came out. A sharp, searing pain shot through him when he inhaled a deep breath. The burn spread across his chest, reminding him of another place, another time, when he was a prisoner, his body encased in a white frame, defenseless against his tormentor's whims. The dreadful memory made him recoil in fear. He cowered to hide beyond the voice's reach. His mind fought to escape to a place far away where he could forget every painful recollection and find solace.

"No, Shonava," said the baritone voice, echoing throughout his mind. "No."

Maashi saw for the thousandth time the light fading from the small female body as it lay limp in his arms, her life slipping away from his grasp. He choked and gasped, and tears filled his eyes. His breathing became erratic. He cried out but heard only moans.

The arms held him, surrounded him, providing critical energy and comfort. The soothing voice continued, "You will live through the pain, Shapinka. You will live."

Maashi fought with all his might to avoid the pain and sorrow, but to no avail. The arms were too strong, the sorrow too vast. He couldn't hide and he couldn't escape. He started to cry like a young pink Chamranlina. At first, a few small sobs, a few more, and then his whole body shook.

It went on for long, agonizing minutes. The sobs and the cries poured out of him. He couldn't stop.

Maashi reeled with shame and dismay.

Sheffrous, trained for twenty, sometimes thirty sequences to control their intense emotions so they could provide sexual favors to the males and even more important, mate with the females, weren't permitted to cry. His mentor, Kokin, had pummeled the rule in Maashi's impressionable mind when he was a young Pure Color. Now Maashi had committed the unforgivable sin: he let the stranger see his tears and cries of despair. Nothing he could say or do would alleviate his shame. He remained silent, trembling, feeling minuscule, worthless. He dropped his head on the other's shoulder and hid his face, waiting for the inevitable punishment.

Pudgy fingers caressed his scalp. Maashi stayed still as stone. He kept his head low and pressed his eyes closed.

The other took Maashi's face between his hands and brought him closer. He kissed his forehead and cheeks and licked his tears. As if speaking to a young Fanella, his deep voice said, "There, there, Shapinka. There is no reason to fear me. I would never hurt you."

Maashi held his breath. Was this a ruse to better punish him? An outburst like the one he did was unimaginable for a mature Sheffrou 8 like him. His shaking intensified. Would he dare open his eyes and gaze at the voice? He inhaled a long breath and peered with caution at the other's face.

The stranger's warm violet eyes showed only kindness. The right side of his face was uneven, scarred by an ugly cut. Maashi didn't perceive any hostility or anger.

He had never seen this Chamranlina.

The other one smiled and this simple action startled the disconsolate Maashi who gulped his saliva. He then kissed Maashi's neck in the customary sign of friendship and respect.

"It's a pleasure to hold you, Shonava."

He picked up Maashi's hand and kissed the tip of his fingers one by one. Maashi shook his head and tried to pull back from him. His crying threatened to start anew, and he didn't want to lose control of his emotions again. He covered his mouth to stop any sound from escaping.

The stranger whispered, "It's futile to attempt to stop the tears." His arms formed a tight circle around Maashi who let out a cry of anguish.

The affection the other displayed was unexpected. Maashi's sobs returned. He cried more quietly this time and after a moment, the weeping slowed and stopped. He glanced at the stranger, who appeared to be waiting for him to regain his composure.

"We, Chamranlinas, feel your pain. There is no shame in crying when the suffering is so great. You are Shapinka. We, Chamranlinas, respect your tears."

Maashi's chest heaved with the effort of facing the stranger. He lifted his head and found the courage to speak. "Who are you?"

The stranger's scarred face opened in a beautiful crooked smile. "I am a Tousanou. I want to be your friend." He ran a finger down Maashi's cheek. "My name is Chendor."

Maashi blinked away the last lingering tears. "Forgive me. Forgive my behavior."

"Don't be ashamed, Shonava," said Chendor. "The tears will help you heal. That's why you were brought here."

Maashi stared at him. "I've never heard of you."

"Only a few Chamranlinas know my name." He patted Maashi's shoulder. "Don't be troubled. Rest now. Sleep. I will stay by your side."

Many hours later, Maashi awoke. Random bits and pieces of recent events flashed through his mind: the sharp prick of a thorn, a repulsive smell, the unforgiving glare of the orange sun, a sense of hopelessness. He attempted to shed light on the maze of his thoughts, but the shadows grew darker.

"Again, my name is Chendor." A warm, welcoming smile lit his mutilated face. He added, "You're in my quarters, thirty levels underground. Under my care, Shonava, you will regain your saweya." He took Maashi's hand and placed it on his ample chest.

Maashi's fingers tingled with the life energy flowing from the quatay, the intricate, erogenous markings on Chendor's chest, markings possessed by all Pure Colors.

Maashi murmured, "You're Sheffrou."

"Yes, Shapinka. I am a Sheffrou 6." Chendor bent his head sideways to best observe him and this hid the deep scar crossing his right cheek.

<*Talinda will not move,* > said an unfamiliar high-pitched voice.

Maashi looked around. There was only him and Chendor in the receiving room, populated by an abundance of blue and turquoise cushions of all sizes on the couch and on the thick gold carpet.

"Come," Chendor said, "we must meet now." He stood and helped Maashi to rise. He supported him as they crossed over to the encounter room looming a few yards away.

<*Talinda will follow. Talinda will obey,* > the screechy voice said.

Puzzled, Maashi followed, scanning the room with wide eyes.

They entered the encounter room decorated in the traditional black and white diamond pattern trimmed with gold. The diamond shapes, small and close together at one end, grew larger in the middle of the egg-shaped room and shrunk back at the other end. The same pattern continued throughout the floor, the walls, and the ceiling. Soft light originated only at one end of the enclosed room and illuminated the pattern above their heads.

They sat down, side by side, on the padded floor, which rippled with every little move. Chendor reclined and gently pulled down Maashi with him. He adjusted the size of the room by pressing controls hidden on the wall beside him. The walls moved closer, and the ceiling came down to rest a few inches above their heads.

Chendor smiled. "Much better, isn't it?"

Maashi didn't say anything. He found the close quarters unsettling. They were both naked and although that wasn't anything unusual, he was concerned Chendor would notice his galloping heartbeat and his erratic breathing. He couldn't shake a troubling feeling of dread. Being Sheffrou, encounter room meetings were an everyday occurrence but, since his kidnapping a sequence ago by the Krakoran, he experienced uncontrollable anxiety whenever he was alone in close quarters with a powerful Pure Color, Sawisha or Sheffrou.

<*Talinda shall obey or Talinda will be punished.* > The high-pitched voice echoed loud and clear in Maashi's mind.

He blinked. "Did you hear? The strange voice?"

"You're confused, Shonava. As you can see there is no one here besides me. Shall we begin?" Without waiting for an answer, Chendor's hands traveled to Maashi's head, shoulders, and chest, feeling every inch of skin and muscle. He nodded, signaling Maashi to do the same.

Maashi mimicked his movements. Chendor's flesh felt cushiony to the touch.

"You're overweight," he said, with a hint of surprise in his voice. In his whole life, he had never seen an overweight Chamranlina, and this one's size was formidable.

Chendor laughed amiably and his chest and belly laughed with him. "I enjoy food and I feed often and as much as I want, which I dare say isn't your case. You're thinner than a Fanella who has never been heavy with offspring."

At the mention of the word Fanella, Maashi's heart thumped in his abdomen. He lowered his eyes. He knew he was thin; feeding was difficult for him. The Krakoran had seen to that. Kidnapped over a year ago and rescued after five grueling months of torture, the enemy had provided just enough to survive and made every feeding a loathsome experience.

Maashi continued to palpate Chendor's gargantuan body as expected in a meeting. His hands felt a deep groove in his neck. It originated below his right ear and ran down his shoulder all the way across his back.

"This is a long and deep scar."

"I got that long ago, more than sixty sequences," said Chendor. "I don't think about it anymore."

"What happened?"

"I was traveling with my Chowlis and a few guards in the main tunnel connecting sector ten to sector seven after a great celebration in the Rashandomora cave. Our group was attacked by the Krakoran." Chendor stopped; his eyes lost their focus for a second. "One of them slammed his appendage on my neck and attempted to pull me away with it. My guards and Chowlis grabbed my legs to prevent the creature from kidnapping me. After what felt like a long struggle, the Krakoran let go, but part of my skull was crushed, and my shoulder and back were burned to the bone. I was unconscious for weeks. The two Sheffrous who cared for me thought I wouldn't survive. It took many sequences before I regained the use of my right arm."

"Sixty sequences ago," Maashi said, his voice low. "The attack occurred before the Rebellion. I remember learning about this."

<His magnificence the Great Hunter will see Talinda now, > the high-pitched voice said. *<Talinda must not speak. >*

Maashi's hands shook. "Did you hear? The high-pitched voice?"

Chendor paused. "I don't hear anything. Are you all right, Shonava?"

"I don't know." Maashi froze. *The voice originated from his own mind.*

Chendor squeezed Maashi's hand. "Several months passed before I recovered from the attack. Since then, I've been living thirty levels below the surface and have never traveled back in the tunnels. I've devoted my life to the healing of injured Sawishas and Sheffrous, like you." He caressed Maashi's cheek. "Shall we continue our meeting?"

He palpated Maashi's right flank. His fingers rested on a small swollen area. "It appears you've been cut by something. It's slightly inflamed but should heal well." He felt Maashi's legs and chuckled. "Long thin legs, small hips, large schloppies." With a wide grin he said, "I hope you aren't offended by my comments."

"I accept your comments in the spirit in which they're offered," Maashi said. "No offense is taken."

Chendor pushed controls on the wall and a yellow pill appeared on the floor beside him. "Take this," he said.

Maashi frowned. "I... don't take chuckies."

Chendor said gently, "Shapinka, I don't use mind-altering substances. This is something to increase your energy level."

Maashi sighed in resignation and extended his hand.

Chendor shook his head to one side. "Open your mouth and I will put it on your tongue." He put the pill between his lips and pressed his mouth on Maashi's.

<*Talinda must eat.* > Maashi swallowed the pill and frowned. A chill of unease ran up his spine. A rush of lingering fear ran through him.

"Thank you, Shonava," Chendor said.

Maashi completed his part of the meeting. Chendor's body: immense abdomen, round hips, full buttocks, and wide muscular thighs elicited a thin smile. He had never been in the arms of a Chamranlina like this one.

Chendor laughed at Maashi's surprised expression. "I see you enjoyed our brief meeting."

"I meant no disrespect with my smile." Maashi felt an immense weariness come over him.

Chendor stroked Maashi's arms. He clicked soothingly and caressed his cheek. "I know what you need," he said in a mellow voice. He bent his head sideways and kissed Maashi's neck.

Maashi sensed the fear intensify in the pit of his stomach. "I'm exhausted. I should leave and get some sleep."

His own voice rang in his head. *Let me go. Set me free.* He remembered pleading with those same words. Flashes from a not-so-distant past bounced in his mind. The thoughts were part of strange memories set loose to torment him. In his vulnerable state, he preferred to avoid an encounter with Chendor. Sheffrous 6 were powerful, dominating, and overbearing. They possessed immense physical and mental strength and could discipline the strongest Sawishas: Purples and Blacks.

Maashi's saweya was so low he feared Chendor would take advantage of him. Although rare, the risk of attack and rape by rogue males or mature Pure Colors was real in a world where contact with females was impossible. The Silver Guards' role comprised protecting Sheffrous from Krakoran and also aggressive males. Sadly, Maashi had been subject to the odious experience twice. The memory was etched forever in his mind. His mentor's rules were explicit: never let your guard down, always remain in control unless accompanied by your Chowlis.

He had to find an excuse to leave.

"Shapinka," Chendor said, interrupting his thoughts, "when was the last time you had an encounter with a Sawisha?"

Maashi struggled to find a suitable answer. A healthy Sheffrou 8 had encounters at least weekly, if not daily, with Sawishas. Their libido surpassed every other Sawisha or Sheffrou's libido. He couldn't admit his last encounter was weeks ago without covering himself with shame.

Chendor's questioning eyes stared into his. "Your answer should be instantaneous," he said in a soft voice. "That you have to ponder what to say is evidence of your lack of a suitable partner. I've been informed by the Elders that since you've been rescued from the Krakoran…"

At the mention of his rescue, Maashi turned his head away. Every time his kidnapping was mentioned, he couldn't breathe as if his chest was being encased in lead. In the last few weeks, his fear and confusion had increased. There had been mention of the Krakoran every day since the attacks the night of the Great Eclipse Celebration four weeks ago. His close friend Tomisho had been taken and Maashi couldn't bear to be reminded of that fact. He blinked and struggled to take in a long breath.

In his unstable state, shadows reappeared in his mind. They filled his brain and obscured his thoughts. His subconscious was protecting him from something terrifying, so terrifying it had been stowed away in an unreachable corner of his psyche.

Chendor hugged him closer. He whispered in his ear, "I know your kidnapping occurred over one sequence ago. I also know that Sheffrous who have been rescued have no recollection of the torture they were submitted to. Over time, flashes of their ordeal cross the mind's protective barriers. This happens at the end of the first sequence and may explain some of your recent behavior."

Maashi's memory of the events of the last few days was invisible to him, as if it lay hidden at the bottom of a pool so deep, so black it was impossible to retrieve them. "What behavior?"

"You left your quarters unexpectedly last week. Your Chowlis searched everywhere to find you. You were recovered on the fourth day, lying in the Goolalong Fields, close to death." Chendor's tone of voice left no doubt about the seriousness of the situation. "Only now, after seven days, you have regained consciousness, but your memory is gone. We still have no clue about the events that triggered your sudden escapade and what happened after that."

Chendor's words confirmed what Maashi suspected. Something of grave importance had prompted him to leave the protection of his quarters to wander in the tunnels. Then, something crucial, perhaps a life-altering event, led him to flee to the surface. He had to find out what it was. To succeed, he had to be alone; only then would he sort out the truth his mind was hiding from his conscious thoughts.

"Forgive me, Chendor, you've been very kind, but I must leave."

Let me go. He remembered his own pleading voice saying that. When did he say this?

"Shapinka, you may rest and sleep all you want after our encounter is completed. There is no reason to fear me. I am thorough but gentle."

Maashi swallowed his saliva with difficulty. He stared at the ripples on the floor to conceal his growing sense of panic.

Chendor clicked soft clicks, as if enticing a young Fanella, and kissed Maashi's face.

"Show me your tongue Chumpi. Show me your tongue," insisted Chendor.

<*Talinda will obey,* > said the high-pitched voice, <*or Talinda will be punished.* >

Who said that? Where did he hear this voice before? Who is Talinda? Frustrated, Maashi shook his head in annoyance.

Undeterred, Chendor took Maashi's face in his hands and his moist lips touched his cheeks, his forehead, and the edge of his jaw. Maashi closed his eyes as a wave of pleasure washed over him. He became alive under Chendor's gentle kisses. Inhaling a long breath of Chendor's spellbinding holoma, his pain gradually subsided. He was grateful for the support of this experienced Sheffrou who knew what he hungered for: great amounts of love and affection. Pleasure was as crucial to his recovery as water was to a thirsty Shoshan.

One by one Chendor's kisses weakened Maashi's resistance. He was so painfully weak and famished. An encounter would infuse a tremendous amount of energy into him. Overcome by desire, unable to resist the Tousanou, he slowly stretched his royal blue tongue out.

Chendor licked it with his own midnight blue tongue. Warm currents of pleasure grew and flowed onward in Maashi's body. Delight overpowered him, and he couldn't refrain from whimpering like a young Sheffrou. Alarmed by his whimpers, acceptable only in his Chowlis' presence, he put his hands on Chendor's shoulders and tried to push him away.

To his consternation, Maashi was no match at all against the powerful Tousanou.

"Have no fear, Shapinka." Chendor lifted Maashi's face upward with his middle finger and gazed into his eyes. "My sole purpose is to help you. Don't be ashamed of your whimpers. They confirm I'm fulfilling your needs." He carefully wrapped his arms around Maashi and held him closer. "I know," he said, "that some mentors train their charges harshly and punish them when they whimper. I've met your mentor, the purple Kokin, and I'm aware of his reputation."

Maashi pulled his tongue back in his mouth and fought to stay in control. "I can't." He blinked tears away. Anger and a sense of purpose arose in him and repressed some of his fear. "I can't possibly have an encounter with you at this time." He stopped. "There is something I must do. Something I must find. Something of great importance."

Chendor caressed Maashi's jaw and said in his unique baritone voice, "You're so pale, Shapinka. You can't succeed in whatever you're trying to accomplish without energy. Let me kiss you until your pleasure overflows. You will feel relief from the hunger and pain I sense in you."

<*Talinda will obey,* > the high-pitched voice commanded.

Chendor bent his head and licked Maashi's chest until his quatay swelled and glowed like a precious jewel under the orange sun. Maashi moaned with pleasure and his fragrant holoma filled the tiny room. He held his tongue in to prevent any sound.

Chendor pulled away and clicked soothing clicks. "Breathe, Shapinka. Don't be afraid," he said reassuringly. "I'll wait until you're ready to continue."

Maashi rested his head against the other's shoulder. He took a long breath in and exhaled slowly, delight spreading in his mind.

Chendor stroked the nape of his neck. "You must understand Shonava. I'm here for you. I won't hurt you, not under any circumstances." With a slow rocking movement, Chendor rubbed his chest on Maashi and held him in a tight embrace.

Maashi's pleasure intensified, and warmth spread to every part of his body. He fought it for a moment, but soon the wave of his climax washed over him and filled his every cell. His skin shone a pale blue in the subdued light of the encounter room, but as his bliss intensified and overcame his last shred of resistance, he glowed a deep iridescent blue, as brilliant as Chitina's night sky before the dawn of a new day.

At last, Maashi lay perfectly still, under the protection of Chendor's embrace. He heard the Tousanou's deep breathing and his powerful holoma saturated the surrounding air, a sign he was also climaxing. Life-giving energy gushed between the two Sheffrous. Maashi imbibed the other's saweya like the dry soil of Chitina soaked up the morning dew. With eyes closed, his mind soared and expanded like a great winged beast. The shadows were ripped apart and the dark clouds drifted so that bits and pieces of hidden memories became visible.

Two eyes stared into nothingness in a young face as pale as moonlight.

Maashi gasped.

"What was that?" said Chendor.

"You saw it too?"

"Yes. As clearly as I see you. Who is it?"

"I don't know," said Maashi as his skin color changed, becoming as pale as alabaster. "I can't remember." Fear and dread pierced Maashi's heart.

Chapter 10

Maashi's methane poisoning stayed foremost in Tamara's mind. She even forgot to inquire about the humans and when she would meet them. She fought to contain the increasing feeling of annoyance that swelled in her as she followed the group deeper into the glowing world of Chendor. This new realm, thirty levels below ground, encompassed an endless series of tunnels and long hallways. Sometimes the ceiling was so low, barely six feet, that it forced the Chami guide to bend down to pass through them. Unlike the tunnels in Maashi's compound, the ones here glowed and shone like the Aurora Borealis on Earth. The guard explained their movements roused the plentiful fluorescent algae growing on the rock walls of this sector. The excited algae emitted flashes of different wavelengths and produced an intense multicolor glow.

With little sleep in the past week, Tamara fought an unusual fatigue. She was short of breath and wheezed at the slightest effort. She had developed an annoying cough and it worsened as the group progressed, passing beside several deep pools, small waterfalls, and fountains. There seemed to be a water element at every turn, and the high level of humidity was exacerbating her unease. Since Maashi's disappearance, she had worried day and night about his fate and her health had suffered; her decreased appetite and poor sleep had taken a toll.

No one knew why Maashi had left in the middle of the night without telling anyone, not even his close friends or Chowlis. A twinge of guilt hung in her mind. Was she the one who had started this sudden behavior with all her talk of a potential traitor? If she had precipitated his disappearance and something awful had happened... The thought gave her palpitations. She shuddered at the memory of the first few days after he went missing; the possibility of capture by the enemy had terrified her.

When they found him in the Goolalong Fields with their dangerous methane pockets, she thought the worst was over only to find it was the beginning of a new ordeal. The Sheffrou was sent thirty levels underground to a special healer, and she knew little about his condition. Her physician reflexes kicked in and she imagined all kinds of scenarios with a poor outcome. She questioned Maashi's Chowlis daily to find out if his health was improving, but they were reluctant to give her any news other than tell her he was still semi-comatose. This made her feel helpless and angry. Only after a long while did Rahma inform her that the Sheffrou was awake and speaking coherently for the first time.

The group arrived in an area which she assumed would be her quarters. The single room, smaller than her previous quarters, with bare walls and low lighting contained one wide backless couch big enough to sit three Chamis, a few reclining chairs and a potted plant with burgundy leaves and dainty pink flowers. In one corner stood the ubiquitous fountain. Thankfully, it was a paltry affair with just a trickle of water which puddled in a basin no larger than a kitchen sink. The water room however, at the end of a short corridor, included a large shower, which they called a choma, with fine jets of water adjustable for any type of stream and intensity and a bathtub big enough for three Chamis to soak comfortably.

She plopped on the couch as soon as she walked in and removed her nateet, the hooded top she wore when traveling. Her body was sore all over and her right foot ached. She couldn't remember if she had twisted her ankle and when, but she was eager to lie down and prop it up.

A Chami of the same height as Maashi but as big as a sumo wrestler entered by a secondary door and stood in the shadows at the other end of the room.

"Welcome to my sector, Tamara," he said with a warm baritone voice. "I am Tousanou Chendor."

"Thank you," she said, straightening up. "I am pleased to see you." She paused, caught her breath, and continued, "I would be grateful if you could give me some news about Maashi. I have traveled a long way to see him." A bout of coughing interrupted her. "I hope to meet him soon."

"Little Fanella," he said, stepping forward, "the Sheffrou is recovering from his exposure to the methane poison and cannot see you today. We are most pleased by your presence and will strive to make your stay as comfortable as possible." He sat on the edge of a chair.

All this arduous traveling to see Maashi and now they refused to let her see him.

Tamara blinked, lowered her head, and fought off the tears that threatened to run down her cheeks. She had been miserable these last few days both physically and mentally.

What a contrast to her life on Earth where, as an Emergency Room physician, she often worked long hours under stressful conditions. That work environment had made her strong and resilient, but here on Chitina, stress, which had been the source of her strength on Earth, just made her weak. The more she pushed herself, the more she lost her inner strength. She feared Maashi's absence affected physically as well as mentally. Maashi had acknowledged and understood how Chitina's world affected her. He had decided her behavior was like a young Sheffrou and that explained her frequent startling outbursts and labile emotional state.

Chendor clicked something, and the guide exited through the other door. Chendor rose from his chair, came closer, and eased his enormous frame beside her on the couch.

She raised her head and scrutinized the Tousanou's wide chest. He wore a beige shirt open at the neck and revealing his quatay, the markings confirming he was Sawisha, part of the elite of Chamranlina society. She cleared her throat and asked, "How is Maashi? Is he improving?"

"His saweya is low," he said, "My Chowlis care for him night and day. Sometimes his mind is clear and other times dark thoughts which we cannot comprehend invade his mind, drain his energy, and break down his spirit."

The words frightened her. She breathed in brief spurts and fought to control a growing feeling of panic. How would she survive in this alien world if something happened to Maashi? She fisted her hands and said in a raspy voice full of anger, "Maashi told me never to go in the tunnels by myself because it was too dangerous and that's exactly what he did. The Krakoran could've taken him..." Her cough resumed, and it took several minutes for it to stop.

Chendor slid his left arm around her waist and drew her to him. His warmth was comforting. "The Sheffrou's health improves every day. He is stronger than he thinks, and I'm convinced he will heal. Patience, little female. I will send my first

Chowli Sateen to tend to your needs until the Sheffrou can see you."

He kissed the top of her head, and a long chubby finger caressed her cheek. He rose and the couch, relieved of the Sheffrou's formidable weight, regained its thickness with a sigh.

"It was a pleasure to see you. You should rest. I will come back later." He turned and left.

A new Chami strolled in. Taller than the Tousanou, with broad shoulders, wearing only a chemcha, their rubbery underwear, he settled on the closest chair and his light almond eyes watched her with a steady gaze.

"My name is Sateen," he said. "I will care for you during your stay. What do you require?"

Tamara cleared her throat. "I would like to drink something warm like broth or soup. Then I want to shower with warm water, not too hot, alone."

Within seconds, he produced a tall glass with an oval opening, like a lumi, filled with a warm liquid and offered it to her. It tasted like vegetable soup with a hint of salt. She drank it, stood up, and walked over to the water room. After undressing, she adjusted the water jets in the white marble shower, washed and rinsed off with cooler water, grunting from the effort required to perform the simple task.

Her mind raced out of control and brought horrid thoughts of Maashi fighting for his life. She would assess his condition herself when she would see him. Perhaps they had overlooked something. Perhaps she could help. Distracted, she hopped out of the water, forgetting the sore right foot, slipped, and yelped when it hit the wall.

Sateen rushed to her side. Flustered by her nakedness and the unfamiliar alien's proximity, she held back her tears and any curses she would have blurted out in normal circumstances. A small trickle of blood from a cut on her foot mixed with the water on the white marble floor.

"You are hurt," said Sateen. "Forgive me for not being fast enough to prevent your fall."

Sateen requested a long towel from the replicator, wrapped her in it, and lifted her in his arms as if she were a babe. He settled her on the couch, examined the injured foot, applied a white ointment on it, which she recognized as a disinfectant of some sort, and skillfully wrapped it in a bandage.

"You may lie down now and get some sleep. I will stay at your side."

Trembling from pain and fatigue, she mumbled a thank you. She reclined on the cushions and closed her eyes. *Maashi. Maashi. Where are you? I miss you.*

Sateen set a blanket over the towel, elevated her foot on a cushion, and settled his long frame alongside hers. Too exhausted to protest, she just sighed. After all, Sateen was only performing what was standard care for a Sheffrou; keep him warm, keep him safe, and never leave his side.

In the glow of the evening lights, Tamara waited for Chendor's arrival. After a two-hour nap, she had spent the day resting and recuperating and now she sat on a chair, her non-injured foot tapping furiously on the floor. She knew little about the Tousanou and what his qualifications were as a healer. Was he certified? A psychiatrist? Both? Was he performing therapy sessions with Maashi or giving him medication? She planned to ask questions but knew Chamis gave answers when ready and divulged information only when they so desired.

Sateen had not left the room and lay sprawled on the couch, studying a new diagram on a virtual computer. He had proposed to swim with her in one of the many pools or to walk around in the adjacent halls, but she was too fatigued to do any activity and instead used the time to write in her diary on her personal pad. She often wrote to Allison, her daughter, as if she had become her confidante. Tamara shared her private thoughts and feelings with her, and this kept her sane in a world where not everything made sense.

Sateen shut his diagram, rose in one smooth movement, and went to the door. He opened it and let Chendor in. They clicked at each other, and Sateen sauntered out a moment later.

Tamara rose from her chair to greet the Tousanou. "Good evening," she said.

"Good day to you, Tamara. I hope you are rested," Chendor said in his rich voice. With a flick of the wrist, he transformed the couch into a high back loveseat that could comfortably sit two Chamis, ample size for the two of them. "Please," he extended his arm toward it, "join me for a tasting."

Tamara sat on the left. She held back a smile at the sudden transformation of the couch. Down here as well as up in Maashi's quarters, the Chamis lived in caves changed at will by holograms. Thus, the colors of the walls, flooring, and furniture could be adjusted to fit the needs of the moment.

Chendor settled beside her, and his impressive physique filled the entire space. "How is your foot? Sateen explained you fell in the choma."

"It feels much better. I guess I'm a little clumsy."

"Please let me know if you feel pain."

Tamara nodded.

He bent down with difficulty because of his immense size to reach a set of controls on the floor. He laughed and said, "I'll make a request to move those up on the wall."

A sweet and fragrant odor surrounded him and filled her with longing. Although familiar, Tamara could not recall where she had smelled it before. All Sawishas and Sheffrous, when mature, secreted a pheromone they called holoma. This helped the males attract the females during the mating process.

Tamara's gaze appraised the Tousanou, an old physician reflex, as he bent over. She followed the deep scar on his right cheek, stretching along his neck and extending down his shoulder. What could have caused this extensive scarring? It puzzled her because her own observations of Maashi's fast healing process had shown Chamis healed extremely well. This must have been a major injury.

Chendor straightened back up. A table appeared in front of them. Seconds later, Tamara heard a light *ping*. The wall opposite them opened and an impressive multilevel tray loaded with food slid forth. Chendor rose easily and brought it over and set it on the table. He looked at her with a twinkle in his eye. "Are you hungry?"

She stirred in her seat and said, "Yes, but this is a lot of food." She surveyed the multiple oval bowls filled with sauces, the green jelly-like mound, many types of nuts and fruits, a pink pudding, triangular crackers, and flat bread.

"I didn't know your preferences, so I ordered a large variety. I'm sure there are a few items you haven't tasted before and that you might want to try." He squinted at her.

She smiled back at him. Her many questions could wait until she finished eating.

"Here." He took a cracker and dipped it in a promising red sauce and offered it to her. "Try this one."

Tamara took the cracker and tasted it. Its sweet and tangy taste reminded her of Mexican salsa. Some of it dripped along her jaw, and Chendor chuckled as he handed her a small piece of cloth to wipe her chin.

"There you are. Now try this one." Another cracker went her way, this one with a blob of pink cream on it.

"Mm, good," said Tamara as she savored the salty crab taste.

"Help yourself. Sample anything you want."

He spread a generous portion of a creamy pudding on a piece of flat bread and took a bite.

Tamara watched him eat, fascinated. Chamis ate in private, never in front of each other. It was considered impolite to do so. This one gulped down his food with obvious delight and did not seem to mind her presence at all.

"Take some more. There is plenty to choose from." He watched her take a cracker and dip it in another sauce. He put two fingers on her wrist and directed it to a second sauce. "Try some of this with it," he said, with a mocking look in his eye.

She took a bite. The cream melted in her mouth like mousse. "Mm. I like it." Another bite and she salivated so much she drooled.

"Tasty, isn't it?" He extended his long middle finger and caught the drool as she lifted the napkin to wipe it off. He brought his finger to his mouth and tasted the sauce mixed with her saliva.

A warm feeling crept up Tamara's neck. Chamis communicated by exchanging saliva. Chendor was attempting to learn more about her. The sampling and tasting continued for some time. Chendor acted like a considerate host. Tamara's stomach filled. She relaxed and enjoyed the meal.

He ingested a good size portion of most of the food and clicked with pleasure as he did. He got a toughi, her favorite fruit, cut it in bite-size pieces, placed one on the tip of his finger, and brought it to her lips. "Take one. You will enjoy it."

She hesitated, then gently took it from him with her lips.

"Do you like it?"

"Yes, toughis are my favorite."

He then sliced a good portion off the green jelly mound, which wobbled wildly but did not fall off the plate. He glanced at her sideways. "How about some loola?"

She took one glance at the green color and wrinkled her nose. "I'm not sure about the green."

He laughed a clear musical laugh, which echoed in the room. "You don't like Greens or just the green loola?"

His joviality was contagious. She giggled and said, "just this one." This enticed her to ask the first question that popped in her head. "What color are you, sir?"

He reached for her hand, bent his head down, and grazed the surface with his lips.

Tamara watched him, mesmerized, and did not remove her hand. She was lightheaded, like someone who had drunk a little too much champagne. Was it the holoma, the food, or both?

He stretched out a dark blue tongue and licked the back of her hand. His gaze met hers. "It's quite acceptable if you don't care for green."

"Oh, you're Sheffrou," she said, suppressing a burp. She thought about her coughing, which had stopped since he walked in the room same as what happened when she was around Maashi. Was it a side effect of their closeness? Was it something they had in common?

His light aroma intensified and swirled around them. She blinked when she identified the odor as the characteristic perfume of the tea olive tree which grew plentiful around her neighborhood on Earth. The memory overpowered her as she inhaled the fruity fragrance, and an irresistible urge to rest her head against his chest overtook her.

"Tamara," he whispered, "may I hold you?"

She looked up in his striking violet eyes and saw only gentleness. The memorable night of the Great Eclipse Celebration when the big Purple had tried to kiss her flashed in her mind. Should she let him hold her? Her inhibitions failing, she bowed her head to show she agreed.

Chendor put an arm around her waist and another under her thighs and lifted her onto his lap. He kissed her forehead and skillful fingers caressed and massaged the nape of her neck. He reached for the pink cream, dipped a finger in it, and offered it to her. She hesitated.

"It's just a little cream."

She let him slide it in her mouth and licked the cream off his finger.

He pulled it out and sucked his finger slowly, savoring the remaining cream mixed with her saliva. With one arm, he loosened his shirt, exposing his chest, and positioned her close to his breast. He reached for a tall glass and offered her some choun.

Tamara licked her lips and sensed a warm blush reaching her neck and cheeks. She had been so lonely these last few weeks. She longed for Maashi's welcoming arms and his mind-altering kisses. The thought made her dizzy with desire. She was certain Maashi would encourage her to let go of her hesitation and feel pleasure. The will to resist faded away as she pressed her lips together and kissed Chendor's quatay.

The Sheffrou glowed, his smooth silky skin changed to a pale blue. He lifted her higher and, with his fingers on her cheek, brought his mouth against hers and kissed her once, twice.

Tamara inhaled deeply, filled her lungs with his glorious fragrance, and her body shivered with pleasure.

"You are indeed Sheffrou. A most special one." Chendor caressed her cheek and kept his head so close to hers she felt his breath on her neck. "May I kiss you again?"

Tamara knew what he meant. One more kiss and she would melt into his arms. That's all she wanted. She rubbed her cheek on his and he kissed her. She opened her lips and his tongue slid in. What a lovely feeling… Her mind danced with pleasure. She inhaled a long breath, arched her back, and savored her sudden climax. The intensity surprised her. She heard his words as if in a dream state. "There. There. That's much better."

He hugged her for a few minutes, waited until she relaxed completely, then transferred her in Sateen's arms who had just entered the room.

He said in a soft voice close to her ear, "No worries. No worries."

Tamara rested quietly. Her coughing was gone. She wondered about what she had observed and felt. Chendor was a Tousanou, a Sheffrou 6, and she had tasted his immense power. Maashi had spent days in his care. Two Sheffrous together. One much stronger than the other. *Was Maashi well? Was he safe?*

Chapter 11

While Maashi recuperated under Chendor's care, Chari spent time in his newly assigned quarters and accessed the complete records of the simultaneous attacks on the Sheffrous the night of the Great Eclipse. He reviewed every detail. He agreed with Maashi's theory that the attacks appeared to have a connection. They had occurred at the same time after the celebration, only groups with at least one Sheffrou 8 were targeted, and they all happened in the tunnels leading back to the compounds. Chari understood the Krakoran launched surprise attacks when the Chamranlinas least expected them, but the scope and preparation required for this level of coordination was beyond anything they had dealt with before. It was a significant finding.

Chari's concerns these past few months rested on the death of the young offspring. The two separate incidents developed over the same period. Without more information, he couldn't tell if there was a link between the attacks and the plague affecting the little Fanellas. The enemy had never targeted offspring before, but instinct told him to keep an open mind. With Sheffrou Maashi incapacitated, there wasn't anyone with the skill and capability of taking his place. Considering Sheffrou numbers were dwindling and with this horrible plague affecting the offspring, the Chamranlina species itself was at stake. Chari snorted. The decision was easy. He vowed to pursue Maashi's quest. He wouldn't rest until he solved both enigmas.

He knew what he had to do. He hurried out in the tunnels and bumped into Chopa who grabbed him and pushed him against the wall. His brow was dark as he yelled, "Where are you going? When can I see the Sheffrou?"

Chari shot him a contemptuous stare. "You have a most unpleasant temper, Chowli." He poked Chopa in the chest with his long, black middle finger. "It's going to bring you a lot of trouble."

"Answer me," hissed Chopa.

Chari said, "I took care of him. He's in a safe place."

"I saw the Silver Guards take him away. They took the elevators down. Where is he? When can I see him?"

"The Elders sent him under the care of a Tousanou, a healer called Chendor. You won't be allowed to see him for a few days. Now, get out of my way, Chowli. I have important things to do."

"You got rid of the Sheffrou with some devious ruse," Chopa snarled, "and now you want to continue to deceive us and pursue your own secret goals. Beware Chari, I will be your shadow wherever you go."

Chari stared at Chopa and ran his fingers through his raven hair. "You don't trust me, and I don't have time to explain things." Chari paused. The young spotted brown might be useful after all. He bent his head sideways and said, "We have little time. If you can travel fast, I'll let you accompany me."

"My first duty is to the Sheffrou. You won't lose me so easily."

"Let's go then." Chari took off in the tunnel and added, "I must question Khon, in charge of internal security. I checked the records, and he was the one commanding the guards the night of the Great Eclipse Celebration."

Chopa kept an easy pace at the other's side. "Why do you want to see him?"

Chari looked back once before sprinting ahead. "Follow me and you'll find out."

They zoomed through the tunnels for only twenty minutes, eliciting some curious stares from the few who were strolling about. They reached the security headquarters: black walls, steel gray floors, long thin desks and virtual screens completed the setup of the main receiving room. Three guards with silver sashes over their black uniforms sat on straight high-back chairs, each one with a virtual image at eye level.

Chari addressed the first guard with a commanding voice. "I am Chari Varian, leader of the Outcasts. I want to speak to your chief of security."

The first guard took one good look at Chari and leaped off his chair. "Chari Varian." He appraised Chari from his faded purple sash to his thick-soled black boots. "This is a rare occasion. I never thought I would see you here, in headquarters."

Chari ignored the guard's comment and said, "Where is Khon? I need to talk to him."

The guard stood unfazed, hands on his hips. "What do you want from him?"

"I have no business with you. I came here for Khon."

The guard turned his head towards another guard who nodded without taking his eyes off his screen. "He's in tunnel number 4 down east side. If you hurry, you might catch him before he leaves for the eastern dome."

Chari nodded and turned to leave.

"Next time you come," the guard sneered, "Stay a while. We can chat about old crimes."

Chari turned and barreled down to tunnel 4. He pulled out his scanner from his belt. It easily located five Chamis straight ahead.

"He's close to here," Chari said and sprinted. Chopa stayed right behind.

Khon, tall and slim, stood out from the others. He watched Chari saunter over. "Outcast," he said, his face expressionless, "what brings you here?"

Chari stopped a couple of feet away from him.

Khon tilted his head. "It's been a while. You haven't changed."

"I want information," Chari said in a deliberate voice, "on the attacks that occurred the night of the Great Eclipse."

Khon stared back at the Ghouli Ghouli. "The official records are available. I have nothing to add."

"I've read the reports and I have only one question," said Chari, his black eyes watching the other guards. "Why did you change the number of guards in the tunnels for the parties that included Sheffrou 8 right before the celebration? Who else knew about the changes? I checked the data and only Sheffrou Maashi was adequately covered."

Khon straightened his shoulders. His face turned gray with anger. "Do you think I wasn't aware of that?" He took a step and faced Chari. "I received orders from Lado, Sheffrou Maashi's Chowli, who had express orders from the Elders, to protect that Sheffrou at all costs."

Chari hissed. "That decision left the other Sheffrous vulnerable."

"I argued with Lado that all Sheffrous needed equal protection, but he refused to change the order."

"Idiot. How could you put all those Sheffrous at risk?" Chari yelled, "your role as chief of security is to protect all of them, not to obey the orders of an assigned Chowli."

The other guards, busy with their evaluation of the parameter of the tunnels, discarded their scanners, came, and stood by Khon.

Chopa stepped closer to Chari's side and made a low hissing sound.

"The Elders know nothing about security." Chari spat on the ground in disgust. "Your lack of judgement put all their lives at risk." He muttered to Chopa, "He's just a pawn. Not worth my time. Let's go."

Chari and the young Chopa located Lado through the Central Databank. Under direct orders from the Council of Elders, they had assigned Lado a new function. His principal duty was to assist the Sawishas, the Pure Colors lords, who controlled the social and political life of their sectors. They found him in a small sector of compound 3 to the east of the Central Compound.

Lado received them in a lavishly furnished receiving room connected to an even greater room. On the walls hung gold crests of prominent Sawishas. Multiple reclining lounge chairs, each with its collection of decorative cushions and pillows, were positioned to favor gatherings of a great number of guests. In every corner, brightly colored water bubbled in multitiered fountains with deep basins. Embroidered throws covered the wide chairs to ensure maximum comfort for their occupants.

Lado received them dressed in silky light gray clothing adorned with a pattern of olive-colored leaves. "Please take a seat," he said. "Would you like a glass of flavored water?"

The two sat but declined the drink with a simple hand gesture.

Chari abhorred opulence. He and his followers had lived for many sequences under challenging conditions and often lacked necessities. He considered excessive luxury an insult.

"We aren't here for a social visit," he stated dryly. "We're searching for answers. What happened right before the attacks on the night of the celebration?"

Lado's face showed no emotion. "Security has completed the inquiry. What more do you want?"

"I will be brief." Chari's lips moved as if he was chewing something, but his lips were bare. "You have stated that the Council of Elders ordered to increase the protection of Sheffrou Maashi's group. Who was the Elder among the fourteen who gave you that order?"

"The Elders work together as one."

Chopa asked him directly. "There is always a leader who pushes the others to follow a course of action. Who was he?"

"I don't know."

Chari spoke in a voice filled with bitterness, "Who did you speak with? Who transmitted the order?"

"I am not at liberty of divulging this. Only a few chosen are privy to that information." Lado rose and took a few steps towards the door. "Have a good day."

Chari sprung out of his chair as if something had stung him. He planted his feet on the plush carpet and fisted his hands.

"Pretend we're part of the chosen few, unless you want us to make an official complaint and have the authorities reopen the case. That night was disastrous for the Sheffrous."

Lado stood expressionless. He stared down at Chari and said in a flat voice. "As you know, you can't easily challenge decisions made by the Council."

"I can assure you," Chari said in an even voice, "we have enough evidence to put you in a most unfavorable position unless you give us that information."

"Of course," Chopa stood and added, "we will be discreet about our source."

Lado's brow blackened. "I don't like threats," he said, "you're mistaken if you think you can intimidate me."

Chari growled. Chopa raised his arm to silence him and said, "Do you know that Sheffrou Maashi was so distressed by the attacks on the Sheffrous that he went on a quest to find a traitor and almost lost his life in the Goolalong Fields?"

Lado's face paled. He swore between his breath, "What?"

"We found him," Chari said, glancing sideways at Chopa, "close to death. He is fighting for his life as we speak."

"The information we seek," added Chopa in a sad voice, "is the one Sheffrou Maashi was trying to find."

Lado lowered his head. "I have the utmost respect for Sheffrou Maashi. I sincerely hope he will heal." He wrung his hands and exhaled a long breath. "All I know is I received orders from Shonava Benshimu Hellowina, the Sawisha in charge of the seventh sector. I think other Sawishas intervened to sway the Elders when they rendered their final decision."

"Thank you," said Chopa.

Lado nodded sideways. His lips were tight, his hands clasped together.

"Sheffrou Maashi is under the care of a Tousanou called Chendor. I can keep you updated on his progress if you wish," said Chopa.

Lado nodded. "Please do."

They left without another word.

"I will contact Shonava Benshimu's first Chowli to schedule a talk and see what we can find," said Chari. On their way back, Chari glanced at Chopa. "I'll keep you informed."

Chapter 12

A stocky guard sporting a short, thin gray and green sash escorted Tamara through the hallways of Chendor's sector. This was the first time Tamara had seen this combination of a light green shirt with short sleeves and navy-blue pants for a uniform. Usually, only Sheffrous wore blue. They reached a two-panel door that seemed built to withstand a formidable blow. Tamara waited as the guard took out of his belt a square-shaped device with engravings on one side and pressed it against the same engraving on the left panel. The door slid open.

"Why is Sheffrou Maashi in an area guarded like a fortress?" said Tamara.

"For his protection," the guard said, "injured or ill Sheffrous are vulnerable, and we must keep them safe. Please hold my hand and do not touch anything." He took her hand firmly in his.

"Please step through now."

They proceeded through three more doors and finally walked into an encounter room, about ten Chami paces wide and twenty paces long. The walls were decorated with waves of multiple shades of blue and the thick carpet was the color of sand.

Out of the corner of her eye, Tamara saw a lone Chami sitting on a couch at the other end of the room. She immediately recognized Chendor. His gigantic size made him impossible to miss.

"Good afternoon, Tamara," said Chendor. "It is a pleasure to see you. You may sit wherever you wish."

"Thank you," she said. The guard took his position by the door. He stood with shoulders held back and hands hooked on his belt, his feet spread two feet apart. She settled on a couch a few feet away from Chendor.

"I'm eager to see Sheffrou Maashi," she said. "I've been told he is not well." She hoped Chendor didn't notice the slight tremolo in her voice. Maashi's health had been foremost in her thoughts ever since she moved into Chendor's sector.

"His health is improving," Chendor said, turning to face her. The couch squeaked as he repositioned his impressive girth. "However, his needs are still great therefore I must ask you to avoid stressing him as much as possible."

"Of course." She wouldn't mention the attacks if that was what he meant. "Can I see him now? Is he available?"

"Yes," Chendor's face softened, and his scar faded. "Follow me."

He stood and led the way out and through a narrow hallway to a small archway. He bent and continued through a different section with a new set of doors.

Bewildered, Tamara shook her head. Such a complicated underground maze. Her heart thumped hard at the thought of finally seeing Maashi.

"You may enter here. His Chowli Chopa is with him."

Tamara walked in. The plush carpet colored with pink, cream, and chocolate, like Neapolitan ice cream made her grin despite her nervousness. The receiving room, the size of a modest conference room contained several couches set close to the walls. She saw Chopa first. He glanced in her direction and nodded sideways to welcome her. Beside him sat Maashi.

"Maashi," her voice faltered. The sight of the Sheffrou took her breath away. She ran to him and halted a few feet away. "Maashi," she whispered, her eyes filling with tears, "What happened?" His face looked different: hollow cheeks, angular jaw, thin brow, all the color of alabaster.

"Hello, Tamara," his gentle voice pulled her to him. "How are you?" He extended his arms, and she flew into his embrace.

"Oh Maashi. What did you do? You're so pale and thin." She touched his cheek and put her arms around his neck, kissed him, and hugged him tight. She felt his fingers in her hair and heard a long sigh.

Maashi circled her waist with one arm. He took her hand in his and kissed her fingers one by one. He touched her face and pressed his lips on her forehead.

"I missed you," he whispered. "So many things have happened in the short time we were apart." He stopped and his brow darkened. "I remember some things and others I can't remember."

"The details will come back to you. Now or later. The important thing is you're alive and you must focus on healing."

Maashi's face brightened in a little smile. "You sound like a physician."

"And you behaved like a naughty young Sheffrou."

"Naughty?" Maashi pressed his lips together and tilted his head in mockery. His grin reminded her of the Maashi she knew. He turned to Chopa. "What do you think?"

"Shonava, what I think is not important."

"Chopa, you're my Chowli. I want to know what you think."

Tamara answered for him. "He would say you look sick and it's all your fault."

"Tamara," Chopa said, "I cannot be disrespectful."

"I heard," said Tamara, turning to face Chopa, "that you were the one who found him with the Ghouli Ghouli Chari."

"Now, that Ghouli Ghouli," stated Chopa with a solemn expression, "is one disrespectful Chami."

"The guy has his faults, I'll admit that," said Tamara, "but he found Maashi and saved him and that makes him a good guy."

Maashi made an approving sound. "Are you an expert on Chamis now?"

"Well," she traced Maashi's jaw with her finger, "I may not be an expert on Chamis, but I know a thing or two about Sheffrous." She planted a kiss on Maashi's chest.

Maashi's expression softened. "Then perhaps you know you're playing with fire, as you like to say." He lifted her head and gave her a long, gentle kiss.

The pleasure warmed Tamara, and she let it seep through her body. She rested her head against his cheek then kissed him back. Her heart skipped a beat. She pulled away from him in alarm. Instead of his usual sweet caramel taste, he tasted like clay, and she sensed a dark, threatening presence. She stared at Maashi whose expression had abruptly frozen. She cried out, "What was that?"

"Sir?" said Chopa. "Is there something wrong?"

Maashi blinked. "I feel like the icy hand of death touched me."

"Should we call Chendor?" Said Tamara.

Maashi jumped off his seat and tightened his grip around Tamara. "Stay away," he snarled at the couch across from him. He clicked and hissed at something they couldn't see.

Chopa approached him and said in a soothing voice, "Shonava, there is no one else here. There is no threat." He discreetly pressed on his left wrist band.

Maashi reeled back and spit in anger. "You will not touch this one."

Tamara said, keeping her voice as calm as she could, "Maashi, put me down. Please, just set me down."

Maashi stepped away from the couch. "Don't be frightened. I won't let it take you."

Seconds later, the door slid open and Chendor stepped in with a guard.

"Shonava," Chendor said, then continued in the Chami language.

Maashi turned and his expression softened when he saw Chendor. In one quick stride, the big Sheffrou came to his side and caressed the nape of his neck. "It's all right, Maashi. It's gone."

Maashi relaxed his grip on Tamara and Chopa immediately guided her out of the room.

With eyes wide, he said, "Are you all right?"

Tamara's heart raced in her chest. "What was that? What happened?"

"The Sheffrou was hallucinating. The Tousanou said he witnessed a few instances of auditory and visual hallucinations. He thought the episodes were infrequent and harmless and they were decreasing."

Tamara shook her head. "This is not good. Maashi may have suffered some brain damage with the exposure to methane. Did Chendor mention anything else?"

"Sheffrou Chendor mentioned the Sheffrou is haunted by a vision: a youthful face with two glowing eyes. He is quite distressed by the vision and Sheffrou Chendor can't figure out what it represents."

They glanced at each other, and Tamara muttered under her breath, "His condition is worse than I thought. It might take a lot of time before he recovers." Her eyes filled with tears. She turned her head away to hide her consternation. Were these symptoms a temporary condition or did Maashi suffer permanent harm from the methane gas? *How long would it be before he recuperated?*

Chapter 13

Chari sat alone in one of the many rooms adjoining the main receiving room in Chendor's domain. He pulled a twig from the inner pocket of his shirt, sat on a high-back couch, and absentmindedly chewed on it.

He surveyed his surroundings; a large oval container set against the far wall was filled with artfully arranged flowering bushes. In a corner of the room, water trickled down a vertical glass sculpture imitating a huge tinqua bush. Chendor's domain inspired serenity and contemplation. It was as if everything here dispelled darkness and despair.

His thoughts traveled back to a time when he had been desperate to forget horrendous events. The twig moved between his lips then stopped.

He had served over sixty sequences ago as first Chowli to a Sheffrou 6 called Shanadou. His time as Chowli had ended abruptly when the Sheffrou and his entourage were ambushed by two Krakoran entities after a night of festivities at the Great Eclipse Celebration. They were returning to their quarters through the tunnels, in an area with no previous sightings of the enemy. The attack was etched in his memory. He had lingered behind to talk with a friend and had rejoined his group moments later only to be the first to witness the massacre that had taken place. Four guards had lost their lives in a desperate attempt to prevent the Krakoran's claws from snatching Shanadou. Two others had succeeded in preventing the kidnapping but paid a heavy price: one dead and one critically wounded while the Sheffrou suffered life-threatening injuries.

The guilt Chari felt from not being there when his Sheffrou needed him the most had followed him like a dark shadow since that night.

The Silver Guards later transported Shanadou to an undisclosed sector, and no one had seen him since then. Rumors said his injuries affected his mind, and he was confined for his own protection. Shanadou, a Sheffrou 6 in his prime mating years, never mated again. Two sequences later, the Rebellion started and then cascaded in a series of events which led to Chari's exile in the Burned Zone as leader of the Outcasts.

Chari never showed any interest in Sheffrous after that. Until now.

In the short time Chari had spent with him, Maashi had impressed the Ghouli Ghouli by his courage and his determination. He saw how he genuinely cared for his Sheffrou friends and was ready to go to extreme lengths to find the truth about the attacks they had endured. Maashi's unique charisma swayed Chari's heart. He could have ignored his qualities and stayed on as leader of the Burned Zone, but he sensed Maashi's motives were pure and felt compelled to cherish and protect him.

Chari ran his fingers through his rough raven hair. *He could become first Chowli once more.* He snorted out loud. The thought was both outrageous and tantalizing. He bit his twig, then his lips stilled, and he grinned.

Chari had to see Sheffrou Chendor. He had to know if Maashi's health was improving. He stood to leave. A light blinked on the wall by the door. He pulled the twig out of his mouth. He pressed on the light and the message appeared in bright blue in front of him. Sheffrou Chendor wanted to see him. Could he join him now in his receiving room?

Great timing. He answered, "Of course," and headed out to see Chendor.

>———<‹‹ ● ››>———<

The door to the receiving room was ajar. A deep baritone voice that sounded eerily like a voice he knew from a long time ago said, "Come in, Chari. Take a seat."

Chari walked into the dimly lit room. The walls were midnight blue except for the one opposite him, which was a gorgeous gold color. A hefty Chamranlina, slightly shorter than him, stood opposite that wall, his back to Chari, in front of a long thin table. He was busy pouring an emerald-green liquid in tall crystal clear lumis.

"I trust you still enjoy the same drink," said Chendor, "I had someone bring it especially for this occasion."

"Thank you for the drink. What are we celebrating?"

Chendor turned around. A pale luminescence outlined his head but kept his features hidden. "My Chowlis tell me you want to schedule a meeting with Sheffrou Maashi and might be interested in becoming his Chowli."

Chari bent his head sideways. Chendor's voice sounded so familiar it was uncanny. "I've given it some thought," he said. *How did his Chowlis find out? Who told them?*

"Maashi is a unique Sheffrou, one you encounter once or twice in a lifetime. I approve your choice."

Chari chuckled. "I'm glad you do."

"However," Chendor said, "there is an old tradition you must comply with when you want to become a Chowli." Holding a glass in each hand, he took a step forward. "Your former Sheffrou must release you from the vows you made." He handed a glass to Chari.

Chari took the glass. He stared at the overweight Sheffrou, standing two steps away from him. A deep scar carved the right side of his face and continued down his neck and right shoulder. His right arm was smaller than the other and twisted while the hand was fully functional and normal. Recognition flashed through his mind. He inhaled a long breath. "Shanadou? Is it you?"

"Changed, older, but it is I."

Chari stood still as stone. Without taking his eyes off Chendor, he said, "They told me you were dead, that you had become…" Chari's voice was icy cold. His eyes thinned and changed to a black darker than the dead of night.

Chendor acknowledged his words with a slight nod.

"So many sequences have come and gone with no news. None." Chari shook his head. Heat crept up his neck.

Chendor remained silent.

After a moment, Chari stirred. "A long time after the attack, I spoke to someone who said you were alive, but your mind was gone. You were living in an undisclosed location for your safety. I never heard anything more."

Chendor's gaze lost its focus for an instant, then he regained his aplomb. "I completely lost my mind for two sequences," he said, "then my body slowly healed. I recovered my brain function but never left my sanctuary. To this day, I experience uncontrollable fear and anguish when I enter the tunnels."

An uneasy silence fell between them.

Chari said in a low voice. "Why didn't you contact me?"

Chendor's features softened. His voice was a mere whisper. "When my body and soul healed, my Chowlis told me you had been exiled in the Burned Zone. It was forbidden to contact you." He paused. "Traveling was out of the question. I thought I would lose my mind all over again." He lowered his head. "I still can't travel."

Chari's words appeared forgiving, but his gaze didn't flinch. "You never liked the tunnels."

Chendor chuckled, as if laughing at a sad joke. "Now, over sixty sequences later, you risk your life to rescue a Sheffrou and that brings us together." His eyes locked on Chari. "Have a drink with me, Chumpi."

Hearing the familiar term of endearment, Chari took a step back and slammed his glass on a table beside him. "I'll pass."

With his jaw set in a scowl, he headed for the door. He turned and faced Chendor. "If the situation had been reversed, I would have moved mountains to find you."

Chendor frowned. His lips moved as if he would reply, but they stilled.

Chari stormed out of the room.

Chapter 14

Cool water sprayed around and above Maashi. He raised his head, and the powerful jets splashed his face and shoulders. He ran long and slender fingers in his hair and massaged his scalp. After several days under the care of Chendor and his Chowlis, his saweya had surged. Warm choun and exercise had toned his muscles and his strength was returning.

Maashi was eager to continue his search for the one or ones responsible for the attacks on Sheffrous Tomisho, Dasho, Ashani, and the unfortunate Choban, on the night of the Great Eclipse Celebration.

Sorrow, like a heavy burden crushing his shoulders, accompanied him night and day. He tried to remember the events that occurred after his escapade, but the memory of those days eluded him and remained indecipherable, a complex puzzle of images and sounds. The child with the glowing eyes haunted his spirit without cease. He was convinced something significant, possibly vital, had happened during the time he had gone missing. To his dismay, the more he fought to remember, the less he understood. His frustration increased.

A little over one sequence ago, after his successful mating with seven Fanellas, he had been captured by the enemy and held five months before he was rescued by the Black Guards, a special unit designed to deal with the enemy. Now, bits and pieces of memories of the time spent as a prisoner of the Krako-ran seemed to surface without warning. Since no Sheffrou had survived long enough to remember what happened during their captivity, Chendor was powerless to help him sort out these troubling thoughts. All he could do was to offer his support and shower him with affection. The gargantuan Sheffrou was confident light would eventually emerge and shine through the shadows obscuring his mind.

Maashi exhaled a long and frustrated breath as he massaged his legs under the choma's hot water. His recent outburst and baffling hallucinations must have traumatized Tamara. He needed Chendor's approval to see her again. Apologies and re-assurance were required. He would see the Sheffrou today.

Someone stood at the door of the water room. Maashi turned around expecting to see a guard but saw a muscular Ghouli Ghouli dressed in black, leaning against the frame of the arched opening, arms folded across his chest. The copper hue of his face emphasized his black eyes and eyelids.

"Hi, gorgeous," said the stranger with admiring clicks. His bold gaze appraised Maashi's naked body. He was a head taller than Maashi, with unruly coal black hair. With an arrogant smile he said, "Chendor and his Chowlis have done an excellent job."

Recognition flashed in Maashi's mind, and he emitted a low hiss. The stranger was Chari Varian, leader of the Outcasts. Maashi stared at him and said, "What are you doing here? What do you want?"

"I was hoping for a warmer welcome after I saved you from death's claws," Chari said in a mocking tone.

Maashi pressed on a control behind him and shut off the water. "I heard you were the one who found me, but I didn't believe it," he said, keeping his eyes fixated on the intruder.

Chari erupted in laughter. "So different from our last time together. This time you're burning like fire. I like that." He advanced toward Maashi and stopped less than a foot away from him. He bent his head to kiss Maashi's shoulder.

Maashi would have none of his kisses. "Stay away from me."

He knew Chari was a Multicolor, but his attitude screamed purple. Purples were bold, insolent, and unpleasant.

Chari clicked softly, as if approaching a skittish Fanella. With long black fingers, he caressed Maashi's forearm. "Don't be shy, Sheffrou."

Maashi pulled his arm away. "You're not welcome here. Don't touch me."

Chari inhaled and said in a low voice, "Your holoma is exciting. Your taste must be exquisite."

Maashi's brow darkened, and he delivered a warning hiss.

Chari cocked his head. "You look well." He bent down, kissed Maashi's neck, and quickly ducked to avoid the fist aimed at his jaw.

"Nice try," he said. He expertly grabbed Maashi's wrists, raised his arms high above his head, and kissed his mouth.

Maashi struggled, but Chari's unyielding hold proved too strong. He couldn't shake him off. He felt Chari's moist lips on his and his taut body against his nakedness. Chari prolonged his kiss until Maashi's member grew hard under him. Only then did he release the Sheffrou.

Chari dropped his gaze below Maashi's waist. His lips curled in a smile. He said under his breath, "I haven't held a beautiful Sheffrou like you in many, many sequences."

"Enough," Maashi hissed. "Get away from me, traitor."

Chari's smile faded. "Sheffrou," he said, "I know you're looking for traitors. I'm not innocent, like a creamy white by any length. I've done many deeds I'm not proud of, but I swear I didn't have anything to do with the Krakoran attacks."

He released Maashi and raised a hand to show his sincerity. "In all my life, I've never willfully hurt a Sheffrou."

"Leave," Maashi glared. "Now."

"As you wish. I will leave but I'll come back and see you soon."

Chari stepped back, turned, and left without another word.

Disgusted at his body's quick reaction to Chari's kiss, Maashi raised his arms in an angry defensive posture and hissed. Too late, his mentor's admonitions came to mind. Don't let your guard down. Learn to defend yourself or you will suffer the consequences. But, as a young Sheffrou 8, Maashi favored diplomacy over aggression and thought he would always be surrounded by Chowlis and guards ready to defend him. Learning different fighting techniques had never been a priority.

He licked his lips and swallowed the saliva filling his mouth. Being a Sheffrou complicated things. His intense and ever-present sexual drive often triggered uncontrollable reflexes. Experienced Sawishas and Multis were quick to notice them and take advantage of him. The copper-skinned intruder seemed to know well Sheffrou weaknesses.

Maashi closed his eyes and exhaled. He had wanted to push Chari away, but to his surprise, froze with pleasure like a Fanella receiving her first kiss. Chari's soft lips caught him off guard. Hidden under his bold, insolent exterior, Chari possessed a tender side and Maashi had felt the Multicolor's gentleness. Disgruntled, he stepped out of the choma. His opinion hadn't changed. Chari was a person of interest in the attacks that occurred the night of the Great Eclipse. He waited until desire left his body and went back to the receiving room. He glanced absentmindedly at the couch where he had left his clothing.

The couch was bare. His clothes, his favorite blanket, and all the cushions were gone.

The brazen Ghouli Ghouli had left with all his belongings.

Bewildered, Maashi stared at the empty couch. If Chari and his people were in such need of basics, they could just ask for them. He would make sure they were provided with all they needed. How disrespectful to grab his things and run like a thief.

Suddenly, he remembered something, and his anger flared. In one forceful move, he flung the mattress of the lounge-chair away and looked underneath. Not seeing what he was looking for, he started a frantic search. He palpated every inch of the mattress, then he looked under the frame of the chair. At last, he exhaled a long-held breath when he found it: a cherished gold chain, a gift from Tomisho. He rolled it between his fingers then held it close to his chest. Tomisho had offered this chain right before the Great Eclipse Celebration as a symbol of his deep affection and friendship. Shaken by the fact he had almost lost the chain, he sat down.

Minutes later, he ordered new clothes by pressing on easy to reach controls on the floor. The clothes appeared through an opening on the wall, folded in a pack. Maashi dressed quickly and put the gold chain in a secure inside pocket of his shirt.

He tied a short royal blue sash around his waist and sat. *Why did Chendor allow this traitor in his domain? More so, why did he let him roam without supervision?*

⊱——⊰‹‹ ● ››⊱——⊰

Much later that same day, Chendor came to see Maashi. The Sheffrou had refused to go swimming with Chendor's Chowlis and was brooding on his couch in the receiving room. At his request, the room had been replenished with a plush blanket and tons of turquoise and blue cushions, his favorite colors.

Chendor sat down opposite Maashi, his ample frame filling the couch. "How are you feeling, Shonava?" he said with a concerned voice.

"I'm well, sir. Thank you for your kindness."

"Are you still hearing voices and experiencing the vision you shared with me the other day?"

"The voices are almost gone. Alas, the vision of the child still troubles me."

Chendor tilted his head to the side. His baritone voice was gentle. "Perhaps it's something from the future or a metaphor created by your mind. With time, you'll be able to explain this enigma. You should rest and regain your strength. Try not to dwell on the vision."

"My strength. Yes." Maashi spread his hands on his knees and remembered his brief clash with Chari. "Shonava," he said, "I must inform you the Ghouli Ghouli Chari Varian came to see me early this morning. I don't want to question your right to invite anyone you wish, but I don't understand why he's here."

At the mention of Chari's name, Chendor's eyes lit up. "As you know, he was the one who brought you here," he said, "I have complete trust in him."

Maashi's brow darkened.

Chendor added, "The Elders were extremely concerned after an initial assessment of your condition showed potential brain damage following the exposure to the methane gas. They have mentioned that several conditions must be met before you're allowed to return to your compound and resume your responsibilities."

"What conditions?"

"Shonava, you must find a first Chowli. Your two young Chowlis, Rahma and Chopa, are excellent but they don't adequately fulfill your needs."

Irritated at the mention of a new Chowli, Maashi raised his voice. "Finding a first Chowli isn't like riding a new shoshan. It may take some time before I find someone suitable."

"Shapinka," Chendor whispered, "there is someone here who is most interested in you."

"Who? I don't know anyone."

"Chari Varian is interested." Chendor paused, as if waiting for Maashi's reaction. "My Chowlis have been in contact with him. He intends to have a proper meeting with you and make a formal request to become your first Chowli."

Maashi's brow darkened. He lowered his head. "I don't want to have anything to do with him."

"I understand. You aren't accustomed to Ghouli Ghouli Chamranlinas."

Maashi murmured. "That's not the reason."

Chendor reclined back on the couch. The thick cushion flattened under his weight. With a cool voice, he stated, "Chari wasn't involved in the Krakoran attacks."

Maashi hissed. "I'm not convinced."

Chendor stretched his long, powerful legs. "Maashi," he bent his head sideways effectively hiding the scar on his right cheek, "when you disappeared from your quarters two weeks ago, Chari was the only one who thought you might have gone to the surface. He went in the Goolalong Fields to find you."

Maashi turned his head away and folded his arms across his chest.

Chendor kept on. "Chari is Multicolor. His purple color dominates but, he also possesses some red, a sliver of pink, and a touch of yellow. Because he is purple, he can perform well as first Chowli and his other colors bring depth to his character. He is an experienced leader, and age has brought him wisdom."

Maashi raised his hand. "Enough. Please. I don't want to hear anymore."

"I thought it was important to describe him and remind you he was the one who saved your life."

"You already told me that more than once."

Chendor patted Maashi's arm. "The decision to choose a first Chowli is entirely yours Shonava, but I should also inform you there is another advantage in choosing Chari. Apart from being a multifaceted purple, he has an efficient network of spies. He has access to details not available in recordings. He might be an invaluable ally in your search for the real traitors."

Chendor lowered his gaze and concentrated on the blue cushion beside him. "You don't have to decide now." He lifted his eyes and his expression changed from serious to amused. "Also, a more pressing matter has come up."

Unable to contain his irritation, Maashi said, "What now?"

"There have been some developments in the mating game."

"I hardly consider mating a game." Maashi said somberly.

Nonplussed, Chendor continued, "If you recall, you were third choice this year. I'm sure you're aware two Fanellas didn't mate with the other Sheffrous. They are ready now. You have been summoned to appear in the third Fanella compound in twenty-six hours. You'll have your chance to mate this sequence."

Maashi was caught off guard. "Two Fanellas?"

"Your reaction isn't what I expected." Chendor's scar took a darker hue. "You don't appear overjoyed."

Maashi sighed. "I'm honored by the request, but the timing couldn't be any worse. I was hoping to meet my friend Tomisho as soon as he arrived. You do know he has been rescued."

"Of course," said Chendor, "but he isn't here yet. The most recent news isn't favorable. The rescue ship is still in hiding. We don't have a good estimate of their time of arrival."

Maashi paled. <*Talinda shall not speak,* > said the high-pitched voice. With a great deal of effort, Maashi said, "Tomisho needs treatment as soon as possible. The rescuers are taking too many risks with his health."

"They don't have a choice, Shonava," Chendor said, "but that shouldn't affect you. The mating is extremely important. You must go. It's an opportunity to restore your standing as a high-ranking Sheffrou."

Maashi stared across the room and said, "The other two Sheffrous are both experienced yet, they both failed. This means the females may not be ready or willing to mate. It won't be an easy task."

Chendor chuckled. "You underestimate yourself. This type of challenge may be just what you need right now."

Chendor rose easily, belying his heavy frame. He walked to the door and turned.

"Get some rest my friend. I'll expect you later in my pool. My Chowlis will be present. In a few hours, guards will accompany you to the Fanella compound."

Maashi watched the door panel slide. He closed his eyes and thought about Tomisho. His friend's booming laughter echoed in his mind. The aroma of his muscular body filled his senses.

He longed for his comforting embrace. *Where was he now?* His ultimate rescue remained uncertain.

He felt trapped. He had a duty to mate, yet the only thing he wanted was to spend time with his friend and find who had betrayed the Sheffrous.

<Talinda shall not move. >

A shiver of disgust ran down his spine.

To accomplish his goals, he might have to associate with Chari, an insolent purple he loathed.

Chapter 15

Tamara sat in her tight quarters on her favorite couch; she loved it because it was low to the ground so she could touch the floor when she sat, and the cranberry material felt like soft velvet. She studied the tray set on a granite table before her. Food in Chendor's sector was varied and plentiful, a feature she fully appreciated. Triangular crackers topped with cream cheese made from choun, several colorful jars of pudding, a comical orange mold shaped like a deflated volleyball, and some olive-size fruit on a stalk like fresh dates competed for her attention. She took a spoonful of pink pudding, swirled it in her mouth, and savored the tart strawberry kiwi taste. She then tried one of the olive-sized fruit. The fruit had a spongy feel but crunched under the teeth when chewed. Interesting.

She reclined and smiled to herself. Chopa had come by and informed her that Maashi was back to normal and was preparing to go to the Fanella compound for mating. She knew how important this was for him and was glad that he could carry on with his duties.

Tamara finished eating her fruit and puckered her lips in annoyance. Humans. Ever since the Chamis had found a ship with two Humans aboard, she thought of them at night before falling asleep and they were the first thought in her mind when she woke in the morning. They were so tantalizingly close, but so unnervingly out of reach. Still in their protective pods, they hadn't been awakened. The Chamis had brought them to Chitina, but she couldn't see them. Not yet.

The Chamis, in their careful ways, had retrieved the small human ship from its decaying orbit around a planet in the nearest solar system. The occupants had most likely been aware of their precarious situation. They sent a distress message to another ship which was picked up by the Chamis, then put themselves in suspended animation. That's the information Tamara got from the Chamis who brought the ship back with them and put it in a stationary orbit around Chitina. She understood the process except the part about the state of suspended animation. No such technology had been invented in her time.

She held a cracker in mid-air; this meant those humans were either from her future, an alternate future, or humanoids not from Earth at all. The Chamis however were convinced they were from Earth because analysis of the DNA of skin cells found on the surface of the pods confirmed their similarity to her DNA.

Tamara had stopped counting how long it had been since her arrival in Chitina. What was the point? There was nowhere to go, and rescue had been impossible. Until now. The presence of the humans had changed everything. She was relieved there were others like her in this sector of space, but that fact alone brought many questions. Who were they? Where were they from? What language did they speak? Would she face the dilemma of deciding whether to stay here with the Chamis and Maashi or leave with them to rejoin her own kind?

She bit her lip and the cold taste of blood hit her. She blinked with the sudden pain. If indeed they were from the future, which was the most likely scenario, this meant her own family, including her precious children, were gone, swallowed by time and space. Tears filled her eyes and soon streamed down her face. She set the cracker on the table in front her, grabbed a hand towel, and wiped her cheeks. David, the oldest, would have to face the challenges of medical school without her counsel. Allison, her golden girl, would have to find her path in life without her mother as confidante. Jonathan, the youngest at sixteen, would live his teenage years alone with his dad. She dabbed at her eyes. In a strange way, she thought little about her husband Nate. Their relationship had been strained, and he wasn't important anymore.

The chime rang. The door opened, revealing a familiar figure. Her lips formed a smile, and she drew her legs under her. "Come in, Chopa. How's everything?"

Tamara had become friends with the tall Chopa, a no-nonsense kind of guy. If one could say that about an alien. Dressed impeccably in Maashi's colors, he bowed to her and said, "Good day to you Chimitanga. What information are you seeking?" Formalities were important for him. Maashi had given her the coveted title of Chimitanga, and this had raised her status in the Chami hierarchy.

"First, sit down. My neck hurts trying to look up at you," she said. "Any news about the humans? When can I see them?"

Chopa sat opposite her and tilted his head to one side. He answered in a measured tone, "They require careful reanimation and must be kept in a secluded location until a welcoming committee is formed to establish contact. This will take time."

"I understand that. Last time I checked you said there was a blizzard going on. Now you're telling me it's going to take time."

"The process of reanimation must be done gradually."

"Damn it, Chopa. They aren't here for a social visit. You can't keep them in their pods forever. You brought them on Chitina without their knowledge." Tamara leaped off the couch and took a few steps. "If they signaled another ship before they went under suspended animation, that ship will come looking for them." She threw her arms up in the air. "Many things can happen when the others locate the ship around Chitina. The humans might consider possessing that ship an act of aggression and attack Chitina. They might not want to establish any kind of communication or collaboration. Who knows?" She worried the humans might consider the retrieval of their ship and the fact that they had accessed the information on board a hostile act.

Knowing that she was so close to a contact also brought a new sense of urgency. But Chamis lived long lives. They never hurried, and this annoyed her terribly.

So many questions popped in her head. Were they really humans? Did they look like her or descendants so far removed from her time that their physical appearance had changed? What were their goals? Did they live in peace or were they at war? With each other or with other aliens? For as long as she had lived, there were wars some place or other on Earth. It wasn't a big stretch to think there was a war going on.

Lost in her thoughts, Tamara failed to notice Chopa was talking. "Tamara? Are you listening?"

"Yes. Sorry. What is it?"

"I must inform you that, when the time comes for an official greeting with the Humans, Sheffrou Maashi will not accompany you. It may take several weeks before his condition is stable enough for him to be allowed out of this area to greet aliens."

"I know. I came to the same conclusion." She frowned and shook her head. "I hope he gets better soon. All this stuff about being poisoned by methane gas concerns me. This whole story of taking off to the surface is unreal. I don't get it."

Tamara remembered how devastated she was when she learned of Maashi's disappearance. His unexpected jaunt had brought tremendous angst and turmoil in his entourage. Why he had taken off in the tunnels at night without his guards was beyond the Chamis' understanding.

Since his rescue, she had quizzed Chopa daily to get the latest information on his condition. She applauded Maashi's progress and despaired when he experienced a relapse. The only time she had seen him Maashi had looked different: thin, frail, trapped in his own bubble, and he had hallucinated. Not at all the loving alien she knew.

"I feel so guilty. I was the one who had suggested a conspiracy theory, the existence of a traitor, responsible for coordinating the simultaneous attacks on three different groups of Sheffrous the night of the Great Eclipse. Somehow, I was convinced of my theory, and I convinced Maashi. In the end, he agreed with me and ran away."

Tamara was closer to Maashi than to any other Chami. He had gained her trust when she first arrived in Chitina. He promised he would always protect and care for her. Her feelings for the Sheffrou were complex, and she refused to admit them. But one thing was clear: she would miss him terribly if she left. His gentle ways, his strength, and the righteousness of his character were the qualities she admired the most. She had not met anyone, on Chitina or Earth, that could compare to him. Her coughing reappeared and continued for several minutes until she took a sip of water. Her cough had improved recently, but today, it bothered her.

Here, safe in this underground haven, Maashi recuperated little by little under Chendor's care, but after her visit with him, Tamara knew he wouldn't accompany her to meet the humans. There were too many unanswered questions and too many holes in Maashi's story. He showed significant amnesia and was prone to hallucinations and terrors. Chendor was confident that with time he would regain all his faculties. Sadly, this didn't help the current situation.

"Tamara," said Chopa, "I will accompany you to see the Humans. You will not be alone."

"Thank you, Chopa. I just hope it's going to happen soon. I need to see them for myself. Waiting isn't something I tolerate well. My patience is stretched to the limit." She watched him as he bowed and left.

Chapter 16

The underground vehicle floated above the rails and zoomed like a silent bullet through the tunnels. All controls were preset, a pilot wasn't needed, and the trip required less than one hour of travel. Maashi sat alone, his back reclined against the plush seat of a private cabin, surrounded by the comfort of soft cushions. The two guards assigned to him were sitting in the next cabin.

He let his thoughts wander.

Mating. Maashi had been given the privilege to mate several times in the last few sequences, and the word evoked a plethora of emotions: exhilarating joy, pure bliss, exquisite pleasure. He was on his way to the Fanella compound and his mood soared.

The youngest Sheffrou ever to be chosen for mating twenty sequences ago, Maashi's official induction had caused an uproar among the Pure Colors. At first, the Council of Elders chose him as the third candidate for mating. This offered the opportunity to try his skills with one or two females who, for different reasons had refused the other Sheffrous. He produced a viable female offspring every time and became a favorite of the Elders. Two sequences ago, he was honored to be selected first. To everyone's astonishment, he mated with the seven Fanellas, and they produced seven offspring. He repeated the feat last sequence. Only the famous Sheffrou 6, Shanadou Aramashan, had accomplished this before him. Maashi bowed his head in a silent homage to the Sheffrou. The terrible attack he suffered had cut short his life as a mating Sheffrou.

Last sequence, Maashi was kidnapped by the Krakoran only one week after his time with the seven females. The Black Guards used all their resources to find him, and they successfully rescued him after five months of captivity. Maashi hissed under his breath at the memory of his ordeal.

He chased away the depressing thoughts and refocused his mind to happier times. He remembered the Fanellas, their delightful aroma, their sweet taste, how his body glowed when he climaxed, and how his skin tingled with pleasure. One Fanella stood out from all others: the graceful and charming Ileana who had stolen his heart. She was the most wondrous female he had ever encountered. She had perfect lips, green eyes speckled with gold, opalescent skin, and the carriage of a queen. He smiled. The exquisite pleasure he had enjoyed in her arms was unequaled. The physical and spiritual connection between them had been complete. Closing his eyes, his mouth filled with sweet saliva as he savored the memory of his last encounter with her.

The Council of Elders chose him to mate with Ileana twice. The second time was even more memorable than the first, but when they parted, Maashi had been overwhelmed with immense sadness. He wanted to hold on to her and never let her go. Tears welled in his eyes at the thought. The longing he felt for her haunted many a sleepless night but in the world of Chamranlinas, the rules concerning Fanellas were unyielding. It was forbidden to become emotionally involved with one Fanella. If his feelings for the slender beauty were discovered, the Elders would never allow him to mate with her again. Maashi knew he wouldn't be permitted to join with her for several sequences since he had already fathered two offspring with her. The Elders maintained rigorous records and they would make sure of that. His chest tightened. He inhaled deeply and his fingers clasped the edge of his seat.

His mind drifted to other sad thoughts: the recent attacks during the night of the Great Eclipse Celebration. He blinked away the tears that filled his oval eyes at the loss of his dear friend Choban, killed by the enemy. The Krakoran had also injured his long-time friend Dasho and snatched two others: the fearless Tomisho and the young Ashani.

Ever since Maashi had met Tomisho at the shoshan race held a few weeks before the Great Eclipse, his saweya had soared. The two Sheffrous had become inseparable; one tall and self-assured, the other kind and thoughtful. Tomisho's loss made living every day without his booming laugh and his ceaseless sense of humor difficult to bear. He cringed at what torture Tomisho would suffer as a prisoner and then recalled that his young pupil Ashani had also been captured. He fisted his hands and held his breath in anger. Sheffrous. Yes, only Sheffrous 8 had been injured, captured, and killed. Their small, privileged group had paid a heavy price in this sequence.

Before the celebration, Maashi was worried about the risk of attack and felt security was lacking. He warned Khon, chief of internal security. Khon's response was polite, but it was obvious he didn't take his warnings seriously. The tragedy Maashi feared became a reality. He couldn't forgive himself for failing to sway the Elders and demand that they cancel the celebration. Sadly, deep down, he knew they wouldn't have listened to him. He was still considered a young Sheffrou at the crossroads between adulthood and maturity, a voice that carried little weight in the Council of Elders.

The vehicle stopped and Maashi was flung back into the present. The doors to the cabin jerked open and an attendant, wearing the standard attire, dark green long-sleeved shirt, and pants, but with a cream sash, stepped in. He bowed to Maashi and said, "Shonava, please follow me."

Maashi stood, stretched his long lean frame like a feline, and stepped out of the cabin. He followed the attendant in the hallway, wondering why a Pure Color cream would be employed at this type of work, well below his capabilities as a counselor and support person. In the prep room, an older Multicolor performed the standard physical assessment and all the data was fully recorded and processed before he was given the final clearance for mating.

At the top of the hour, Maashi followed the cream and boarded the elevator, which brought them up to the surface. He entered alone in an enclosed area located under dome 3, separate from the Fanellas' living quarters and specifically prepared for the mating process.

The Chamranlinas had constructed the clear domes two hundred sequences ago to protect the Fanellas from the desert landscape and attacks by the enemy. They designed them intending to create an environment to promote the Fanellas' well-being, hoping to increase their fertility.

Whereas the Pure Colors and the Multis lived in the bare dark surroundings of the underground tunnels and caverns, the females lived above ground during daytime under a cotton-candy pink sky, generated by the dome and retreated in caves at night. The Chamranlinas had hoped that living underground would ensure the protection of the Pure Colors against the enemies but, considering the recent devastating attacks after the celebration, that long-held belief had proven to be false.

Maashi contemplated the large open field with lush vegetation and mature trees designed to provide shade and a minimum of privacy. As usual, the couple would be under continuous scrutiny by the Gray Feeders with hidden cameras to ensure everyone's safety.

The Fanella, of course, was already in the mating arena but as was the custom, was hiding and waiting for him to flush her out by sprinting to catch her. Maashi nodded his head to one side and listened. He wasn't in the mood for running. He used to think the habitual game of hide and seek between the couple was amusing, although a lot of energy was spent trying to locate and entice the elusive female to approach the male. Now, with so much at stake, including his goal of finding who betrayed his people, he couldn't help feeling it was a pointless exercise. Without the protection of a chemcha, his protective underwear, considered futile in mating, running while only wearing his pants would cause friction and undue pain, not a favorable preambule for a successful mating.

He walked for half an hour amidst the shapely trees and an impressive variety of flowering plants saved from extinction and brought to Chitina from their home world Chamtali. Centuries ago, their beloved home planet underwent a change in orbit because of the gravitational influence of a rogue planet far out in space. The new orbit moved Chamtali slightly closer to their sun and, over two hundred sequences, the climate changed, and the world they knew became dry and arid. Chamranlinas found a way to escape the dying planet with the help of special Sheffrous called Ishkibu who could travel through wormholes and thus found Chitina. They took with them as many plants and animal species as they could to start a new colony in this world.

Maashi stopped and scanned the area carefully. He chose a shady spot under the thick canopy of a large tree, settled on the burgundy moss covering the ground like a soft carpet. There, he waited. Since he was the third choice for mating, he concluded that if the Fanella was willing to mate, she would come to him of her own accord. She had to know this was her last opportunity to mate this sequence.

From the corner of his eye, he noticed movement on the right. About two hundred feet away, he saw her. She was naked as were all females and partially hidden behind bushes, and thinner than any female he had ever seen. As she got closer, Maashi noticed she was limping. *How could this be?* He couldn't find a satisfactory explanation for this. Any injury should have been noticed and treated by the Gray Feeders. She came closer, and he gasped at her appearance. *So thin! Why?* Fanellas were always thin, but this one's shoulder bones and ribcage protruded through her skin. Her legs appeared to be two sticks. Maashi moaned in anguish at the sight.

Was she not getting enough food? Was she being punished, or worse, coerced in accepting the mating? He hissed under his breath. There had been a lot of conjectures about the increased rate of miscarriages in the last twenty sequences. Her exaggerated thinness could lead to problems with carrying a pregnancy to term.

She hesitated, and Maashi felt compelled to click softly to entice her to approach. As she got closer, he called out, "Come. Come, Shapinka. I am here for you."

She advanced slowly, her gait uneven, her eyes furtive.

Maashi's brow darkened. From up close, she looked barely old enough to conceive and her hollow eyes suggested she may be sick.

She bent down, kneeled close to him. He inhaled her fragrant skin and shivered with desire.

With pleading eyes, she said, "Please don't hurt me. This is my first time. The others they were big. I got scared. I thought they would hurt me. I screamed, and the Grays took them away."

Maashi thought for a moment that even using the utmost precaution, she seemed so small it would be difficult not to hurt her during joining. He whispered, "Gentle one, come. Let me hold you and feed you."

It took a lot of soothing clicks to convince her, but after a few minutes, she consented and lay down her head on his chest to breastfeed. Feeding the Fanella was an intrinsic part of mating. Choun had a calming effect on the female, and it increased the physical connection between the couple.

Maashi fought a strong urge to hold her tightly against him. Instead, he continued his clicks, tilted his head back, and savored the pleasure of her closeness. His fragrant holoma imbued the surrounding air. He waited, knowing the powerful pheromone would increase her desire and tempt her to mate. The Fanella at first took small rapid gulps of the warm choun but then took long swallows of the sweet liquid.

Laying still, Maashi watched her feed. Minutes later, she was done and sat back up. He felt she stopped not because her stomach was full but because she had exhausted his supply of choun. He himself could not reach his ideal weight even with Chendor's generous feedings.

She looked up at him and said with a resigned voice, "Do we have to do it now?" And her stomach made a grumbling sound which reminded Maashi of Tamara who always seemed to be hungry.

"Would you like to share some food with me first?"

Her almond eyes opened wide, and she whispered, "I would be honored, Sheffrou."

Maashi pressed on a bracelet given to him earlier by the cream attendant and ordered fruits and puddings. "The food should be here in a minute," he smiled, "and you may call me Maashi."

The door to the enclosure opened and a Gray Feeder brought a tray laden with fruits and puddings. He set it down in front of them and left without a word.

"Please, Shapinka, help yourself."

Without hesitation, she grabbed a pudding and an oval scooper and gulped down mouthfuls without tasting. Maashi took a scooper but ate slowly so he could observe her. She gobbled down three puddings and a fruit before he had swallowed his first spoonful.

"You seem hungry, sweet one. Are you getting enough to eat?"

A shadow flickered in her eyes, but she quickly recovered and said with conviction in her voice, "I am healthy and stronger than I look. I will carry an offspring for you."

Unconvinced, Maashi asked again, "Is anybody threatening you? Did anyone hurt you?"

With a look of alarm, she shook her head to one side. "No one. No one, sir."

"Very well," he said, not reassured. "You can leave some food for later and I can order more to take with you to share with your sisters."

"Thank you," she said, avoiding his gaze.

When he got to the bottom of his jar, he put some on his finger and offered it to her. "Here," he said in a gentle voice, "taste this." She let him introduce his finger in her mouth and tasted it.

She made a delicate smacking sound with her lips and said, "Tastes good."

He put some more on the tip of his finger, and it slid off and dropped on her chest.

"Oh. It fell," he said, feigning surprise.

"You did it on purpose," she said and giggled.

Maashi smiled. "Maybe I did." He caressed her cheek with his hand and bent down and licked the pudding off her chest. "Can I hold you close?"

She bent her head sideways to signal him to proceed, and he put his arms around her and sat her on his lap. He touched her shoulders and put two fingers under her chin and raised her head to his mouth and kissed her. Once. Twice. Then she opened her mouth, and he slid his blue tongue inside. She let him feel her and she swallowed his sweet saliva.

A warm rush sped through his veins, but he refrained from showing his elation. He wanted to prolong as much as possible the preliminaries before the actual joining. To be successful, he would need to be gentle and patient with this young female.

He cradled her right ankle and massaged it between his hands to ease the pain and swelling. "What happened to you?" he said.

Her large almond eyes dove in his and she said, "I tripped on something yesterday when I was running away from the other male. It didn't swell until today."

"May I lick your ankle?"

Her brow darkened in puzzlement. "You think it will help it heal?"

"Yes, of course. Just lay back." Maashi brought her foot way up and slid his long tongue out and licked the ankle under her watchful eye.

After a moment, she closed her eyes and moaned in contentment. Maashi ran his fingers the length of her legs and said in a low seductive voice, "Such beautiful legs, such perfect skin."

She peaked at him under her thin eyelashes and spread her legs so he could touch her thighs and he did, gliding the tip of his fingers on her inner thighs. He then caressed her buttocks and in between her legs until she cooed with pleasure.

He clicked and with his softest voice, said, "It is time, gentle one. Let me do what I must."

She kept her gaze fixated on him and opened her legs.

He introduced two fingers in her long narrow vagina, breaking and stretching the small curtain of skin at the entrance.

The female gasped, sat up, and cried out, but he quickly introduced his tongue where his fingers had been and flooded her with his saliva. She sighed and reclined back on the soft mossy ground and moaned with delight.

Maashi continued licking her until she panted heavily and then he pulled his tongue back in his mouth, introduced his erect member. His powerful holoma wrapped the couple in a sweet-smelling mist. Their energy rose as they held each other in unison. Maashi shared his climax with her, making sure she experienced the same level of pleasure he did. The seduced and sated female clung to his body. Maashi turned on his back and held her against his chest for the longest time, kissing her hair and caressing her shoulders and arms. He repeated the mating twice before the allocated time was over.

<Talinda shall not move. Talinda will give pleasure. The Master Hunter will be pleased.> The now familiar high-pitched

voice clamored in Maashi's mind. He gasped as he finally understood. HE was Talinda. He was the one who had to obey orders or be punished.

At last, Maashi remembered who spoke with that voice. It originated from an alien creature associated with the Krakoran. The foot tall creature possessed a hard exoskeleton and eight legs. It could crawl over and around Maashi who lay trapped in a rigid white structure like an armor with openings only over his head and genitals. It used thin graspers located under an appendage (its mouth?) to fondle Maashi's genitals and stimulated him until he climaxed. At that precise moment, the Krakoran connected with Maashi with long thin filaments so he could share Maashi's pleasure. If Maashi failed to cooperate, the little creature punished him by burning him with a sharp stinger at one end of its body. The small creature worked in symbiosis with the Krakoran who, incapable of feeling pleasure by themselves, hunted Sheffrous, kidnapped them, and brought them back to the colony to share with them.

Maashi sat up, his head spinning with the sudden realization of the details of his captivity. If the Krakoran was pleased, the little creature fed him by inserting his thin rear end in Maashi mouth and excreting a soft reddish substance. Maashi had no choice but to swallow the secretion, which was the only form of sustenance he was given. He had to ingest the excrements or starve to death.

The cream color attendant arrived at that moment and led a bewildered Maashi back for a final physical check. When the exam was completed, Maashi sat alone in his assigned quarters, trying to make sense of the jarring memories of his kidnapping. Being held motionless, encased in a white structure like a coffin in a completely white room was torture for a powerful Sheffrou used to swimming freely in the swift, flowing rivers and the crystalline pools of Chitina. But the ultimate humiliation of sharing his pleasure with the Krakoran made Maashi's stomach heave in disgust. With the memory vivid in his mind, Maashi took long breaths to calm his distress. He crossed his arms over his chest and sat still, willing the images away.

A few minutes later, the cream came and settled beside him. With a cunning expression unexpected in a cream, he leaned close to readjust Maashi's sash and whispered in his ear, "Sir," he said, "I'm here in place of the usual attendant to warn you. Trouble is brewing."

Maashi tilted his head sideway as his brow darkened. "What do you mean?"

"I must inform you the second female has refused to mate with you."

"What? Why?"

"Because of the rumors that you illegally entered one of the Fanella compounds and created havoc."

"What? What havoc?"

"I'm sorry, sir, but that is all I know. Communications between the Fanella compounds and all other compounds have been upended for several weeks by order of the Council of Elders."

Maashi's eyes thinned to slits. He hissed in anger. "That first Fanella was injured and emaciated. She looked like she was starving," he said. "Do you know anything about her?"

"No, sir. I will attempt to find out. But I know something of the utmost gravity is going on. I am convinced the Elders are aware but are refusing to divulge the information to the general population."

A cold chill of impending doom spread through Maashi's body. "I see." Maashi was crestfallen. The nightmarish vision of the young face with the two eyes staring into nothingness flashed in his brain. His mouth went dry. *What calamity was unfolding as he was kept distracted with mating?*

The cream affectionately held his hand and squeezed it. "Let me accompany you back to the transport vehicle."

Maashi followed him. As he stepped into the transporter, the cream said, "Stay safe, sir. Danger lurks in every corner. If you need a trustworthy companion, call me. I will be honored to serve you. My name is Sacha."

Maashi nodded.

The return to Chendor's sector felt much longer than the trip to the Fanella compound. The vehicle zigzagged endlessly through the darkness of the underground tunnels. A dark cloud enveloped Maashi's mind.

Did he really go to the Fanella compound? What happened there? Why was the vision of the young face with the two glowing eyes haunting him ever since he had been rescued from the Goolalong Fields? If there was something wrong with the Fanellas, then all Chamranlinas might be in peril. He needed to know more. *How could he find out? What should he do?*

Chapter 17

The classic black and white diamond pattern on the ceiling, walls and carpet cast a faint glow on the two figures present in the encounter room. Maashi rested on his side, his jaw set, his eyes fixated on Chari. He was not pleased.

Under Chendor's care, Maashi's health had improved and his saweya had increased. His discharge from Chendor's care depended on several conditions, one of which was to find and bond with a first Chowli. Only then could his charissa, his 'joie de vivre', be restored to a healthy level. Maashi was impatient to leave. He had to find out more about the Fanellas' situation and continue his search for the one responsible for the attacks on the Sheffrous. He had vowed to find the traitor, and he wanted to resume his quest as soon as possible.

Chari was a strong candidate for first Chowli: Multicolor Ghouli Ghouli with purple dominant, he also possessed prior experience with a high-ranking Sheffrou. After spending sixty sequences in the Burned Zone, he had paid the price for fomenting the infamous Rebellion. The Elders had allowed him to move back in the main Chamranlina society if he so wished, and they restored his full rights as citizen. He was strong physically and mentally and could provide emotional support and sexual gratification both essential to a Sheffrou 8 like Maashi.

Even with these qualities, Maashi disliked him. He was bold, independent, insolent, and above all, purple.

Maashi's reluctance to choose Chari Varian, even though he was convinced it was a choice the Elders would approve of, stemmed from his long-standing dislike of purples. As a young Sheffrou, Maashi had been trained by a strong-willed purple Sawisha, Kokin Cronobutin. He was harsh, vengeful, and sometimes cruel. From that day onward, Maashi hated purples. He treated them fairly but could never bring himself to accept them as friends. Taking Chari on as Chowli was a big step.

"Maashi," said Chari, "we've been in the encounter room for three days and we've had numerous encounters as required by tradition, but I'm not satisfied."

"What more do you want?" Said Maashi, in a cool, flat voice.

"Your body responds to my caresses, but your heart is frozen like the ice atop the Chizoo mountains."

Maashi turned sideways to better assess his new Chowli. He rested his head against his elbow. The movement made the mattress ripple, creating a wave which traveled all the way to the ceiling. "I'm responding adequately to your stimulation."

"Adequately? Nonsense!" Chari snorted.

The startling sound reminded Maashi of a shoshan.

"I'm not some male you're servicing, Maashi. You must establish a deep connection with me."

"I can't do more," Maashi said, "not now." Since his kidnapping by the enemy one sequence ago, he had been reluctant to engage in deep encounters and this had prevented him from choosing a new Chowli. As a prisoner, he had been forced to do unspeakable acts and his shame barred him from sharing this with anyone.

Chari's gaze mocked Maashi. "This means I have to try harder."

"I have accepted you as Chowli. We have spent the required time in the encounter room. We should leave." Maashi started to rise.

Chari grabbed his arm and held him down. "We're not leaving until I'm satisfied."

Maashi eased back on the mattress and stared at the black-and-white pattern on the ceiling. Perhaps by showing patience, he could appease Chari. "What do you want?"

"Trust," Chari said. "I want to know what makes your heart flutter, what excites you, what you care for above everything else. I want you to drop your guard and truly show me your soul."

"There are things I can't share. Not now. In due time I---"

"Maashi, there are also things I refuse to share, but you have to show some feeling, some emotion. Otherwise, there won't be a bond between us."

"In time we will connect."

"I can't accept that."

Chari spoke under his breath. "I'm prepared to risk my life, my reputation, and my close friends for you, Sheffrou. I take this first Chowli bond seriously."

"So do I."

Chari stated in a grave tone. "I don't see that."

Maashi's brow darkened. He sensed Chari's frustration, and he understood it. He wanted more and had the right to demand more. Maashi exhaled a long breath.

"Chari," Maashi said, keeping his voice low although no other could hear him, "I've experienced difficulties with deep encounters ever since I've been rescued from the Krakoran," he paused, "and I've stayed away from them."

"Difficulties?" said Chari. "Tell me about them. Show me."

Maashi raised his voice. "I can't just blurt this out."

"Did you experience the same difficulties with Chendor? I'm sure you had deep encounters with him."

"It's different with Chendor. He's forgiving," Maashi said, "gentle."

Chari took Maashi's head in his black hands and kissed his lips.

"Show me your tongue Sheffrou," he demanded, "show me."

Maashi's stomach twisted with growing fear. He might fail in his attempt to secure a first Chowli if he didn't comply and risked unspeakable shame if he did. Also, he couldn't shake the immense sadness he had been feeling ever since his rescue from the Goolalong Fields. His growing fear of losing control of intense pent-up emotions changed into a sick feeling when he realized he didn't have any other choice than to obey.

He lowered his eyes, opened his mouth, inhaled, and slowly stretched his striking royal blue tongue.

Chari kissed the ten-inch tongue and then licked it inch by inch. He twirled his own tongue around it and glided up and down. He moved closer to Maashi and slowly positioned his lower body over the Sheffrou to prevent any escape from his embrace. His copper skin glowed a fiery hue under the light of the encounter room.

Maashi's pleasure soared, and saliva filled his mouth until the excess drooled from his lips. He fought to control his emotions, his most private thoughts. He trembled under Chari's weight. Pleasure and fear mixed, threatening to shatter the wall he had built around his intimate feelings. His mind scrambled to free itself and run from the intense and unrelenting stimulation. The pleasure slowly engulfed Maashi. Like someone drowning in quicksand, he fought and screamed.

The only sounds he heard were feeble whimpers. Once they started, he couldn't stop them. Shame replaced all pleasure even though his body continued to respond until he reached the expected climax, and his body glowed an intense blue. At last, the whimpering stopped.

He had failed. Whimpers were unforgivable. He felt naked, worthless in the arms of the purple. There were no words strong enough to convey his shame. Even more unforgivable, the memories he had fought to hide had escaped and scattered about like broken glass. His weaknesses and all his wrongs were exposed. He was convinced Chari's critical mind would seize the opportunity to belittle and punish him. He knew from experience asking for forgiveness was unacceptable and would be another element held against him. How he remembered his mentor Kokin's burning glare, his supreme contempt at the slightest whimper. The punishment would be severe.

Maashi panicked. "Please let me go. Please. Please." He pulled away, but Chari's hold was unshakable. He cried, pleaded, and wailed like a child.

"Tsh. Tsh. Tsh," clicked Chari. His arms enveloped Maashi, his copper body covered the Sheffrou like a glistening blanket. He liked his tears and caressed his neck. "Do not fear me Shapinka. Cry if you need to."

Trapped under Chari, the distraught Maashi shook and whimpered without control.

Chari turned sideways and positioned the troubled Sheffrou's head on his shoulder and caressed the nape of his neck. He clicked soothing clicks.

After a long while, the sobs stopped. The tears slowed to a trickle. Only sighs remained. Maashi waited for Chari's rejection. He tried to say a few words, but they caught in his throat, and nothing came out. He hid his face away from Chari's searching gaze.

Chari kissed his cheeks and whispered, "Feeling better?"

The gentle voice threatened to trigger a new downpour of warm tears. Maashi felt guilt slicing through him. "Forgive me Chari," he said in a trembling voice, "I have brought shame on myself."

"Shapinka, most precious one," Chari whispered in Maashi's ear, "there is nothing to be ashamed of." He sat up, held the Sheffrou's head in his hands, and looked into his eyes. "We're not at the Draharma trials here. A little whimpering is nothing."

With silent desperation, Maashi searched Chari's face. His eyes appeared forgiving, and he didn't appear offended by his outrageous outburst. He asked, keeping his voice low, "Aren't you angry with me?"

A soft chuckle was his answer. "Chumpi, sweet one," Chari said. "Why would I be angry? Because you cried in my arms? Because of your whimpers?"

Maashi lowered his gaze. "You must think I'm unworthy. My behavior is unacceptable. I am Sheffrou, soon to attain maturity. This behavior would never have been tolerated by my mentor."

Chari licked Maashi's remaining tears and kissed Maashi's neck to show his boundless affection. "Shapinka, as your first

Chowli, I am here for you. I will be the shoulder to cry on, the support to lean on, the friend to share your pain. I welcome your tears. I want to hear your cries." Chari turned and rested on his back, keeping the dejected Maashi safe in his copper embrace. "Rest, Chumpi. Do not fill your head with silly fears. Sleep. Don't worry. There is no shame, no punishment. Not now, not later."

Maashi shuddered. Exhausted by the intensity of his outburst, he took one last look at Chari's face. He saw only kindness. He nestled his head on his chest. Within minutes, sleep took him.

Chari placed a soft kiss on the Sheffrou's forehead and then pressed the controls on the floor of the encounter room. "Rahma," he said, "I need you in here."

The encounter room door opened an instant later and Rahma popped his head in.

"Stay with the Sheffrou," said Chari. "Make sure he sleeps well and feed him when he wakes up. I have to go."

Rahma's gaze questioned him, but he nodded. "I will not leave his side."

"Good." Chari quickly exited the small room and went back to the receiving room where he came face to face with Chopa.

"Is everything all right?" asked the young Chowli.

"Yes," answered Chari as he quickly gathered Maashi's clothing and personal blanket and put them in one large bag.

Tomisho's gold chain fell to the floor. In one swift movement, Chopa picked it up.

"What is that?" asked Chari who noticed the chain.

"It's a gift from Sheffrou Tomisho. Sheffrou Maashi is very fond of it."

"Keep it for him then," said Chari.

Chopa grabbed Chari's wrist and with a cold voice, said, "Why are you taking his clothes?"

"I'll explain later. I have to go." He reached the exit in two strides. He turned and said, "Don't let anybody in unless you're sure of their loyalty. I'll be back as soon as possible."

Chopa stood holding the gold chain. He watched Chari leave, and his eyes changed to black slits.

Chapter 18

T he two-paneled door opened without a sound and Tamara and Pini entered. *Nice room* thought Tamara. Bright lights flooded the turquoise walls streaked with dashes of coral and pink. Several long couches were overflowing with ivory-colored cushions embroidered in gold. White marble side tables positioned throughout the room completed the décor.

Maashi lay on a couch close to the far wall. His shirt, a size too large for his slender frame, accentuated his thinness. Rahma hovered over him. He fluffed up a pillow, positioned it behind Maashi's back, and covered his long legs with a blanket.

Maashi raised his arm in protest. He shook his head to one side. "That's enough, Rahma. I'm fine."

"Yes, sir," answered Rahma, his brow dark with concern.

Tamara quickened her pace and went to the Sheffrou. Pini, her young companion, recently allowed to join her in Chendor's sector, followed right behind.

"Maashi," she said, "how are you? I was so worried about you. They said you were upset after the mating."

At the sight of her, Maashi's expression softened. He extended his arms to welcome her. "It's a pleasure to see you little one."

His eyes were the color of rain-filled clouds and his open shirt revealed gray blotches on his chest.

She sat right beside him and took his hand and kissed it. He took hers and pressed his lips to her palms.

"How are you feeling?" She said, "How did the mating go?"

Maashi tilted his head sideways. "It is completed." He looked away. "I was expecting a surge of energy after the mating, but somehow I feel drained. I guess my saweya isn't strong and I need more time to recuperate."

"Have you been eating well?" Tamara said. She touched his cheek. His skin was pale like a wax mannequin and his holoma had a slightly unpleasant smell, like an overripe fruit.

Rahma answered her. "Sheffrou Maashi is eating better today, but he is dehydrated. He should drink more choun."

"Perhaps Sheffrou Maashi would prefer water," said Pini, who had remained standing close to the door. "I'll get some fresh water." He quickly exited the room.

Tamara's gaze traced Maashi's hollow cheeks. She frowned.

"I don't think Rahma," Maashi's mouth eased in a small smile, "will ever be satisfied with how much choun I drink."

Tamara grinned, but she sensed something was off. Maashi looked sick. In a more cheerful tone, she said, "What's the news about the females? Do you know if they're pregnant?"

"I heard," said Rahma, "that the first one is pregnant, but there is no evidence of pregnancy on the ultrasound evaluation."

"Perhaps it's too early to tell," said Tamara.

Maashi dropped his head back on the pillow behind him. "This shows a high probability of miscarriage." His brow darkened. "And the second Fanella changed her mind and refused to see me."

"That's too bad," said Tamara.

Pini walked back in and gave a glass of water to Maashi. "Have some water, sir," he said.

Maashi obediently took a sip. He thanked the young pink who had retreated to the back of the room. He turned toward Tamara. "How was your trip? Did you meet the Humans?"

Tamara shook her head. Seeing Maashi's poor condition, her adventures didn't seem so important anymore. "I haven't seen them. A major blizzard is raging. Everything is canceled until further notice."

Pini said, "The risk of facing the blizzard was too great, sir. Chopa decided we should postpone the trip."

"That was a good decision. Too many sad things have happened." Maashi closed his eyes for a few seconds.

The door opened and Chopa strolled in with his head held high, his shirt and pants impeccable, and his sash tied in a perfect flat knot. "Shonava, I come bearing excellent news."

Rahma and Pini turned and stared at him.

Chopa smiled and said, "I have new information about the first Fanella. Her ultrasound confirmed she is pregnant with twins."

"Congratulations, Maashi!" said Tamara. She hugged him and kissed his cheeks. All three Chamis clicked and came to kiss his shoulders.

Maashi smiled. "Thank you all. I hope she will progress well. I know the Fanellas have been experiencing problems with their pregnancies, including premature deliveries."

"You must remain optimistic, sir. I am sure the Gray Feeders will take excellent care of her," said Rahma.

"Your sash is crooked, Maashi," said Tamara. "Let me readjust it." She reached for the sash on each side of him and her fingers felt a bulge on his left flank. "What's that?" She lifted his shirt and examined the swelling. There was a brownish discoloration, and a sharp point pierced the surface of the skin. A yellow streak coursed down all the way to his hip.

"Maashi, something like a big chard is sticking out of your skin. The area shows some swelling and is infected. Let me remove it for you."

Chopa bent down to look at it. "I see what you mean." He locked eyes with Maashi and said, "Sir, if you agree, I will let Tamara proceed."

"Yes," said Maashi. "Tamara can take care of it."

Chopa nodded. "Let me order what you need." He pressed on the floor controls beside him and a tray with a sharp blade, a bottle of disinfectant, tweezers, and sponges appeared.

Rahma observed how she handled the instruments then, apparently satisfied, sat down, and said, "Where did you get that, sir?"

"I don't know," said Maashi who tilted his head sideways to watch the procedure.

Tamara washed her hands with the disinfectant she had seen the Chamis use and cleaned the affected area with care. She pulled on the protruding chard with a pair of tweezers. A piece broke off and a bile yellow liquid oozed out.

"Darn," exclaimed Tamara, "I'll have to cut the skin to remove this thing. It's bigger than I thought."

"Here," said Chopa, handing her a blade, "use this."

"Do you have a local anesthetic?"

"That won't be necessary," said Maashi, "just proceed."

Tamara shot him a serious look. "This will sting."

"I understand," Maashi said. "Go ahead."

Tamara cut the swollen area, and putrid fluid drained from the opening. She frowned. "Wow, that's a lot of drainage. Don't move. I got a grip on the chard." She pulled a brownish green fragment an inch and a half long.

Maashi winced. "Thank you."

Chopa stared at it. "Interesting." He opened a clear container and presented it to Tamara. She dropped the piece in it. "It appears to be a thorn," he said. He also took a sample of the bile yellow fluid. "I'll analyze both with my friend who works at the main lab."

Rahma stared at it. "Where did that come from?"

"I think something scratched me on that side. It was a while ago," said Maashi. "I can't remember when or where it happened."

"We should leave the wound open so the pus will drain. The incision should heal well. It doesn't require any stitches," declared Tamara.

"Yes," agreed Chopa. He cleaned the wound and applied a clear gel-like dressing that solidified on contact.

A chime rang, and the door opened. Chari strolled in dressed in a short-sleeve black shirt, thick-soled black boots, and a new purple sash with a thin wave of pink and yellow. He stopped a few feet away from them. His copper skin flashed under the vivid light of the receiving room. He said, "Congratulations Maashi on your successful mating. I just heard the news and wanted to be the first to offer my compliments."

"Thank you, Chari," said Maashi. "Everyone, please welcome Chari Varian. It is my pleasure to inform you I have accepted his request to be my first Chowli."

Rahma and Chopa exchanged a concerned glance, then stood. They clicked at Chari, stepped closer, and gave him a hug. A moment later, Pini said, "First Chowli is a great honor and a grave responsibility. Sheffrou Maashi needs a strong first

Chowli. I wish you well in your new function, Chari Varian." They embraced each other. Chari kissed Pini's cheek. "Thank you, Pini."

Tamara observed the scene without saying a word. First Chowlis were close to their respective Sheffrous. This meant less time with Maashi, and she would have to share him with a new rival.

Chari turned to look at her. With a voice devoid of emotion, he said, "Chimitanga, good day to you. Perhaps we can have a proper meeting sometime soon."

Tamara raised an eyebrow at the term 'meeting'. She had no intention of carrying out a meeting, which implied intimate physical contact with him or any other Chamranlina.

"Verbal greetings will suffice, Chari," said Maashi. "Tamara doesn't take part in meetings. In her world, that would be quite unacceptable." In a pleasant tone, he added, "Rahma, Chopa, and Pini have already congratulated me, but I thank you for your wishes."

Chari grinned as if amused by a private joke. Then his gaze locked on Chopa's two containers. "What are those?"

"Something Tamara found and removed from Maashi's flank," Chopa said. "I was going to get it tested."

Chari's lips moved as if he was chewing on something. "Where was it?"

Chopa nodded to Maashi and lifted his shirt to show the fresh dressing on his side.

Chari made a soft hissing sound. "The Sheffrou and I were together a few days ago. I didn't notice anything." He added in a dry tone, "Please keep me informed of the results of your findings."

The door chime went off and one of Chendor's navy blue and green guards appeared, carrying a large package covered by a thick black cloth.

"Shonava Maashi," he said, "Master Kokin Cronobutin wishes you a prompt recovery and sends you a gift as a symbol of his affection. May I bring it in?"

Maashi's expression changed. His mouth stretched in a thin line. He grew paler. He waved his hand and said, "You can set it over there. Thank you."

Tamara didn't like this surprise gift. *What was Kokin, a significant figure in Maashi's past, up to now? Was he trying to redeem himself?* She had seen the purple Sawisha only once. He had provoked Maashi's ire by insulting her and questioning her presence at a private evening of celebration. The memory sent a chill of trepidation up her spine. Tamara noticed how Chari's brow darkened. *Was there a connection between Kokin and Chari, Maashi's new Chowli?*

The guard walked in and set down the package on a low oval table a few feet away from Maashi. He took off the cloth over it and stepped back.

The three-foot tall glass sculpture shone under the room's bright light.

Maashi screamed. "No!!!" He gasped and put his hands around his throat and shrieked, "Talinda shall be punished." He grabbed the side of the couch and bent over. His chest heaved, and he vomited.

"Maashi!" Tamara ran to him.

Chopa and Rahma jumped by his side. Rahma produced a wet cloth and wiped Maashi's face. He clicked sharply at the guard. Chopa put his hand on Maashi's stomach to check his pulse.

Tamara turned and yelled, "Get this thing out of here."

Chari jumped in action. He grabbed the black cloth, covered the sculpture, lifted it, and bolted out of the room.

Pale and trembling, Maashi stared at the ceiling and didn't respond to his Chowlis' clicks. He rested on his side and remained silent.

Chopa said, "Tamara, the Sheffrou will rest now. Rahma contacted Chendor, and he is on his way. Please leave with Pini."

She didn't like being dismissed, however Chendor seemed to be the one most qualified to care for Maashi. There wasn't much more she could do. She took Maashi's hand in hers and whispered, "Stay safe Maashi. I'll be back later." Her heart in turmoil, she left the room with Pini on her heels.

Down the hallway, the door to a small receiving room was opened wide. She glanced inside and saw Chari. He stood, one hand on his hip, his back turned away from her, staring at the sculpture. She entered the sky-blue room, devoid of any furniture except for the one marble table where the sculpture stood. Pini followed in.

Tamara carefully circled the sculpture and scrutinized it.

Pini said, "I have never seen anything like it. What does it represent?"

Chari growled. "Maashi appears to be familiar with whatever it is."

"It looks like some kind of creature," Tamara said.

Chopa joined them and said, "There are no creatures resembling this sculpture on this world or on Chamtali."

Chari ran his fingers in his unruly hair. "Maashi has traveled beyond Chitina. Perhaps he saw a creature like this when he was a prisoner of the Krakoran."

Tamara frowned. She approached the sculpture but didn't touch it. "See here," she said, pointing with her finger, "This white part looks like a head with mandibles. These long segments with black stripes could be legs, and this part here looks like a stinger ready to strike. It reminds me of a cross between a wasp and a scorpion."

"A stinger," said Pini, "do you mean something that could inflict pain?"

Tamara's hair raised on ends. "Yes Pini, pain or a burn, or even inject poison, like scorpions."

Chopa's brow darkened. "Do you have creatures like these in your world?"

"Yes, we do. But they are much smaller, no bigger than my little finger, however some are deadly. If this is its actual size, this creature could inflict terrible pain and could also be lethal." She shook her head. "It looks so real."

"Why would anyone send something like this to the Sheffrou?" said Pini.

"Why indeed?" growled Chari, "and yet it was sent by his former mentor, Kokin." He took a step closer to the offensive sculpture.

Tamara said, "There's definitely something wrong with this gift." She stood, hands on her hips, and couldn't take her eyes off the sculpture. "I know Maashi didn't seem to be close to his mentor. In all the months I've been here, to my knowledge, Maashi has had no contact with Kokin except once, and believe me, it wasn't cordial." She shook her head. "Why would Kokin send something now?"

"Perhaps," said Pini, "Master Kokin heard that the Sheffrou is ill. What I do not understand is why he would send him an odd-looking sculpture."

"It looks like it's encased in a flexible clear plastic." Tamara's eyes thinned. "I don't like this. It reminds me of a Greek gift," said Tamara.

"What is that?" asked Pini.

"Some trick or ruse. Something dangerous. We need to be careful. This thing might be alive, just in some type of stasis. If this is the case, it would be risky to keep it here." She rubbed her chin and stared at it. "Guys," exclaimed Tamara in a commanding voice, "You need to get rid of it. Send it as far as you can. If it's not alive, it might also be a bomb."

"A bomb?" said Pini who stepped back a few feet.

"An explosive device," answered Chopa who pulled a three-inch long object out of his pocket and scanned the sculpture.

Chari hissed in anger. "The little female appears small and insignificant," he growled, "but her mind is sharp. Under our present circumstances, we must take every precaution to protect the Sheffrous. There are several Sheffrous in this sector."

Chopa raised his arm. "Wait, the sculpture is emitting radiation. Tamara is right. It may be an explosive or even a recording device. We should be cautious."

Tamara raised her voice. "You need to move it out of here as soon as possible. If it's a bomb, it might be set to detonate soon."

"I agree," said Chari. He covered the sculpture with the black cloth and ordered the others. "You two, take Tamara and leave now. I'll take a guard and I'll move this thing up on the surface in an isolated area where it can't harm anyone."

"Be careful," said Tamara.

Chari stared at her. "I will."

They each left, taking separate paths.

Chapter 19

Back in her quarters, Tamara took a shower to calm her nerves. She recapitulated the events of the past few weeks in her mind, events she had difficulty understanding. First, Maashi disappeared for three days, which drove her, Rahma, and Chopa mad with worry. Then, the Ghouli Ghouli Chari Varian, leader of the Outcasts, showed up unexpectedly. With Chopa's help, he rescued Maashi from the Goolalong Fields, notorious for their methane gas pockets under Chitina's dry surface. It was odd that Chari was the one who found him because Maashi had put Chari on his list of suspects in the attacks.

Brought under the care of the Tousanou Chendor, Maashi appeared to make good progress in regaining his health, so the Elders agreed to send him to mate. He came back with a fever, looking out of sorts. Tamara diagnosed an abscess on his left flank and drained it. Then, Kokin, his former mentor with whom Maashi didn't entertain good relations, sent him get well wishes with a sculpture. When he saw the strange-looking gift, the Sheffrou panicked and passed out.

Tamara scrubbed her skin raw under the hot water. She told herself she had to remove any trace of that foul-smelling fluid that oozed from Maashi, but deep down she was furious with him. She was upset about his infection and because he announced to everyone he chose Chari as his first Chowli.

She closed her eyes and let the water run down her face and hair. The life she had hoped for on Chitina was unraveling like a loose ball of yarn. Maashi, it seemed, would always be one step beyond her grasp. At first, her main rival was Sheffrou Tomisho. He was loud, boisterous, and full of himself, sometimes to the point of arrogance, but Tamara eventually felt sympathy for the friendly giant.

Now, Maashi had chosen Chari as Chowli. She understood Maashi's companions considered him an intruder and were reticent to include him in their closed circle. With all these individuals vying for the Sheffrou's attention, her status as Maashi's love was in peril. Jealousy surged in her heart.

Tamara was also worried. Chari's cunning personality could hide his real persona. Was he a skilled traitor biding his time, deceiving everyone? Could he hurt Maashi? Put his life in danger?

The remote chance of leaving with the two humans to start a new life didn't seem so far-fetched anymore. This meant abandoning the search for the wormhole which brought her to Chitina and removing any possibility of a reunion with her family. Tamara sighed. She could only speculate about the humans and their connection to her world.

Unfortunately, her scheduled meeting with them had been postponed because of foul weather. A blizzard was a blizzard she thought, on Earth or elsewhere.

She dried herself carefully and chose a pale lavender outfit. No more turquoise except for the ever-present sash. It would be lavender and khaki this week. She put on her sandals and settled on the couch in her receiving room. She heard the chime.

It was Pini. Again. Didn't he have a life? She started to cough and grumbled out loud her discontent. These quarters were too humid. Something here didn't agree with her.

She pursed her lips. She had always dismissed concerns about her health because she rarely caught any viral disease even though she worked long shifts in the Emergency Room. Here, however, her instincts warned her to be careful. Germs in this world could lead to unknown diseases which might be serious. She made a mental note to consult with Maashi at the earliest. If that wasn't possible, Chopa might provide the needed information.

"Come in Pini."

Pini strolled in and bowed to her.

"I've told you many times, Pini. You don't have to bow to me."

"Pardon me, Tamara, but you are Ishkibu, and it would be unacceptable not to bow."

"Just because you call me Ishkibu Sheffrou doesn't transform me into royalty or something." She shook her head when she saw his face and neck pale at her words. "Anyway," she said with a gentler tone, "why are you here?"

"Sheffrou Maashi has requested your presence. I am here to accompany you."

Tamara jumped to her feet. "Why didn't you say so? Let's go."

About ten minutes later Pini opened the door to Maashi's receiving room.

"The Sheffrou is expecting you." He bowed and let her pass.

Maashi sat alone. He was wearing a simple khaki shirt and dark brown pants.

"Come, Tamara," he said in a steady voice.

Tamara walked closer and checked his color. His face wasn't pale as before, and his eyes had regained their warm amber tint. Reassured, she sat beside him.

"Shapinka," he whispered, "I'm so sorry about what happened earlier. That gift from my former mentor upset me terribly." He exhaled a long breath.

"Are you feeling better now? Your color has improved."

Maashi smiled. "You're very perceptive, Tamara. I do feel better thank you."

He took her in his arms and settled her in his lap. "I have been plagued by flashes of disturbing events from the past. They pop in my mind and trouble me. Sadly, I'm unable to control them. Some are quite unsettling. Chendor says I'm stronger than I think and that overall, I'm dealing well with these memories." He chuckled. "I can't say I agree, but I appreciate his confidence in my abilities."

He caressed her head and let his fingers slide down her auburn hair. "Such soft and shiny hair," he said and smiled. "The last few days must have been difficult. I know I'm responsible for part of it."

"It couldn't be helped. Circumstances, for whatever reason, weren't favorable. Even worse, we had to cancel our trip to greet the humans." She frowned. "You also ran into all kinds of adventures, some good like the mating, some bad, like your abscess." She caressed his neck, then looked up at him. "I have a question."

"What is it?"

"I don't understand why you took Chari for your first Chowli. I know it's none of my business, but I thought he was on your list of suspects."

Maashi took a moment to respond. "It's complicated," he said in a soft voice. "Let's say I erased him from my list of suspects. I think he can actually help me find the real culprits."

"I see."

Maashi touched her chin and brought her face closer to his. "You usually say that when you don't agree with me," he whispered and kissed her forehead.

Tamara felt her face flush. "You know me well."

Maashi rubbed his silky cheeks against hers and kissed her once more. Tamara chuckled with contentment. She loved how incredibly soft his skin felt.

"Maashi, what do you do to me?"

"I want to please you, little one."

He reclined on his back and held her on his chest. The amber in his eyes glowed. He showered her face with kisses. He unfastened her shirt and let his fingers glide over her skin until she shivered from the pleasure of his touch. With a simple wrist signal, he lowered the lights in the room.

He put his hand between her legs and rubbed her gently until she moaned. He pulled her clothes off, and she lay naked over him. The surrounding air became heavy with his fragrant holoma, the perfume he exuded when he felt pleasure. Tamara inhaled the sweet, warm caramel aroma she had grown accustomed to and became dizzy with desire.

With long, slender fingers, he caressed her thighs and then paused. He gazed at her and asked with glowing eyes, "Yes?"

"Yes Maashi, yes."

He bent his head and rubbed his cheek on her thigh. His warm breath made her skin shiver. He licked in between her legs with his long, luscious tongue.

Tamara cried out. "Oh, please, please kiss me."

He pressed his mouth on her and his tongue reached deep inside and licked her.

The world swirled and spun. She moaned softly as she relinquished all control and pleasure engulfed her. Her mind floated. She felt warm, as light as a feather. "Oh, I missed you so much Maashi."

Maashi pulled away and exhaled a long-held breath. He rested on his back beside her. His skin glowed an iridescent blue. He turned his head to glimpse her face, extended his arm, reached out, and brought her closer.

"I miss holding you, sweet one," he said. He embraced her with both arms and content, closed his eyes.

Tamara's mind was freed from all its worries. If only life could always be this simple. Light as a bubble, she drifted away in a vast blue expanse far from the world around her, as if it didn't exist. Only the safe and infinite blue nothingness existed.

Chapter 20

"Damn you, Patel. How could you make such a mistake? I tol' you to send a distress signal to our command ship on a secure channel and you sent it across the whole sector," said Lieutenant Yoon as he paced the small receiving room where they were held. He pulled at the hair of his sparse goatee and ran his hand in his thinning hair.

"I'm sorry," said Vidal, his copilot, as his eyes scanned for the hundredth time the bare room, which contained only two couches and one low table. "I was concerned about our orbit around tha' M planet. It wasn't right. My instruments kept fluctuating and I couldn't determine our exact position."

The lieutenant fumed. "I can't believe the signal got picked up by fuckin' clickin' aliens we never encountered before. Our translator can't process their clicks and they are not responding to any other alien language. Damn. What are we goin' to do? How are we goin' to contact our command ship? I don' even know what they did with our pods."

"Ya," said Vidal. He undid the elastic band holding his wavy black hair together and tied back his hair in a neat ponytail. His thick black eyebrows went up as he added, "We're in a pickle. They left us with our short-range communicator and it's useless. Can't reach anything."

The two-paneled door slid open, and an alien came in bearing a tray containing bottles of clear fluid, an oval platter with fruits and several jars of pudding.

Vidal jumped to his feet and approached the alien.

Lt Yoon cried out. "Stay away. Don' touch him. We don' have protective gear and his germs could be dangerous." He stared at the alien and said, "When can we leave? Why are you keepin' us here?"

The alien, taller and more muscular than the humans, wore a multicolor sash. He clicked a few words.

"You need to send someone we can communicate with. Send someone else."

The alien tilted his head to one side, clicked, and stepped forward.

The lieutenant raised both arms and in a strong voice said, "Stop right there. Don' come any closer."

The alien straightened, set the tray on the table, and left.

Lt Yoon stared at the door and shook his head. "I don' see any hinges or any control mechanism. I don' know how we'll get out of here."

"We need to find a way soon," said Vidal. "We'll 'ave to be creative."

Chapter 21

Tamara had showered, dressed, eaten a light meal of creamy choun, cheese, and crackers with toughi, her favorite fruit, a blend of apple and pear. Now, as she waited for Chopa, she paced her room with arms swinging at her side and then paced some more with arms crossed on her chest. Would she finally meet the humans today? She knew that the Chamis were bringing them to an easily accessible location, and that Chopa would accompany her to see them. That was it.

Chopa hadn't been forthcoming about specific details concerning them. He said they were healthy males, and they were more anxious and unsettled by the hour. The Chamis had to post a guard at the door because they figured out the controls on the door frame and left their assigned quarters several times to wander off in the tunnels. One of them had a small device and tried to contact their main ship but was unsuccessful because the signal was too weak. Chopa confirmed communications between the two species remained a problem.

Tamara's palms were sweaty, and every little sound made her jump. Her heart thumped in her chest, and she found it difficult to take a deep breath.

One moment she was excited and wanted to see what those humans looked like, question them about their life, where they were from, how long they had been traveling. The next moment, she felt overwhelmed, frightened, and worried that they would not meet her expectations. Would they offer her a way back home? How long ago had it been since they left Earth? How far was Earth? Even if it took a few years, she might go back to her world, see her family again. At the thought of her family, her heart sank, and tears blurred her vision. It was all she could do not to burst out crying. It had been more than six months since her arrival on Chitina and she no longer had outbursts of despair and uncontrolled sobbing. There was only a feeling of emptiness in her heart and longing in her soul.

She had many questions but what if they didn't understand her language? If they did manage to converse, would they believe her story? Even if wormholes were a frequent occurrence, she didn't know if they were considered reliable enough to be used for space travel. She wished it were the case. But what if her arrival on Chitina was an extraordinary event, and therefore almost impossible to replicate? Maashi had mentioned months ago that Ishkibu Sheffrous could travel through wormholes but didn't say if they could use those reliably.

What about her life here with Maashi? She had adapted to the Chami ways and shared a powerful bond with a Sheffrou who was considered the most promising on Chitina. She had almost given up hope she would ever go home. She had accepted the fact that she would stay here forever. Now, everything had changed. Like in a card game, an ace had popped in her hand and had overturned her odds of winning. So many thoughts whizzed in her mind that her head spun. She inhaled deeply, slowly exhaled. Chopa's voice startled her.

"Good day to you Chimitanga," he said in a tranquil tone. "Are you well? You look nervous."

"I'm fine," she said, wondering why she didn't hear the chime when he came at the door. "Just eager to get this meeting over." She shook her head. That didn't come out the way she intended.

"Tamara, this is a greeting. Not a meeting. Also, I must inform you that a guard will be present to ensure your safety. Our goal is to keep you from harm. The males are becoming more agitated. We think the lack of proper communication is the cause of this behavior. We could not approach and kiss them to establish an adequate physical link with their body fluids."

"Yes, I figured that," Without proper language, this whole process would quickly become a circus. *Great. They're already upset.* She shook her head. Obviously, the two men would not be inclined to let the Chamis kiss them to establish proper communication.

"Chopa, I was referring to this meeting as a human meeting, not one like the Chamis do." The memory of her first meeting with Maashi, when they both undressed, touched, and felt all over each other's bodies, flashed in her mind. This wouldn't be anything like that.

He tilted his head to one side. "You must remember to keep two arm's lengths away from them and avoid touching them. We have confirmed that they carry microbes with which we are not familiar. Those may be harmless to them and to us Chamranlinas because of our potent immune system, but the microbes could harm you."

"Yes. Yes. The germs. I understand."

Chopa nodded sideways in agreement. He straightened his shirt, adjusted the already perfect knot of his sash, and said, "Let us go then." He strolled to the door, and she followed. The guard standing outside joined them. They walked along a hallway decorated with alternating cerulean blue and apple green stripes, no doubt Chendor's preference, and continued through a series of tunnels with walls with a rough surface and low ceiling, just above Chopa's head. In normal circumstances, Tamara would've commented on the tunnels' tight space, but this morning, her mind was preoccupied, and she concentrated on keeping up the pace with the two aliens.

The group took an elevator to reach a much higher level and followed a well-lit hallway to a series of chambers connected by narrow corridors. The wall colors, dove gray and khaki, were much brighter and the same style as the one in Maashi's quarters, and she started to relax. She squared her shoulders and took a deep breath to prepare for the meeting as they entered a receiving room the size of a spacious living room. The room was all tan color and devoid of furniture. A two-paneled door slid open on her left and a new guard entered, followed by the two humans.

They appeared as surprised by her appearance as she was by theirs. They were both tall and lanky, well over six feet, their long arms reaching below their knees, no doubt a consequence of living in an environment with lower gravity than Earth. Dressed in standard edition Chami shirt and pants which emphasized their slender build, their deep-set eyes and pale, grayish skin color gave them a sickly look. The taller one had Asian traits, a goatee, and his long hair was drawn in a tight bun over the top of his head. The other one had a darker skin tone and warm brown eyes with thick eyebrows. His hair was also long and tied loosely in a ponytail.

They immediately advanced in her direction and started talking in a language that sounded like gibberish. The guard positioned himself in front of them, blocking their path. He clicked something, and they stood still.

"Hello, welcome to Chitina," Tamara said. She smiled and fought the sudden urge to walk over to them and shake their hands. "My name is Tamara Walsh. I'm from Earth. Can you understand me?"

They glanced at each other and the Asian one pulled out of his khaki shirt a small sleek device, no bigger than a cell phone, to translate her greeting in their own language. He spoke, and the device responded. "My name is Lieutenant Yoon, James D. and my associate is Patel, Vidal. You speak an ancient American English dialect. How is this possible? And what are you doin' with these aliens?" He gestured to Chopa and the guard.

His question confirmed Tamara's greatest fear. They were indeed from a distant future. The realization triggered a visceral reaction. Her hands shook and a loud humming buzzed in her ears. She clenched her hands together and said, "I'm from the United States of America," she stated that with an emphasis on the word America. They both frowned at her. "Early twenty-first century. I fell into a wormhole, and it brought me on this planet. The aliens are called Chamranlinas. They rescued me and have been caring for me."

The two glanced at each other and proceeded to a rapid exchange in their language. Lt Yoon said using his translator, "That's impossible. You're probably one colonist jettisoned from the Yervaland ship. They ran into serious difficulties a few months ago and sent a good number of passengers out in space in survival pods. Most have been recuperated, but unfortunately, not all. These aliens probably detected your pod and brought you here."

Patel became animated and said, with exaggerated hand gestures which reminded Tamara of marionettes held by long strings. "Spendin' a prolonged period in a space pod plays with your mind and that's why you' confused."

Tamara shook her head. "I'm not confused. I'm from Earth. Not from a spaceship."

Lt Yoon stared at Tamara and said through his device, "It is our duty to verify your story, but either way, you cannot stay here with those aliens. We've never been in contact with them before and can't communicate. We don't know if they're friendly or not and where they stand with the coalition of planets rules and regulations. The Extraterrestrial Alliance will not authorize your stay." He pointed to the Chamis with his arm, "As soon as our main ship arrives, we will leave. I'm hopin' they'll let us go without any trouble and you'll come with us."

Tamara declined to comment. She needed time to process the implications of his statement. Instead, she asked the foremost question on her mind. "How far is Earth from here? How long have you traveled?"

"Why are you asking this?" Lt Yoon said. "Even if you're confused, you know very well we're in the Magellan system."

Tight-lipped, she said, "What year is this?"

Patel's eyes widened. "The space year is four hundred seven," he said. "The Earth year is two thousand five hundred seventy-seven."

Tamara gasped. Over five hundred seventy years ahead of her time. The room danced before her eyes. Her chest tightened. Her head felt squeezed in a vise. If he added anything more, she didn't see or hear it.

Chopa put a gentle hand on her shoulder. She heard his voice as if in a dream. "Thank you. That will be all for today. The guard will direct you back to your quarters."

The humans left with suspicious looks on their faces. Tamara looked up at Chopa. "Take me back. I want to see Maashi."

Chopa led the way, and she followed. With a loud ringing in her ears, she walked back in a daze. *What was she going to do?*

Chapter 22

Maashi lay pensive, resting on the wide couch of his receiving room, surrounded by gold embroidered cushions, his long legs stretched out in front of him. He held a lumi to his lips, unfurled his tongue, dipped it in the warm choun prepared by Rahma. His Chowli didn't mind milking the choun from his breasts and prepared a tall glass every day for him. He lapped the liquid, swirled it in his mouth, and swallowed. He savored the sweet taste which brought memories of happier times when life was simpler, when his main preoccupation was deciding how to best enjoy the many pleasures offered to him; a time of fun and playful games with his former first Chowli Ashra, a Multi with green as the dominating color and a dash of pink. They had shared over forty sequences together before his own kidnapping.

Sadness rose inside him, and like an overflowing vase, spilled over. Tears ran down his cheeks as he recalled the night of his kidnapping. The deadly attack against his group happened just a little over a sequence ago in the winding tunnel leading to the Seventh Compound. Ashra plus another Chowli and several guards lost their lives trying to save him from being captured. Alas, they failed. Maashi was injured, kidnapped, and never saw his Chowlis again. The trauma and the torture he endured for five months at the hands of the enemy had aged him more than the previous twenty sequences of his life.

Maashi couldn't remember much of the time spent as a captive of the Krakoran. His mind had contained those memories with such effectiveness that until the last few weeks, he couldn't recall anything at all. Although it was a bewildering condition, that protective mechanism had kept him safe from reliving the trauma of his kidnapping.

Recently, Runshama or flashbacks had manifested themselves and had shaken his confidence; visions of being bound in a casing of smooth unyielding material for days at a time in a room bathed entirely in white: white ceiling, immaculate white floor, and walls. A totally alien experience for someone used to swimming freely in the cold, clear water of Chitina's underground pools scattered among the dim tunnels.

His eyes thinned as he remembered something else that filled him with fear and confusion: some type of giant helicoidal structure that rose twenty levels high above ground. Like a huge wheel with spokes, it connected to different levels above a horrifying pit filled with crawling creatures. Every few days, he was pushed and prodded with a rod as hot as a burning coal until he crossed on the spokes above the looming pit and reached the giant structure. A pervasive stench of blood and carrion wafted from the deep pit. Pity for the unfortunate who tripped and fell off the narrow spokes, for they would be devoured instantly in a feeding frenzy. Until this day, Maashi was stricken with terror every time he saw a random object which appeared to twist and turn like a helix.

With his long fingers, he slowly wiped the tears that had surged with the painful longing for his Chowlis. His gaze settled on the elaborate fountain across the room. He tracked the drops of water as they trickled down from one opalescent marble vessel to the next and gathered in the elaborately carved oval basin, big enough for an adult Chamranlina to bathe in.

He pondered the last few weeks spent under Chendor's care. The huge Sheffrou had been the epitome of kindness and patience. With his help, Maashi's mind had finally cleared after days of confusing visions. Some he remembered and then understood important facts: his trek through the tunnels to see Chari Varian leader of the Outcasts, and the brutal beating at the hands of the outcast guards. He remembered standing over a deep dark pit with Chari at his side, but then his memory blurred, replaced by a feeling of despair so great that even now, his chest hurt at the mere thought of it.

He had pushed his mind to the limit, and he still could not recall Chari's words and what caused the terrible realization that life on Chitina was doomed, hopeless, without a future. His brain had erased his words as completely as the wind erases footprints on the dry soil of Chitina. The only thing that remained was the chilling vision of two eyes staring at him from a young face. The confounding thread of events that began with Chari led to the moment he was found close to death in the Goolalong Fields.

What did Chari say to him that could bring about such despair? Maashi had seen little of him these last few days. He wanted to ask the Ghouli Ghouli, but the answers scared him to the point he decided I was best to wait for an auspicious moment to prod him with questions. Chari possessed a sharp mind and could easily evade his questioning if he so wished. Maashi would have to catch him with his guard down.

Lost in his thoughts, he paid no attention to the door chime and was startled by the sudden appearance of Chendor's gargantuan shape. He stood before him wearing midnight-blue pants and a simple white shirt which exposed his quatay.

"How do you feel Shonava?" Said Chendor, his eyes gentle and concerned. "Are you pleased with my Chowlis today?"

Maashi fixated Chendor with an intense gaze. The giant Chamranlina was an enigma. The Tousanou's behavior was beyond reproach but today, his kindness was irritating. "I am as well as can be," he answered, "after hours of being pleasured by your two Chowlis. I could not wish for companions as thorough and attentive as them. Their devotion is irreproachable." He lowered his eyes and watched the air bubbles rise and disperse in the basin across from him.

"I sense sarcasm in your voice." Chendor eased his corpulence on the couch close to Maashi and his holoma settled around him like a translucent veil. The olive tea tree fragrance floated in the air and reached Maashi. "Are you still haunted by the vision of the two piercing eyes? The one that has been the source of so much pain and despair?"

"The vision is ever present," answered Maashi. At the mention of the vision, he set his glass of choun down on the granite table beside him with such force it clanged.

"With time and rest, the meaning of the vision will reveal itself. I'm convinced you will solve the puzzle." Chendor kissed Maashi's shoulder to appease him. "Perhaps you saw it during a time of extreme stress when you were captured by the Krakoran. You should not torture your mind by questioning it without cease." Chendor took Maashi's hand in his and caressed his long, slender fingers. "You are still thin. Would you like something to eat?"

Maashi frowned, and his eyes darkened. "Pleasure and food. Food and pleasure. Does your life consist only of these two things?"

Chendor chuckled. "Although these may seem trivial to you, they, and psychotherapy are effective in treating many cases of trauma such as yours."

"There are things more important in life than food and pleasure. Someone told me this once and I realize she was right."

"She? A Fanella said that? Who?"

"Not a Fanella. Tamara, the little human female, told me that. She is also the one who made me understand that the most recent attacks by the Krakoran on the night of the Great Eclipse had to be coordinated by one or more of our own people."

"Oh." Chendor emitted a mocking grunt, but with Maashi's serious expression, he refrained from showing more hilarity. "That is a grave accusation, Shonava. Unless you have proof of your theories, no one will take you seriously."

"A Chamranlina had to be involved." Maashi said in a tone which left no doubt about his conviction. "I didn't believe it at first, but I have given the facts significant consideration. Those three attacks on the same night were coordinated with the utmost precision in time and place. The enemy targeted multiple groups of Sheffrous, with a level of sophistication not seen before. The odds of this happening are extremely low."

"I see. The facts were not presented to me that way." Chendor rubbed his hands together as if he wanted no part of this dirty information. "Tell me, is this conviction the reason you left your quarters a few weeks ago to go to the Burned Zone? Why did you seek Chari Varian without informing your Chowlis?"

"I went to see the leader of the Outcasts to get answers. In my ignorance and naivete, it never occurred to me that my visit would be interpreted as an act of aggression and that his guards would attack me." Maashi set his hands on his knees. "I thought that Chari might have been involved with the attacks by the enemy. If not, perhaps he could provide pertinent information and he might reveal clues that would help solve the puzzle."

Chendor grumbled and readjusted his position. The couch protested with creaking sounds. "Chari led a rebellion that caused a rift between the Ghouli Ghouli race and the main population of Chamranlinas. His goal was to recover rights his people had lost many centuries ago. But I refuse to think he could have been involved in the betrayal of his people."

"All the same," said Maashi as he spread his fingers on his knees, "I went to see him and was found days later, close to death, in the Goolalong Fields." Maashi's amber eyes flashed with anger. "Chendor," he said, "you have also suffered a horrible attack by the Krakoran. You almost lost your life and have been permanently disfigured. This happened dozens of sequences ago. Why have you been hiding deep underground since then? I had never heard of your existence until we met recently."

"I resent what you're implying. I'm not hiding." Chendor raised his arms up high and bounced on the couch with surprising ease. "Why would I put myself in a position of ridicule in front of my peers?" Chendor cocked his head to one side, rendering his scar less visible. "I knew the Council would refuse to consider me for mating and my scars were a constant reminder to every one of my sad fate. I deemed it best to continue my life in the deep underground, away from inquisitive eyes. My skills as a healer are well developed, and I have been working as a Tousanou for dozens of sequences. And, I might add, you benefited from my care."

Maashi straightened, and his voice found new vigor. "You are a Sheffrou 6. There are so few of you. You possess incredible strength, both physical and mental. Your voice could have tremendous weight among the Sawishas. Why do you hide with your perfect Chowlis in this perfect falsehood of a life?" Maashi's amber eyes glowed. His brow darkened. "Why didn't you rise to the challenge of finding the truth when I was kidnapped one sequence ago? Perhaps the most recent attacks could have been prevented. Why did a Sheffrou die needlessly, two others were kidnapped, and another severely injured this sequence? Where were you?"

Chendor hissed. "You're overstepping the proper boundaries between a guest and his host, Shonava. I resent your comments. I have suffered so much that to this day, I can't travel in the tunnels without losing my mind."

Maashi stood and stared at Chendor like an opponent sizing up another at a wrestling match. "A very convenient excuse to relinquish your responsibility of finding the truth to help the others."

Chendor's eyes thinned with anger. "You have the right to speak your mind." Chendor lifted his large frame off the couch. "I think your stay here is ending. I will arrange a transfer back to your own compound at the earliest. Good day, Shonava." Chendor held Maashi's gaze then tuned and left.

Chapter 23

"I will contact Sheffrou Maashi," Chopa said, "he will see you later today."

Tamara nodded and stepped in her receiving room in silence. As soon as she was settled in, Chopa left. She knew he would inform Maashi in person of her request.

Tamara slumped on her favorite cranberry couch and secured a soft cushion on her lap. Her chest felt constricted, and her temples throbbed. She stared at her surroundings: the beige walls, the brown carpet with teal swirls, the granite tables, the little fountain, and the dark burgundy plant set in the corner and her eyes filled with tears. This place wasn't home and the two men from the spaceship didn't convey a feeling of home either. There wasn't anything familiar she could relate to.

The humans were from a time so far ahead of hers that they were completely disconnected from the world she had known. A time when space travel was common, where humanity had already settled on other worlds, and where meeting alien life wasn't an extraordinary occurrence.

Adapting to their way of life would be a challenge as much as trying to adapt to the Chamis' society had been. More than that, they didn't understand she was from twenty-first century Earth and mistook her for a lost colonist. A fact that meant numerous possibilities. A colony existed nearby, colonists looked like her, and a ship on its way to the colony had experienced a major adverse event. This only increased the difficulty of explaining to them her arrival on the Chamis' planet. It seemed traveling in space through a wormhole was unheard of. To make matters worse, they were convinced she had been in a pod retrieved by aliens and therefore it was their duty to rescue her from their hands. If she had seen this in a movie, she would have laughed. Sadly, this was reality, and she couldn't see the humor of it all. How much pressure could they exert on the Chamis to force them into releasing her under their care?

These two individuals were so different from her people. Had they spent their lives in space, in some engineered artificial environment? Had they ever experienced the freedom of standing in a meadow surrounded by forest, the fresh smell of the ground after a rainfall, the salty air of the seashore, blue skies with puffy clouds? Were they raised and influenced by different values and morals? Tamara shook her head. Even their appearance, tall and thin, with abnormally long limbs, reminded her of patients with Marfan syndrome. The way they moved felt surreal like puppets controlled by strings. They were the aliens.

What should she do?

She coughed, sneezed, and said aloud, "Haven't these guys ever heard of a wormhole? They didn't listen to me. They paid no attention to what I said." She sneezed multiple times and scurried over to the water room. "I swear this place doesn't like me." She removed her sandals, stepped on the slick granite floor of the water room, and growled, "They think I'm a colonist." They had stared at her like she was inferior, and she had sensed their contempt. The next unexpected but violent sneeze sent her flying headfirst. She slammed the opposite wall and dropped limp on the floor.

An aroma of warm caramel tickled Tamara's nose. She licked her lips. A thin film on them tasted like pecan pralines. Calm, peaceful thoughts spread in her mind. She remembered the little candy shoppe on Meeting Street in Charleston where they gave out samples of candied pralines in summer. She smiled. Her tongue touched something soft, warm, of delicate texture: Maashi.

She opened her eyes, and her gaze was lost in the bright amber of the Sheffrou's large oval eyes. He retracted his royal blue tongue back in his mouth. His face was so close she could feel his cool breath on her cheeks.

"Mm," she said, "You taste like my favorite candy and your holoma smells wonderful."

He wrapped his arms around her in a protective embrace. "How do you feel, my little Chimitanga?" His long middle finger traced the contour of her jaw. He kissed her temple and his lips lingered on her cheeks.

"My head feels like it weighs a ton." She looked around and realized she was back on her couch, snuggled in his lap. His chest was bare like it had frequently been in Chendor's sector.

Maashi smiled and held her up higher and reclined further back on the couch, so she lay on him, her head nestled on his quatay, the ivory markings on his upper chest.

He whispered in her ear. "I missed you."

"I missed you too." She rubbed her cheek on the silky skin of his torso. "These last few weeks have been dreadful. I was so worried. When you went missing, I imagined the worst. I thought you had been kidnapped." Her voice choked. "I cried every day."

"Forgive me, Shapinka. I was foolish to leave like I did. I knew the Ghouli Ghouli wouldn't be welcoming, but never expected them to attack and beat me the way they did."

"You could have gotten killed." She shook her head. "How are you feeling? Are you still experiencing hallucinations? Headaches?" She reached for her temple. "Oh. I'm a little dizzy myself."

He took her head in his warm hands and gave her a pro-longed kiss. Then another. His chest heaved with a deep sigh. "I'm better." He slid a hand under her shirt and massaged her back with soft circular strokes.

She sighed with the pleasure.

He played in her hair with long fingers then lifted her chin upward and scrutinized her face. He clicked and said, "You have an impressive bulge on your forehead."

Tamara wriggled to free her right hand and touched her head. "Ouch! I must've hit my head hard when I slipped in the water room. I don't understand. There's something about this sector that doesn't agree with me."

He bent down and pressed his cheek on the swelling then kissed her forehead. "This will decrease the swelling." He nuzzled her neck just below her ear.

"I was so preoccupied with those darn humans." She withdrew from his arms.

"Yes," he said. "I sensed your frustration. Is that why you fell?"

Tamara straightened and back rigid, said, "They didn't believe me. They didn't believe I fell in a wormhole. Plus, they acted like they had been violated. Such suspicious and unpleasant characters. They even think I'm a colonist from one of their ships jettisoned in a pod."

With gentle fingers, Maashi felt her body, arms, and legs searching for injuries. He found a bruise on her elbow and on her right knee and, when he rolled up her pants, exposing her ankles, he noticed more bruising. "You twisted your right ankle." He held it in his warm hand then massaged it. "Better now?"

"Maashi," she said, "didn't you hear what I said?"

"Yes. I heard. Why are you so angry, Tamara?"

He tilted his head to better judge the condition of the ankle. Then he rubbed the balls of her feet in a slow, circular motion. "Tamara," he said in his musical voice, "didn't you expect the two males to react the way they did?"

"Frankly, I didn't know what to expect, but I'm puzzled. They seemed so different."

"Imagine a reverse scenario. What if your ship had been seized, towed with a tractor beam, and you had been transported on the surface of another planet, awakened, and put in a cell without any way to contact your own people? Wouldn't you behave the way they did? They are upset with reason. They don't know who we are. We have never met aliens like them."

Tamara opened her mouth to say something but stopped short. After a moment, she stated, "I see what you're getting at. However, they didn't listen to anything I said. Their minds were made up, and they treated me like I was insignificant." She grumbled. "I'm not used to being ignored and my statements questioned. I don't trust them."

He massaged her ankle once more, paused, and said, "First impressions are most important, especially when dealing with alien species. If the Elders had consulted me, I would've recommended a different course of action."

"Like what?"

"I think we shouldn't have intervened with their ship's orbit and kept our distance. They sent a distress signal and rescue was likely on the way. We could have contacted them later when the situation wasn't urgent. Now, their ship is in orbit around Chitina, and another ship is being lured here."

"Why is that a problem?"

"We Chamranlinas try at all costs to avoid attracting other alien species to our home planet."

"Because you don't want to attract your enemies, the Krakoran? But they already know your coordinates. They know where you live."

"There. Your ankle is back to normal." He carefully released her leg. He glanced at her. "It's complicated."

"Why?"

"There are now other species who wish to capture and sell our people to the Krakoran and the Rodenegad."

"Why would they do that?"

"Sadly, it's true." He looked down and spread his fingers on his knees. "Some species will pay a high price for Chamranlinas slaves. Multicolors are indefatigable workers and Sheffrous are sought as sex slaves."

Maashi looked away. His eyes lost their color.

"I'm sorry." She put a light hand on his chest. "I never thought about it that way."

She shook her head in annoyance. "The humans think I'm one of their colonists, to the point they might try to take me with them against my will, thinking they're saving me from aliens. What am I going to do?"

Maashi said in a low voice. "I know you wanted to meet them but, between trying to explain your most unusual arrival here, and our own well-intentioned but ill-thought actions, we have created disbelief and mistrust; not a good way to establish adequate relations."

Tamara couldn't think of an appropriate response. She let out a long sigh, then stared at him. Maashi's eyes grew bigger. All color drained from his face.

"Maashi? What's wrong?"

"A small body. A young face with two glowing eyes staring into nothingness."

"Still haunted by the vision of the face with two eyes?"

Maashi set Tamara aside and stood. "The vision follows me night and day." In a hushed voice, he said, "I know what it is. It's an offspring. A young Fanella. I think she's sick."

The door chime rang. Chopa walked in. Maashi, still as a statue, did not acknowledge his Chowli's arrival.

Chopa approached the Sheffrou, "Shonava, are you well?" He put an arm around Maashi's shoulder and held him tight, a concerned expression on his face.

Maashi slowly turned his head to face him, his face as pale as if he had seen a Krakoran. "What is it, Chopa?"

"Sir, I have important news. News that may cause concern."

"Yes." Maashi's voice sounded faraway.

"The thorn Tamara removed from your side has been analyzed. It's from a cookra plant, the one that produces chorila nuts."

"Those plants," said Maashi in a slow deliberate tone, "don't have thorns."

"You're right, Shonava, but this is a new variety. I don't know where it originated from. We are searching with the central computer of the colony to pinpoint where these plants are growing. They are not showing up in the main records."

"That's weird," Tamara said. "Do you think there's a glitch in the records?"

"No, I do not," said Chopa, indignant. His brow darkened, "I do not understand it."

Maashi slid out of Chopa's embrace and took a few steps away from them and turned. "I remember leaving my quarters. I went to see Chari Varian, leader of the Outcasts, then somehow traveled to the Goolalong Fields. Chopa, you confirmed there were faint traces of my holoma in the tunnel close to the entrance to the Fanella compound, the one next to the Central Compound."

"Yes, Shonava. The scent was there."

Maashi's eyes shone. "That's where I went. The attendant who took care of me when I was summoned for mating said there were rumors I had gone there and created havoc. That's where I saw the little Fanella. The one in my vision. The vision is powerful, relentless." Maashi put a hand on his temple, took a step forward then stopped abruptly and gasped. He roared, "It's a warning. Something is terribly wrong. I must find out what it is. I must go there."

"Shonava," said Chopa, "You know that even in regular circumstances, Sheffrous and Sawishas may not enter there and doing so may result in serious consequences. In recent weeks, without giving the general population any explanation, the Elders have cut off all communications between the Fanella compounds and the outside." He paused and added under his breath, "I can try to request an authorization for a visit. However, I'm convinced your request will be denied."

Maashi's voice resonated in the small receiving room. "But it is imperative I find out what's wrong. I think the little Fanella is sick."

"Maashi, slow down," said Tamara, "you need to think this through." She was worried about the sudden turn of the conversation. "You can't take any more risks."

"Shonava," Chopa said, "if I may ask, what did Chari Varian tell you that prompted you to go to the Fanella compound even though you knew that if you got caught, you would be severely punished?"

Maashi tilted his head to one side. "I can't remember what he said to me. I was indisposed."

"Indisposed, sir?"

"Yes." He glanced sideways at Chopa. "Let's just say the reception from his men had been brutal."

Chopa's body stiffened. "That explains the injuries we found before you were brought here under Sheffrou Chendor's care. You had been poisoned by the methane gas, but you were also close to death from severe hemorrhaging. Now I see why Chari came to your quarters to inquire about you and was so intent on finding you." Chopa's voice faltered. "He knew that your life was in danger. No one could figure out where you had sustained those injuries. Chari did not disclose that his men beat you and didn't say anything about what he told you." His eyes thinned to black slits.

"Chopa," Maashi said, "what's most important now is that we must find out what is going on. The Fanellas might be in trouble. This must be attended to immediately."

Tamara bounced off the couch. "Maashi, I can help. I can go to the Fanella compound." She glanced at both. "I'm sure Lady Ileana will see me. She must know something." Tamara welcomed the opportunity to leave, if only for a little while. The diversion would give her time to sort out how she felt about the humans and help her decide whether to stay on Chitina or leave.

"I will send a special request to the Elders right away," said Chopa, "with your permission, sir."

"Yes, do so. I need to find Chari. I want answers," said Maashi. "I plan to leave Chendor's sector as soon as possible."

Chapter 24

One group of Fanellas lived in the area located right next to the Central Compound where Maashi lived. Above ground, a translucent dome the size of a football stadium covered the surface which served as recreation area and greenhouse. The Chamis grew a wide variety of edible plants and flowers in a climate-controlled environment which mimicked their original home world, the wondrous planet Chamtali. Without the protective dome, few plants could survive on the desolate surface.

The Chamis had established a colony on Chitina after their own world became inhospitable to life. A rogue planet wandering in deep space had come too close to Chamtali and caused a slight deviation of its original course around their sun. The change in orbit created an instability that translated into intense volcanic activity. Within two hundred sequences, their world changed: The surface water evaporated, and the land became dry and arid, exposing the Chamis to more frequent attacks by their enemy, the Krakoran. They had no choice. Face extinction or search for another world to emigrate.

The exact number of Fanellas who lived in that compound was kept secret for reasons that eluded Tamara's understanding. All she knew was that Lady Ileana, a lovely green-eyed Fanella, lived there. Maashi had told Tamara of his love for the enchanting Ileana. He also explained that if anyone found out about his feelings for her, the Elders would never let him see her again. While Tamara had been disheartened by his revelation, she promised never to reveal his secret.

Tamara vividly remembered the first time she met Ileana in the greenhouse months before. What a lovely place. The dome above created a magical world of cotton candy pink sky, abundant flowers, and luxuriant vegetation. She had been enchanted by the female, the epitome of grace and femininity. Tamara shook her head in disbelief. So many things had happened since then: The Great Eclipse Celebration, the coordinated attacks by the Krakoran which killed many Chamis and the conclusion that a traitor was the culprit. Maashi disappeared not long after and now, since his rescue, he was haunted by the vision of a young female.

One of Chendor's personal guards accompanied Tamara through the tunnels to the Fanellas' underground quarters. They soon reached the main entrance and crossed the first obstacle, a massive metallic door at least twelve feet high and ten feet wide secured by twelve locks on each side wall of the tunnel. The guard sent a signal by pressing a code on a thick bracelet on his wrist. The door opened and Tamara entered the welcoming room where she was transferred to the care of a Gray Feeder. He was one of many gray Multicolors who traveled daily to the surface to expose his skin to the orange sun. Through a process like photosynthesis, the Chamis produced choun, a creamy substance like milk they fed to the females. This prevented them from leaving the protection of the dome and risk being attacked and kidnapped by the enemy.

Tamara followed the Gray Feeder and entered a narrow tunnel which led to a smaller door. After a short walk, a large open cave with several secondary caves stretched in front of her.

The lighting in this strange underground reminded her of dusk on Earth, just after sunset. "Oh, I can't believe how gloomy it is in here." The comment escaped her lips before she could stop it.

The Gray Feeder who had greeted her stopped and tilted his head to one side. He didn't say anything but simply showed the way by extending his arm. She frowned when she realized he was wearing steel gray shirt and pants, an unusual color, worn by the Chamis only in times of mourning.

He took off, and Tamara trotted behind him to keep up. After a hundred feet, she slowed down because of the irregular ground and observed the surroundings. The walls of the cave had a dull washed-out look, and an obnoxious, pungent odor permeated the air. She noticed a few islands of vegetation growing in big twelve feet wide planters which contained clusters of tall stalks with purple flowers like sunflowers. They seemed to be the only ones growing in the low light.

She walked over to examine one of them and covered her nose. Up close, the acrid smell was overpowering. She examined it and frowned when she saw thorns every few inches on the main stalk. She made a mental note to ask for a sample before leaving.

Two Fanellas walked past her with glazed eyes and vacant stares. They wore elaborate turbans, and their bodies were wrapped like mummies in dark color clothing. One almost bumped into Tamara as if she hadn't seen her at all. What a strange contrast to the gorgeous gowns the Fanellas had worn at the Great Eclipse Celebration. That night, they looked like fairy-tale princesses with their colorful makeup that made the eyes glow and the delicate flowers braided in their hair cascading down their backs.

The Gray Feeder clicked at Tamara and entered a straight tunnel, which led to a secondary cave. This smaller cave possessed several portals, and the guard pointed to the last one on the left.

Tamara nodded and said, "Thank you."

She walked into a receiving room with an embroidered carpet on the floor, two wide couches overflowing with dark green cushions, and several small granite tables. A blue globe the size of a football set on one table emitted a pleasant glow.

Tamara waited a few minutes and Lady Ileana came in through a side doorway. Tamara, remembering her exquisite beauty, her warm smile, and charming ways, gasped at her sight. Wearing a turban and a steel gray shapeless dress, Ileana approached quickly. She clasped her hands together and said, with hollow, hopeful eyes, "Welcome back, Shapinka. It is a pleasure to see you. Are you bringing the cure we so desperately seek?"

Tamara took a step back and cleared her throat. "It is a pleasure to see you also," she said. "I come looking for answers. I have many questions."

Ileana's face and neck paled. She brought her hands to her chest. She moved her lips, but no sound came out.

"Lady, what's wrong? What happened?"

"Don't you know?" She whispered. Her eyes darted from side to side. "The Sheffrou was here. He saw our predicament, our desperation. Where is he? Where is the help he promised?"

"I'm sorry," Tamara said, "Maashi's been sick."

"No! Not him as well." She flailed her arms about her. "How is he? Is he still alive?"

Tamara shook her head vehemently. "He's all right now. It's a long story."

"Then let me kiss you. This way I will reach in your thoughts and learn what happened."

Tamara nodded in agreement. She was reluctant to engage in a French kiss with the lady, but she knew this would be the best way to provide her all the information about Maashi's adventures and bring her up to date with his current situation.

Ileana sat on the nearest couch and opened inviting arms. Tamara sat on her lap and braced herself for her kiss. She noticed how extremely thin she was, like an anorexic patient.

Something dreadful had happened.

Ileana took Tamara's face in her hands and pressed her lips on her mouth. She introduced her tongue inside and licked her mouth and palate. This lasted a few minutes. She paused long enough for Tamara to inhale a few times, then kissed her again. At last, she retreated and wiped away tears. Up close, Tamara noticed how her translucent skin sagged under her eyes and around the corners of her mouth, making her look old and exhausted.

"We believe Maashi came here," said Tamara, "but he can't remember a thing. What happened?"

"The Sheffrou slipped in the compound unnoticed over three weeks ago," Ileana said in a tired voice. "Chari Varian had revealed to him our dire situation against express orders by the Elders not to mention the plague to Sheffrous." She stared at Tamara with an intense expression. "You must understand. The one and two-sequence old offspring were all Maashi's. When Chari told him about the plague, he refused to believe the terrible news. He came at great risk to see the young ones and find the truth. Sadly, there was little he could do and to this day, the cause of the plague is still unknown."

Tamara sat in stunned silence as the lady gave her details of a sickness that started close to three months ago. "The young one-sequence old became weak, lethargic, and stopped eating. Within weeks, two of them had died. A mere two weeks later, three more were gone, including one two-sequence old. The mothers became frantic. They were desperate for a cure. I, myself, lost my youngest, the little Shanta." Ileana looked away and wiped her tear-filled eyes. She looked weary and pale. "Our best healers, our Elders, even the Outcasts couldn't find a remedy. The news of our plight reached across the colony, but the Elders were adamant. We had to keep the information secret from the general population, the Sawishas, and Sheffrous, especially Maashi who had fathered the one and two-sequence old. They wanted at all costs to avoid a panic, or some type of rebellion like we experienced around sixty sequences ago."

"We are powerless to stop the disease. Now, there is only one child left. She is my daughter Shalina and Maashi is the father. When Maashi came, he held her in his arms for hours and her condition improved." Ileana's eyes lit up.

"While the three of us were together, someone called the Silver Guards. I found out later it was my oldest daughter, eighteen sequences old, who sounded the alarm. You must understand, many have blamed Sheffrou Maashi for the sickness because all the ones who died were his offspring. But I know other Fanellas were sick as well." She lowered her head as if in silent prayer. "Maashi was devastated by the news. I could tell how his heart broke when he held his last offspring. Sadly, he had to leave at a moment's notice. The Silver Guards were approaching fast. Being caught in a Fanella compound entails a serious punishment. He removed his shirt and wrapped the child in it. He left strict instructions to feed her only fresh choun by Gray Feeders who went to the surface daily. When he left, he promised me he would find a remedy to heal the little one and would be back soon, but I heard nothing after that."

"One Gray Feeder who has connections with Chari Varian smuggles from time to time some of Maashi's clothing with instructions to cover the child in them. Every time, she seems to improve, but she remains weak and inactive. I have already lost my youngest and I worry night and day that this one won't survive." She wrung her hands in misery and desperation.

Tamara couldn't think of anything to say that would console her. She took one of the lady's hands and kissed it. "I'm so sorry."

Ileana embraced her. Tamara considered having a brief contact with the child. It was possibly risky for her. No one knew what had caused the plague, but she decided it was too important not to see the child. She said, "Can I see your daughter?"

Ileana nodded sideways and lead her to a back room with light blue walls and pastel color cushions. As Tamara examined the room, a faint but pleasant aroma tickled her nose: Maashi's holoma. The little girl lay silent and listless in a sea of cream color shirts and pearl-gray pants. Tamara recognized them. They belonged to Maashi.

The child turned her head when they entered, and Tamara stopped at the entrance, astonished at the sight of her. The little one was Maashi's vision come to life: a young face, two glowing eyes staring into mid-air. Her light chestnut hair was adorned with small bows and delicately folded sky-blue shapes, which reminded Tamara of origami.

She approached her and sat close without touching her. "How are you little one? What's your name?"

The child glanced at her mother who came and sat on the other side of the couch. She clicked at her daughter and the child responded with one word, "Shalina."

"Such a beautiful name. I hope you get well soon."

Ileana translated. Shalina nodded sideways.

"Do you feel any pain? Is something hurting you?"

She glanced at her mother. They clicked at each other. "No, she doesn't feel pain."

"We'll let you rest now," Tamara said. "I need to speak to your mother." Tamara wanted to give her something to remember her by. She thought of the perfect gift. She unclasped the gold bracelet Maashi had offered her when he gave her the title of Chimitanga and asked Ileana, "Can I give her this? This was a gift from Maashi. I'm sure he would love for her to have it."

"You are so kind and generous." The lady touched Tamara's shoulder. "Thank you. She would be honored to wear it."

Tamara handed the bracelet to Ileana who fastened it onto the child's wrist. Shalina blinked and looked up at them. She smiled as her mother explained the meaning of the gift. She settled comfortably on the cushions and held her arm close to her chest to examine the bracelet.

"My daughter needs rest. Thank you." Ileana rose. "We should go now."

"Of course." Tamara smiled one last time at Shalina and followed the lady back in the receiving room. She sat on a couch and said, "We need to talk."

They spent the next two hours discussing the signs and symptoms on the sickness, how it had first manifested, and if other individuals were affected. Tamara asked about the food they ate, the fluids, and the choun. She even inquired about the tall pungent plants she had seen and requested a sample. The lady explained they were provided by a young purple called Noolin who worked as an assistant for Master Kokin Cronobutin, Maashi's mentor when he was a young Sheffrou.

At the mention of Master Kokin, Tamara cringed. She hadn't forgotten how he had insulted her and Maashi in front of Maashi's guests. Thankfully, a massive green Sawisha called Benshimu had intervened to save the situation. Kokin had no other choice but to leave under the harsh clicks coming from the guests. She saw Benshimu once more at the Great Eclipse Celebration and couldn't forget the fiery hot kiss he gave Maashi.

Ileana told Tamara that Noolin had encouraged them to consume the nuts, stating they were an excellent source of protein for the youngest offspring during the long winter months. She said he also gave them plant cuttings so they could grow them. Unfortunately, the plague started a few months later and despite all their efforts, including providing ample nuts, the offspring died.

She lowered her head in her hands. With a face devoid of color, she pleaded, "If there is anything you can do to help, anything at all, please do. We feel hopeless."

Too choked to respond, Tamara squeezed her hands hard and nodded. *Did the thorn she removed from Maashi's side come from the same plant that produced those nuts? Was there a connection between the nuts and the plague?*

She rose and turned to leave. The Gray Feeder was at the door waiting to bring her back. She left with a heart heavy with sorrow and a small pouch offered by the guard containing plant cuttings and nuts.

Chapter 25

The lights dimmed in the tunnels, showing early evening. Chari shadowed by Chopa had been traveling for several hours when they reached the seventh compound, domain of Shonava Benshimu Hellowina. They had progressed at a good pace but had remained silent during the whole trip.

The stunning news Tamara had brought back with her about the fate of the young Fanellas had saddened Chopa beyond words. Their species was in peril. The Sheffrous were under constant threat of attack by the enemy, the mature females weren't ovulating, and the offspring were dying from an illness no one could explain. Such a strange yet almost apocalyptic scenario.

Chopa's heart went out to the little females and to their mothers who had suffered so much. Watching any creature die a slow death was difficult enough. Seeing your own offspring wither away must have caused unbearable pain. When Chopa disclosed the news to Chari, the Ghouli Ghouli acknowledged the information without showing emotion. He explained that he had been sworn to secrecy by the Elders but had known about the plague for some time.

Chopa couldn't help but think that Chari could have shared the news with the Sheffrou in the last few weeks, thus sparing him the torment of the relentless vision of the young face and glowing eyes.

Chari slowed his pace and turned to Chopa. "We're approaching the compound. Let me address the guards."

They came upon a large circular opening wide enough to let five Chamranlinas walk abreast, with a fifteen-foot-tall marble column on each side of the opening. A large gold crest of Sawisha Benshimu encrusted in each column contrasted with the emerald-green color of the stone in the fading evening light.

A guard wearing a green attire with a multicolor sash stood by the door. Chopa noticed he didn't show any concern about their showing up without prior notice. Then he saw the multiple recording devices mounted all around the door, confirming the lone guard could summon reinforcements in the blink of an eye.

"Greetings," Chari said in an even voice, "we are here to see Shonava Benshimu Hellowina."

"The Sawisha's door is always open for visitors," the guard said. "Who shall I announce?"

"My name is Chari Varian. My companion is Chopa."

The guard took two steps back and waved at Chari. "Please follow me."

They both entered through the wide door. Another guard welcomed them in and led them through an arched hallway to the main receiving room.

Shonava Benshimu held a high-ranking status among the Sawishas because of his physical strength and endurance and his reputation as a tough but fair negotiator. Chopa admired the elegance of the room, which, although smaller than he expected, characterized Benshimu's status. One wall made entirely of green marble richly veined with gold contrasted with the other walls, which were all white marble with silver streaks.

Shonava Benshimu joined them as soon as they walked in. Big, muscular, like a classic high-ranking green, he wore a cream shirt embroidered in the front with a bold pattern of vines and dark emerald leaves. His sash was a lighter green color with a thin gold wave to assert his status as a mature Sawisha.

"It is a rare occurrence to greet one from so far away," he said in a welcoming voice to Chari. He locked eyes with Chopa. "It's a pleasure to see both of you. Without you two's perseverance and determination, we would never have found Sheffrou Maashi. No one would have thought of looking for him in the Goolalong fields. I am extremely grateful to you both for the risks you took and what you accomplished. It's a feat I'll never forget."

Chari and Chopa bowed and stepped closer to kiss Benshimu's shoulder.

"I don't understand," Benshimu said, "why Maashi left his quarters without any protection and how he got lost in the Goolalong Fields, but I know he was devastated by the death of his close friend Sheffrou Shoban. A terrible loss such as this can make anyone behave in a strange fashion." Benshimu's face lit up. "Please, take a seat," he said with enthusiasm. "My Chowli will bring refreshments."

After they sat and were given a glass of tougui juice, Benshimu whispered in a sad voice, "Sheffrou Maashi..." He shook his head and a lock of chestnut hair fell on his forehead. "I miss him very much. Please enlighten me. Tell me about him. How is his health?"

Chopa saw genuine interest in Benshimu's eyes. He remembered how the Sawisha had been a great help in coordinating search parties and communications between the compounds in the days following the Sheffrou's disappearance.

"He is recuperating in good hands, Shonava," said Chari, "as you probably know, he is under the care of a Tousanou named Chendor."

Benshimu nodded sideway in a slow continuous motion. "I've not heard much about this Tousanou. All I know is he lives in secrecy thirty levels below the surface, and he's quite skilled. I wish Maashi a speedy recovery. He has already suffered so much." Benshimu stilled his head. "Why was Maashi in the Goolalong Fields? Was he in trouble? Does anyone know?"

Chari cut to the point. "It's a long story Shonava. One Sheffrou Maashi should convey to you himself one day. I'm here to find out more about the reasons why he left his quarters without any notice to his Chowlis. Do you know if Sheffrou Maashi has enemies? Do you think anyone would want to harm him?"

Benshimu's growl shocked Chopa. "These are difficult times," he said with a strong voice. "If you had asked me this question two sequences ago, I would've mocked you. But now, with the attack on Sheffrou Maashi one sequence ago, and the horrible attacks which occurred this sequence on the night of the Celebration, I have grave concerns." Benshimu took a tall glass of juice in his hands and stared at it. "The Krakoran are relentless and I think our defenses are seriously lacking. After these events, we need to reevaluate all levels of security. The monitors and the guards positioned throughout the compounds are clearly not effective against our enemy. I've brought this matter to the attention of the Council. Shonava Kokin suggested we put together a committee to study the situation."

Benshimu's brow darkened. He took a gulp of his juice and set it down beside him.

At the mention of Kokin, Chopa held back a hiss of disapproval. He wasn't fond of the old purple. "Sir," he said, "you don't seem to approve of a committee."

"I've been an ad hoc appointee on the Council of Elders for a few months only, but I have learned important lessons. One is that assigning a critical task and especially one of this magnitude to a committee slows down the decision-making process by prolonging the time needed to evaluate all the facts, and snuffs the power out of it." Benshimu rubbed his big hands together as if he were crushing something.

"Shonava," Chari said, "with all due respect, we would like to ask a few questions about the security the night of the Celebration."

Benshimu lowered his head and stared at the floor. "It was a sad evening."

"Yes, sir." Chari paused, set his glass on a side table, then said, "We saw the records, and Lado confirmed their accuracy. They show that you ordered Khon to increase the security for Sheffrou Maashi's party. Is this correct?"

"Yes, it is. When Shonava Kokin strongly suggested that we do so, I agreed right away. It was our duty to protect our most prolific Sheffrou. There was no question in my mind. Any attack on Maashi would've been catastrophic."

"Sir," said Chopa, "forgive me for asking this, but were you aware that this reallocation of guards decreased the protection of the other groups?"

Benshimu tilted his head sideways. "Shonava Kokin assured me that the other parties would be well protected." He paused and rubbed his jaw. "Kokin has been a member of the council for many sequences. I didn't question his judgment. I'm sure he made an honest mistake in his assumption that a great number of guards were available." Benshimu paused. "I've pondered for days over this matter. Unlike others who are talking of betrayal or a premeditated plan by a traitor to endanger the life of Sheffrous, I concluded both were inconceivable. We are all part of the great Chamranlina race, and we are all sworn to protect Sheffrous." He picked up his glass and gulped down the last of his juice.

"However," he said in a slow, apologetic voice, "in retrospect, I'm partially to blame. I should've been more vigilant and should've assessed the distribution of the guards myself before issuing that order. Sawisha Kokin is advancing in age and may have misread the situation. I have disclosed that fact at the inquiry."

Chopa set a light hand on the green's arm and said, "Sir, you harbored no ill intentions. In your mind, protecting Sheffrou Maashi was primordial. We respect that."

"Thank you for the information," said Chari, who stood up and discarded his glass in the recycler.

Benshimu rose from his seat and said, "Please keep me informed of Maashi's condition. He is very dear to me."

"Yes, of course," said Chopa, "we appreciate your time and concern. It was a pleasure to speak with you."

They bowed and left without another word.

Chapter 26

The morning light spread its faint glow along the wall of Chopa's small receiving room. As the new day dawned, the opalescent radiance gained strength and intensity. A five-note chime signaled Chari's arrival.

"So," Chari said, out of breath as if he had been running, "it took you a while. Did you find anything?"

Chopa didn't like the Ghouli Ghouli's condescending attitude. Even though Chari was older than him by more than 80 sequences, almost twice his age, he hated being treated like he was an ignorant twenty-something. If Sheffrou Maashi's safety hadn't been at stake, he would've dealt differently with this rude and overbearing Multi. However, time, circumstances, and the need to elucidate troubling events compelled him to remain polite and cooperate with Chari.

"I've been working to connect the thorn that was removed from Maashi's side to its plant of origin. After several attempts, I determined its chromosomal structure and found it is a variant of a common plant from Chamtali, our mother planet."

"A variant?"

"Yes. The original plant, called cookra, grows as high as an average Chamranlina and produces six-inch-wide purple flowers with a yellow center and tan nuts we call chorila nuts, a good source of protein for both shoshans and Chamranlinas."

"I know about Cookra plants. What about the variant? Any particularities about it?"

Chopa straightened his chocolate-colored shirt. He wore Sheffrou Maashi's colors with pride and always strived to look impeccable. "That's where it becomes interesting."

Chari cut him off. "I don't have time for details. Give me the relevant facts."

Ignoring Chari's comment, Chopa continued. "Tamara went to the Fanella compound and brought back with her samples of stalks with thorns like the one we removed from Sheffrou Maashi's side. This confirms the presence of these variants in the Fanella compound. The variant has thorns whereas the original plant doesn't and its spotted nuts are indistinguishable from the original but they contain small amounts of zanil, a rare poisonous chemical."

Chari banged his fist in the palm of his other hand. "Poison." He paced the length of the small receiving room back and forth. He pulled out a fragrant kego twig from his inner pocket and inserted it between his teeth. "Where did this plant come from? There aren't any plants on the surface and none in the tunnels." He chewed on the twig, which bounced up and down between his lips as he tried to solve the apparent riddle.

"There are numerous gardens in the Fanella compounds," said Chopa. "Apart from the thorns, the adult plants of both varieties look identical. It's possible both plants grow side by side."

Chari chewed fiercely on his twig. "They grow only in the Fanella compounds, therefore hiding in plain sight among the other variety. How did the poisonous variety appear? Some spontaneous mutation? There are controls designed to prevent this kind of thing from happening. What if both varieties were ingested by the Fanellas?"

Chopa's eyes widened. "That would be dangerous. The poison is especially potent in the young. Zanil causes lethargy, loss of appetite, and mental apathy."

Chari stopped dead in his tracks and stared at Chopa. "What are you saying? Could these nuts have been given to the young Fanellas, the ones who died?"

Chopa felt his heartbeat slow down. He answered with difficulty, his mouth suddenly gone dry. "Tamara said they were a gift from Shonava Kokin brought by his assistant, a purple called Noolin. If the little Fanellas were fed the wrong nuts," he said, his face losing its color, "over a period of weeks or months, the zanil might have been capable of killing them."

Chari slammed both hands against the wall. "We tried," he growled, "we tried so hard to find out why the little females were dying. If we had been granted access to the Fanella compound, perhaps we would have noticed the thorny plants... but we weren't given permission and never found the cause of the plague. Damn it." He lowered his head, and his harsh breathing could be heard across the room.

Chopa, in shock, felt the blood drain from his body, and stood frozen in place, as if his likeness had been carved in ice.

Chari's chest heaved in a long sigh. He hissed for long minutes. He said in a low, ominous voice, "I need to send a message to my contact in the Fanella compound. I want to confirm the Fanellas eat both types of nuts." He paused. "I don't understand how the variant plant could've slipped through the controls." He left without another word.

＞——≺ ‹ ‹ ● › › ≻——≺

By midday, Chopa received a message from Chari. "Meet me now in my quarters. Don't talk to anyone."

Chopa left immediately. He crossed paths with Rahma in the hallway and asked him, "Are you going to see Chari?"

Rahma was quick to respond. "Yes, he called me. Did you find anything?"

Chopa meant to answer yes but stopped short. "Not much."

Rahma gave him a quizzical look. Chopa gave a slight nod and sped up. Rahma followed right behind him.

The door opened as soon as they came upon Chari's quarters. He welcomed them in with a big smile and open arms. "Come my friends," he said. "We finally have time to have a proper meeting. I have something special planned for you."

Chopa frowned.

Rahma hesitated.

This prompted Chari to hug Chopa and whisper in his neck, "I have important news." Aloud, he said, "please, taste my favorite drink, a liquor from the tinqua plant. We shall celebrate Sheffrou Maashi's recovery." Chari handed them a clear glass filled with an emerald liquid.

"Come," he said with enthusiasm, "we shall enjoy some time together in the encounter room." He led them in, and they followed.

As soon as the door closed and they were shielded from the ever-present recorders, Chari sat on the rippling floor and set his glass down. He adjusted the controls; the colors settled on a light blue and pale cream. He ran his fingers in his unruly hair. His expression changed from cheerful to deadly serious.

"I have important news," he declared. "This must stay between us. Lives may be at stake." He waited for them to nod in agreement. "Lady Shanaka, long-time friend of Sawisha Kokin, received the nuts of the variant chorila as a gift from Kokin. His assistant Noolin brought them and told her to grow the plants and feed them to the little Fanellas to provide them with extra protein during the long winter months."

Chopa's airway tightened. "What? How can this be?"

Rahma, unaware of their most recent findings, answered his friend. "I've made inquiries and found Shonava Kokin has a passion for botany and the study of alien creatures. He has several pupils working with him, including a young purple assistant called Noolin who is friends with Chola, a member of our group."

The other two stared at him with such intensity that Rahma said, "What?"

Chopa wanted to inform Rahma of their recent findings but, overcome by sorrow, he lowered his head and kept silent.

"What's wrong?" said Rahma.

Chari said in a low voice, "Let me kiss you and bring you up to date." He bent down, kissed him, and then backed away.

Rahma covered his face with his hands.

Chari sat back, picked up his drink, and took a long sip.

Wiping the tears off his cheeks, Rahma hissed. "I can summon my followers. We can storm Kokin's compound and take him and his assistants in custody."

"Not so fast," Chari said in an ice-cold voice, "there is more."

The two friends glanced at each other and held their breaths.

"Kokin is the one who sent that strange sculpture to Maashi," he paused. "While you were busy finding information," he nodded at Chopa, "which has serious ramifications, I reached out to my contacts to find more about the sculpture." He paused, pulled a twig from his inner pocket, and inserted it between his lips. "Tamara said it could be an alien creature. She was right. One guard, captured by the Krakoran many sequences ago and later rescued, recalled seeing these creatures. They work in association with the Krakoran. He couldn't tell me much, but he remembered they could inflict terrible pain."

Rahma's chest swelled with indignation. "Kokin sent a likeness of one of these creatures to the Sheffrou. What disrespect! What impudence!"

Chopa hissed. "He sent it when Sheffrou Maashi's saweya was so low we feared for his life."

"It's logical to think Kokin knew about the poisonous nuts and about the existence of this dangerous alien creature." said Rahma.

Chari, in a somber tone, declared, "We can assume his ultimate aim was to harm, perhaps even kill Maashi and his offspring."

Chopa's eyes grew bigger. "That's horrible."

"Why would he do such a thing?" said Rahma. "He was the Sheffrou's mentor. He took care of him for so many sequences."

"You two are young. You didn't live through the Rebellion," Chari said. "There were intense arguments, bloody fights, and hundreds were sent to the Burned Zone as Outcasts. But not everyone was sent. Some were in their prime mating years like Kokin. He had a large group of powerful Sawisha followers and with his evil tongue threatened the Elders' control over the colony by constantly questioning their motives and their value in Chamranlina society. The Elders caught him at his own game when they demanded he prove his loyalty to the colony by becoming a mentor to a promising young Sheffrou."

"Sheffrou Maashi?!" exclaimed Rahma, eyes wide. "I never knew that."

Chari nodded. "Kokin was allowed to stay only if he stopped interfering in the decisions of the Council and become a mentor. From that day, Kokin was confined to a small sector and his fate depended on the success of a Sheffrou he had never bonded with. I'm convinced that's how his hatred of Sheffrous developed and grew. Ten sequences later, an agreement was reached between the most powerful Sawishas and the Council of Elders."

Chopa cut in. "The Sheffrou Mating Edict. Only Sheffrous could mate until the number of Fanellas rose significantly. The Elders argued for months before they reached an agreement, and it became law. Every Pure Color from that moment on was sworn to abide by that law when they came of mating age or were exiled to the Burned Zone as an Outcast."

"Some Sawishas protested with vigor against that law." Rahma said. "I remember from our formal teachings one of them was Kokin. The Council of Elders gave him permission to live in the colony, but he never mated again."

The three went silent as they acknowledged the gravity of the situation.

"I must add to the list of accusations," said Chopa in a somber tone, "Kokin was the one who convinced Shonava Benshimu to change the allocation of the Silver Guards the night of the celebration."

"Souls of my ancestors!" exclaimed Rahma. "Maybe Kokin has a bigger plan. Maybe he wants to eliminate all Sheffrous!"

"You're exaggerating Rahma," said Chopa.

Chari raised his hand. "He might be right. We need to consider this possibility. If this is the case, Kokin may be extremely dangerous. We must take all necessary precautions."

"My friend Chola," said Rahma, "might be able to help us."

"How?" said Chopa.

"He is close with Noolin. He can mingle in Kokin's entourage, get access to the laboratory where they conduct their experiments, and invade his files. I'll tell him to retrieve any information about the cookra plants and transmit them to us. If I explain to him what's at stake, he'll do the job. He's got the bold personality of a purple. No insult intended," said Rahma who glanced sideways at Chari.

Chari shook his head. "I don't take offense for trivialities. But you must inform your friend he must be discrete and avoid detection at all costs. You must also warn him of the dangers he may face."

"I know him. He'll do it."

"Should we contact Khon," said Chopa, "the chief of security?"

"Absolutely not," stated Chari. "We don't know who we can trust."

"I agree," said Rahma, "but I have total confidence in my close followers."

"Very well," said Chari, "We must put together a carefully laid out plan. I have a few ideas. Let's go over them."

Chapter 27

Tamara looked over her small quarters. She wouldn't miss the low ceiling, the plain ivory color granite walls, and the slick floors, which didn't bother the Chamis but for her was the source of frequent falls and bruises. Nodding to herself, she muttered under her breath, "I'm so happy to leave this place and go back to Maashi's quarters."

She folded her warm nateet with care and slid it in her bag along with a change of clothes and a second pair of thick soled footwear that she refused to send to the recycling. She carefully wrapped in a small blanket her personal tablet which never left her side. Maashi had given her that tablet when she first arrived on Chitina to help her get familiarized with their language and keep notes for future reference.

"Fold five times the seam at the top and grab both top corners and click the lock." Pini's instructions on how to fold the waterproof bag had been precise and accurate. Funny how she couldn't wait to see the young Chami again. It had been awkward at first to have him follow her like a puppy, but now she was lonely without his constant presence. Patient to a fault, he would fill her in on all the gossip and proved to be an inexhaustible source of information. A few days ago, Pini told her he was being sent away. She shook her head in annoyance. She hadn't heard anything else about him since then.

Tamara couldn't wait to leave. Maashi had informed her they planned for an early departure. Chendor's underground sector, located thirty levels below the surface, filled with eccentric sculptures, elaborate fountains, and hallways glowing with fluorescent colors contrasted with Maashi's soft-lit quarters, and seemed to hide mysterious secrets and unseen dangers. She had always been clumsy and, as a child, was prone to bumps and scrapes but, ever since she had arrived here, she had slipped, fallen, and hit herself much more than would be acceptable even for her.

Maashi was late. More than usual. Tamara suppressed a feeling of unease. When she worked in the Emergency Room, she learned to trust her instincts and they rarely failed her. Now her instincts told her she needed to leave as soon as possible. Bad vibes lurked here.

Right then, the door chime rang and Maashi, wearing khaki, the subdued color he wore when traveling, strolled in accompanied by Chopa.

"What took you so long?" said Tamara. "You said you were going to be here at first light."

Without acknowledging her comment, Maashi clicked something, then said, "Are you ready, Tamara?" With cloudy gray eyes, he searched the room as if expecting to see someone else.

"Never been so ready to leave a place; too spooky down at this level." She picked up her bag and swung it over her right shoulder.

"Are you expecting someone, sir?" said Chopa. He straightened his impeccable chocolate shirt, speckled with salmon drops, something he did when anxious.

"I thought Chari would be here to accompany us," said Maashi. He set his gaze on Tamara's luggage but did not look at her directly. "Do you have everything you need?"

"I'm ready to go." She glanced at Chopa. "Where is Rahma?" These two friends were inseparable. When you saw one, the other was never far behind.

Chopa gave her a slight bow and said in a low voice, "Rahma is waiting for us outside the confines of the sector with several of his companions. They will escort us on our way to the Sheffrou's quarters."

"Good," said Maashi, "Sheffrou Tomisho is scheduled to arrive in the next few days, and I want my quarters to be ready to welcome him. Come, Tamara. Let's go." In two long strides, he reached the door, exited, and she and Chopa followed. As soon as Tamara took her first breath of the damp hallway air, she started to cough.

Maashi turned toward her with a worried look, and she waved him off with her hand. "It's better. Don't worry. It's not bothering me as much as it did before." She rushed her pace to keep up with them and said, "Will Tomisho be staying with you?"

"The Council of Elders," said Chopa, "is meeting today to discuss this. My sources told me new facts have been brought before them."

At once, Maashi's pace slowed, and he glanced at Chopa. "What do you mean? What new facts?"

Chopa avoided Maashi's gaze and said, "I am sorry to say I have no clue what they were referring to."

Maashi let his eyes linger on Chopa for a minute then resumed his trek.

They followed a serpentine hall and passed a gurgling fountain with a six-feet wide basin filled with pebbles and shells of lichi, a tasty mollusk Tamara had enjoyed earlier in the season. Further down, the hall widened and opened into a large cave the size of a conference room. A grand marble fountain with a deep basin lay in the middle. The ground was uneven in this cave, and the ceiling was only a couple feet higher than the Chamranlinas, a feature Tamara disliked. It made her feel ill at ease, trapped.

A few Multicolors mingled around the fountain. As soon as Maashi arrived, as if on cue, three Silver Guards, recognizable by their short silver and black sashes, entered and stood at attention in the middle of the cave. Right away, a fourth guard appeared and positioned himself in front of the others, blocking Maashi's way. Then Chari marched in from a side entrance wearing all black. He stared straight ahead without acknowledging the Sheffrou, positioned himself alongside the guards, and crossed his copper arms on his chest.

Something wasn't right. Chari failed to greet the Sheffrou. A shocking insult. Tamara kept her eyes riveted on Chari. *What was that irritating Ghouli Ghouli up to now?*

The fourth Silver Guard took one step forward and produced a device the size of a cellphone. He read the text on it in a cold, expressionless voice. "To all Chamranlinas, this is an official proclamation from the Council of Elders."

As soon as he said this, Sheffrou Chendor flanked by two personal guards entered through another opening on the far side of the cave. A tall, emaciated individual, partially hidden by Chendor's enormous frame, followed closely behind.

The gargantuan Sheffrou stopped close to the grand fountain, yards away from where Tamara and Maashi stood. Chendor appeared to be waiting for something and avoided looking at them. Tamara squinted at the tall individual behind him who wore a khaki shirt and pants. There was something oddly familiar about him. She took a deep breath and bit her lips. *Was it Tomisho?*

Before she could ask Maashi, the Silver Guard continued in a strong voice, "Shonava Maashi Torrenadanga, you are accused of treason resulting in the murder of Sheffrou Choban Chimilan, severe bodily harm to Sheffrou Dasho Fontina, and the kidnapping of the Sheffrous Tomisho Sannalachan and Ashani Shamanoon on the night of the Great Eclipse."

"What?" Maashi raised his head. With shoulders pulled back and fiery eyes, he said with a thundering voice which echoed throughout the cave, "This is absurd! Who dares to accuse me? Everyone knows I had nothing to do with these attacks."

The guard glared at Maashi. "The accusations were made by the Ghouli Ghouli Chari Varian and by Sheffrou Tomisho Sannalachan, both present today."

Chopa hissed, raised his arms, and fisted his hands.

"You! Traitor!" Maashi lunged at Chari. Two guards jumped on Maashi, the third one on Chopa who, caught by surprise, couldn't shake him off. Maashi shoved one guard with so much force that he flew in the air and landed with a hard thump on the cave floor. The second guard held on to the struggling Maashi's shirt and it tore in half. Maashi landed a terrific blow on that guard's face. He swayed but held on to the Sheffrou.

Dumbfounded by this unexpected event, Tamara's jaw dropped open as she watched Maashi battle the guards in a fight he was bound to lose. Chari stood still as a statue; his face devoid of any expression as he observed the spectacle. Tamara saw Maashi's gold chain, Tomisho's gift, fall out of his shirt pocket, and get trampled on the uneven ground. The guard who was thrown quickly bounced back on his feet and snapped a metal bracelet around Maashi's right wrist and his own. The second guard did the same. It was over.

Maashi's brow was black with anger. He raised his head and fixated the motionless Chendor across the room. "Are you also part of this odious scheme? What do you say?" It was only then that Maashi noticed the Chami standing behind Chendor. He jerked the bracelets, fought to raise his arms, but was prevented from doing so by the guards who held him. He mumbled some words Tamara didn't understand and then called out, "Tomisho? Tomisho? Is that you?"

The tall and thin individual behind Chendor kept his face hidden and didn't answer.

Maashi yelled, "Chendor, what have you done? You're hiding my friend from me. You promised I would see Tomisho as soon as he was brought here." Chendor stood somber and silent, like a smoldering volcano.

Maashi persisted, louder this time. "Tomisho, answer me." In a defeated voice, his breathing shallow, he lowered his gaze and added, "What have they done to you?"

Chendor raised his head and for a moment locked his eyes with Maashi's. He didn't say a word and left by the same opening he had entered, shielding with his ample girth the thin Tomisho walking behind with his head held low. Chendor's guards followed.

The fourth Silver Guard continued his speech, "Sheffrou Maashi, you shall be confined in solitary detention until further notice by the Council of Elders. Absolutely no contact with anyone is allowed while the accusations are being assessed."

Maashi's face paled. He hissed and stared at Chari. "What is the meaning of this? Why are you accusing me? You're my first Chowli. What kind of Chowli would betray their Sheffrou this way?"

Tamara, at first shaken by the unexpected turn of events, recovered her composure and tried to calm him. "Maashi," she said, "This must be a misunderstanding. Go with them. Chopa and I will figure this out."

Chari stared at Maashi and did not respond. He signaled to the guards. "Take him away. Let's be done with this." His pupils were small slits. His face showed no other emotion than hatred. He turned and left by the same back opening used by Chendor.

Tamara watched with a sinking heart the guards take away the furious Maashi. It was all she could do to hold back tears, but she was determined not to give Chari the satisfaction of seeing her cry. She shook with fear and dread.

What had just happened? Why did both Chari and Tomisho accuse Maashi?

This made no sense. Even the usually impassive Chopa appeared to be stunned. His face had paled to the color of alabaster. He stood straight as a rod with his hands fisted.

Something was terribly wrong.

Tamara was shocked. She stood still and her mouth went dry. Since the first day she saw Chari, she didn't trust him. He was an individual who hid his true self behind multiple layers of secrets, lies, and deception. She started to trust him only after he rescued Maashi from the methane fields. Now this.

Tamara took a step, bent down, and feigning to adjust her sandal, picked up the gold chain laying on the ground, and discretely slid it in her pocket. Accompanied by Chopa, she went back to her quarters. He averted his gaze and didn't say anything. He looked stricken and seemed in shock like she was. His only comment was, "I will contact Rahma. We will sort this out."

Tamara recovered enough to ask, "What will they do to him? Will there be a trial?"

Chopa tilted his head sideways to consider her question. "The facts will be presented to the Council by representatives of both sides. The Elders will debate the accusations and reach a decision. It will take about a week."

"But Maashi's innocent. He didn't have anything to do with those attacks. You know it and I know it."

"Proving it or disproving it may be impossible," said Chopa. "The Elders may consider demanding Rue-Shan; a fight until one is incapacitated or concedes defeat. Sheffrou Maashi will have to win against an opponent chosen by the Sawishas to prove his innocence."

"A fight? But Maashi is not in good shape. He's still recovering from his time spent in the methane fields and the abscess caused by the thorn." She wiped the sweat off her forehead. "What happens if he loses?"

Chopa lowered his head and said, "He will never mate again and will live in shame for all time."

"Damn it!" She paced the room, grabbed the first cushion in her path and threw it on the wall. "I can't believe it. This is terrible."

Chopa commented in a flat tone, "The decision of the judges is final."

Tamara nodded. There was nothing else to say. Chopa bowed and left.

Overwhelmed by fatigue, dizzy with frustration, she let her small frame drop on a couch the color of dark grapes. She grabbed a cushion and held it in her arms. Maashi must be pale with rage right now. These last few weeks had been dreadful, and now this new twist of fate might be enough to drive him crazy. There was nothing she could do to help. He wasn't allowed to see anyone. She could only hope he would calm down after a few hours and meditate to find a solution to his predicament. He had endured worse circumstances and had proven his resilience. He would have no other choice but to face this new challenge.

Tamara pulled open the bag containing her few belongings and took out her little pad. She wrote to her daughter Allison. Ever since her arrival on Chitina she had found comfort in writing. She had been stranded in this world for over six months now. Her first impressions of the Chamranlinas were of peaceful beings living in fear of attacks by their giant amoeba-like enemies, called the Krakoran, roughly translated as the Untouchable because any physical contact with their long filaments could inflict terrible pain. But, as time went on, she realized that their society possessed a rigid hierarchy. The struggle for survival and the relentless competition for mating shaped their everyday lives. Even the females suffered. They were kept isolated in four compounds inaccessible to the main population. They were allowed contact only with infertile males, the Gray Feeders.

She had been told that Chami society wasn't always this way and centuries ago, male and female could mix and live together in harmony. But, in the last few centuries, their species changed and the Pure Colors, the ones with their single-color tongue, were the only ones capable of reproducing. The Multicolors, except a small subgroup called Ghouli Ghouli, were all infertile.

Now a new pattern was emerging. The fierce competition for mating attained surprising heights as Sheffrous fought each other to gain advantage. Tamara thought she knew Maashi well, Tomisho well enough, and didn't think either would willingly get involved in a scandalous betrayal. But then, she had witnessed only a few events and had been a part of their lives for a short time. How could she judge them? They weren't human and couldn't be held to human standards of behavior. Would either be capable of orchestrating the attacks that killed one Sheffrou, permanently disabled another, and caused the kidnapping of two more?

She pulled out Maashi's gold chain from her shirt and examined it. It had been crushed in the middle but was still in one piece. Bruised but not broken. A good omen? She hoped with all her heart it was.

Tamara rose and paced the length of her receiving room, hands on her hips. They had been so close to leaving Chendor's sector with its glowing serpentine hallways and thousands of fountains. Tamara couldn't wait to return to a normal life in Maashi's compound. How she longed to spend precious time alone with the Sheffrou in his own quarters where the environment was comfortable, not cold and humid like here. Now, Maashi was accused of consorting with the enemy, imprisoned without access to his Chowlis, and he had to prove his innocence to the Council. What a mess!

Tamara dropped on the couch again and attempted to calm her anger and disappointment by taking deep breaths. She held the gold bracelet in her right hand. She rolled it back and forth between her fingers. When she was a child visiting her grandparents' country house, she used to love rolling spruce needles between her fingers. The sap would cling to her hands and the evergreen smell would follow her all day. Such a peaceful time, so long ago. The memory brought a little smile, and she relaxed her shoulders.

She studied the situation at hand.

Maashi was in trouble.

Someone was trying to frame him and without realizing it, the Sheffrou was fueling the fire. His erratic behavior in the last few weeks hadn't gone unnoticed by the Sawishas, Greens, Reds, and Purples, who seized each opportunity to destroy his reputation. Many of them were envious and resentful of the fact that only Sheffrous could mate. Tamara knew that every room was monitored night and day, and anyone could access the recordings.

On Earth, Maashi's erratic behavior these last few weeks would have been classified as psychotic. He experienced vivid visual and auditory hallucinations. He spent days without eating, intent on searching for the identity of a young face visible only to him. Were it not for the excellent care he received with Chendor, his condition might have worsened. Tamara frowned. In fact, his detention, although undeserved and humiliating, prevented him from diving headfirst into more trouble. Were it not for that, he would certainly have tried to break into the Fanella compound to see Lady Ileana and the little Shalina.

Tamara slid to the edge of her couch. She rubbed her forehead and took a sip of choun from a glass she had set on a side table earlier that morning. Her gaze settled on the small vertical fountain which stood in the corner of her room. Apart from her bushy burgundy plant, the fountain was the only decoration in her room. The water trickled down a quartz sculpture resembling a small plant with delicate branches. Light from within illuminated the structure and brought it alive.

It occurred to her then that the two who had brought forth the accusations against Maashi were a friend, Sheffrou Tomisho, and Chari, someone he had met recently and had accepted as his first Chowli.

Maashi and Tomisho were inseparable before the attacks, and Tamara couldn't believe that Tomisho would turn against him. Was he influenced or coerced to blame Maashi for his kidnapping by the Krakoran?

Chari was a Ghouli-Ghouli and an enigmatic character. She couldn't determine his motives or his ambitions. He had left a negative impression the first time they met, but he was the one who rescued Maashi from the Goolalong Fields and brought him under Chendor's care. Since then, Chari seemed to be fond of Maashi and looking out his welfare. Why did he accuse Maashi of plotting the attacks with the enemy? Did he possess information he couldn't divulge to the others? Tamara was sure he had devised a plan. What was it? And was this plan for or against Maashi?

She rose, took a few steps, and came a foot away from the glass fountain. An irresistible urge to break it overtook her. She raised her hand to strike but stopped in mid-air. Instead, she poured her glass on the top of the quartz and the choun spilled over the crystalline sculpture. Its glow faded, and the fountain went dark. She sneered with satisfaction. "There. That's better."

Chapter 28

Maashi sat on the single lounge-chair of the detention room. Four days after his arrest, his initial anger and bewilderment had decreased. There had to be a logical explanation for those extraordinary accusations from his friend Tomisho, and Chari Varian who had the audacity to become his Chowli.

Tomisho couldn't have been back on Chitina more than two days. Maashi had been waiting for his arrival for several weeks and the only way he escaped Maashi's keen extra-sensory perception was because he stayed concealed by Chendor's powerful aura. Somehow, the giant Sheffrou was implicated in a scheme with Chari which required Tomisho's cooperation. Chari was hiding something. Maashi was sure of it. He had put his trust in the Ghouli Ghouli. Would he come to regret it?

A succession of muffled sounds came from behind the door. Maashi stood and waited. He wasn't allowed any visitor. Who could this be? The door slid open.

Chari bounded in the room. As soon as Maashi saw his copper skin, he hissed with anger. "You! What do you want? How dare you come in here?" He lifted his fists, ready to strike.

Chari shot a furtive look behind his back, closed the door, and said, "Quickly, give me your clothes. We have little time."

Maashi growled and charged the incoming Chari who easily pounced on him, grabbed his wrists, and rammed him on the closest wall.

The Sheffrou struggled and spit in disgust.

"Simmer down," said Chari. "Don't you understand?" He blurted out. "We had to put you away for your own protection. Weeks have passed since I found you poisoned with methane. Don't you remember what I told you in the cave beside the pit, back in the Burned Zone?"

He paused for the time it took for one breath, locked eyes with the fuming Sheffrou, and kissed him. A long, hot kiss. He backed away and licked his lips. "Damn you," he said, "You taste sweeter than any other Sheffrou."

Maashi's face paled. "What are you saying? My nights are filled with horrific visions." His eyes shone with tears. "Then it's true. I thought they were only nightmares. My offspring are..."

"Dead." Chari hugged him fiercely then took Maashi's face in his hands and kissed the tears that rolled down his cheeks. "Yes, it's true." He added in a softer voice, "I didn't know at the time they were all your offspring. Had I known, I might not have divulged that information." His brow darkened. "But there is still one clinging to life."

Hearing this, the Sheffrou started sobbing. Chari kissed him again and hugged him tight. Maashi breathed in and out and after a few minutes, his cries decreased.

"Maashi, listen to me. You must be ready for tomorrow's trial."

"What?" Maashi cleared his voice. "What kind of trial?"

"I don't know exactly, but you must win. At any cost."

Maashi searched Chari's face with widening eyes.

"Do whatever it takes. Do you understand me?"

"What are you saying?" Maashi wiped his cheeks.

"You must win to save the last offspring." He took one step back. "You are her only hope. She is clinging to life, and you are the only one who can save her. Now quit crying and hand me your clothes."

Maashi untied his short sash, removed his shirt, dropped his pants keeping only his chemcha, and gave them to Chari.

Chari grabbed the lot and turned to leave. "Don't let us down, Maashi." He took one step, changed direction, planted a last kiss on the Sheffrou's lips, and ran out of the room.

Chapter 29

Tamara stood on the shore of the impressive underground lake supplying the Gorganna Gorge. The water shimmered like thousands of diamonds under the light of gigantic white globes eighty feet above. In the shallows, the water gently lapped the banks; further out, under the calm surface, two underwater streams converged and created a powerful current which churned, tossed, and propelled the inexperienced swimmer towards the mighty Gorganna Gorge. She knew this well because Maashi had saved her from drowning months ago when she got pulled under during what was supposed to be a simple morning swim.

The incessant rumble of the cascading waterfall drummed in Tamara's ears and the hair on her arms stood on ends. A mere five weeks ago, Tamara had foolishly run away in the tunnels and was pursued by a Krakoran, the formidable but elusive enemy of the Chamis. She tried to escape and became trapped on a ledge overlooking the dangerous falls. Maashi risked his own life to rescue her as she hung precariously over the gushing water. The memory brought back the terror she had felt, and her heart thumped in her chest. Without Maashi's intervention, she would have been killed, or worse, kidnapped by the enemy.

Today, Maashi had no choice. He had to dive in the falls and risk his life to win an absurd competition. Tamara's anger boiled. Why did Chari accuse him of planning the attacks per-petrated by the enemy on the night of the Great Eclipse? *Didn't Maashi suffer enough?*

Maashi, wearing only his chemcha, stood silent and solemn between two Black Guards. His intense amber eyes gazed at the restless crowd gathered in the cave to witness the trial. A few Sawishas were there to see him fail. His success at mating had been the source of envy for others not so fortunate.

Some Sawishas were in attendance to fulfill an official func-tion, including the big green Shonava Benshimu Hellowina, First Lord of the Seventh Compound, who had showed his affection for Maashi many a time. Today, intertwined with Ben-shimu's forest green sash was another silver one showing he was an official observer of the competition. The venerable emer-ald green Shonava Shitan Garavella, an experienced and distin-guished lord who ruled the Western Compound with Sheffrou Tomisho, also wearing a silver strand on his sash, scanned the perimeter and directed a squad of eight Silver Guards to their posts.

Accompanied by Chopa and Rahma, Tamara felt like a helpless observer among the crowd of Chamis. Both Chowlis wore Maashi's colors, a fudge-colored shirt with salmon drops and light gray pants. Chopa's watchful eyes kept track of the slightest movement in the crowd. With a darkened brow and tight lips, Rahma remained silent, but Tamara knew his si-lence hid his repressed anger at his inability to intervene and help Maashi. The Sheffrou glanced in their direction but didn't acknowledge them. His doing so would give credence to the rumors that they were his accomplices.

Maashi's friend, Sheffrou Tomisho, thin and pale, flanked by six guards, stayed apart from the other spectators. He flashed a contemptuous stare at anyone who dared to look in his direction. Chari, arms crossed on his chest, his expression unreadable under his dark brow, chewed his characteristic kego twig a few feet away from Tomisho. His copper skin shone under the light of the globes and contrasted with his tight-fitting black attire. Sheffrou Chendor was absent. Few knew of his existence, so the fact he wasn't there didn't raise any comments. His fear of venturing in the tunnels prevented him from traveling outside his own section. He had become supreme master but also a prisoner of his own secluded world.

Maashi's opponent, a young red Chami called Hamra, stomped the ground like a shoshan stallion before a race. The Red had volunteered to compete against Maashi. The two had been involved in a fight weeks ago, when Hamra had insulted Tamara. Hamra had won the altercation and Maashi had to make a shameful retreat after his opponent broke his arm. The Red paced back and forth and waved to the crowd with a confident grin. He puffed up his chest, flexed his arms and stretched his muscular body forward and sideways.

The Elders had deliberated for days the unthinkable accusations against Shonava Maashi of plotting with the enemy. The deadly attacks of the night of the Great Eclipse Celebration had dealt a blow to all Chamranlinas: one older Sheffrou and numerous Silver Guards had been killed, another Sheffrou had been severely injured, and two other Sheffrous along with three Silver Guards had been kidnapped.

The Elders had listened to recordings of witnesses' statements and other individuals in charge of security. They decided there was no proof that Maashi had conspired with the Krakoran in the combined attacks on that night. Yet, they couldn't exonerate him because although there was no direct evidence of his participation, the Sheffrou would have benefited from the elimination of potential rivals in the competition for mating. In their great wisdom born of shared centuries of governing, the Council of Elders recommended a test of strength and courage. They strongly believed that fate controlled significant life events and that they should let it determine Maashi's destiny.

Chopa explained to Tamara how the trial would unfold. "Shonava Maashi and a volunteer opponent, Hamra, will dive in the Gorganna Gorge and swim the treacherous course until they reach the calm waters of the smaller pool one mile downriver. The first one to complete the course will be declared the winner. If Shonava Maashi wins, all accusations against him will be dropped and he will hold on to his title of First Lord of the Central Compound. If he loses, he will live in shame and never be considered again for mating."

"If his opponent Hamra wins," he said, his face rigid, "Hamra will gain the title of Shonava, and will receive compensation including gifts and suitable quarters to match his new rank."

"What are Hamra's chances of winning?" said Tamara, her voice filled with concern. "After all, Maashi has been exposed to methane, and he recently developed sepsis caused by the abscess on his side. He isn't in his best shape. These falls are dangerous." She bit her lip and blinked away the sudden wetness in her eyes.

Chopa put a light hand on her shoulder. "Physical shape and youth may render one more reckless. Sheffrou Maashi is an excellent swimmer and has more experience than his opponent. It's more important in this kind of run to steer away from obstacles rather than face them head on and risk injury."

"What happens if there's an accident? Who's going to rescue them?"

"Don't worry, Tamara," said Chopa. "The Silver Guards will observe the swimmers throughout the course with the help of monitors. If they see one of them is in danger, their designated swimmers will not hesitate to jump to their rescue."

Meanwhile, Rahma had ventured close to Maashi, whispered something to him, and rejoined them. "The event will be broadcast all over the network," he said. "We should be able to see the race right here, on a virtual screen on the wall of the cave. If the Sheffrou needs help, I will dive in."

"No, you will not." Chopa's voice cut him short. "This will infuriate the guards. Wait for the end of the run like everybody else."

Rahma stared in Chopa's face, and Tamara understood he connected with him telepathically. Chopa turned his head away and said, "Come over here, Tamara, if you want to see them dive."

She took her position and gritted her teeth as everyone settled close to the edge of the water.

Maashi knew the course well. Seventy sequences ago, he jumped in the Gorganna falls, risking life and limb to prove his courage and his excellent physical shape. He foolishly thought this would increase his chances of being chosen for mating. He escaped without injury, but this wasn't always the case for the ones who dared the feat. Such displays were banned after one Sawisha lost his life attempting to do the same.

He remembered how the fast-moving water of the deep underground lake sped until it poured down a hundred feet, then churned and cascaded in a long tunnel that ended abruptly when the waters plunged another thirty feet. The roaring water then became a torrent and continued its course for a thousand feet until it reached a fork where only the right side was wide enough to let a Chami through. After that, the current slowed down in a calm pool, and one could reach the banks easily and step out.

A large tympanic drum had been brought from the Rashandamora cave for the event. Three beats would signal to the competitors to get in position, two to get ready, and then one final beat on the drum would signal to jump in the water. Maashi fought to control his thumping heart. He inhaled deeply to prepare himself. There was no turning back. Little Shalina depended on him.

He had one goal in mind: to stay alive. If the situation were favorable, he would do his utmost to win the competition, but he refused to put his life in peril. A dead Sheffrou can't solve anything. A live one can still find a way to prove his innocence. It was imperative to save his last offspring, and the thought lay foremost in his mind. He wasn't in top shape, but the last five days had given him a chance to eat well, rest, and recuperate. He was a strong swimmer, but strength and speed were not the only factors in this type of run. Mental acuteness and fate would determine the winner.

At the final sound of the drum, Maashi dove in the cool water. With sure and easy strokes, he reached the falls and went down headfirst, arms extended and slightly spread out. He dodged the bigger rocks, but at the last moment, his body flipped sideways, and he flailed for a brief instant. This brought him too close to the rocky side, and he felt a sharp edge cut his right leg just below the hip, leaving a long gash. The pain was severe but not excruciating. He swam sideways for a moment then regained his aplomb. With his senses on high alert, he continued the run.

Hamra plunged to the left of Maashi and went straight down for the first half of the fall but hit a boulder on his way down. He lost control and tumbled head over heels. He wasn't hurt but was stunned and disoriented as he reached the bottom of the falls.

Maashi fought to stay on course in the fast-moving rapids and kept his head above water to make sure he veered to the right. He saw Hamra ahead of him, struggling with the current. Soon the stream divided in two. A large rock formation jutted out four feet above the surface on the left. Hamra was headed right for that rock. Maashi screamed in warning, but his voice was lost in the roar of the rapids. Hamra rammed the boulder and cried out in pain. Soon after, his body floated aimlessly, reminding Maashi of a young offspring swimming without any control.

Concentrated on watching his opponent, Maashi didn't see a group of rocks right ahead and, at the last moment, he twisted and turned his body to avoid them. He clenched his jaw in pain when they grazed his already injured right leg. When he checked again, Hamra was out of sight. The smaller second waterfall was fast approaching. Hamra had not resurfaced. A sick feeling invaded Maashi's mind. *What if he was in serious trouble?* Before he got too close to the falls, he dove under. His mind sent telepathic signals right, left, and up ahead to locate Hamra.

The red had gotten wedged in between two underwater boulders. Maashi reached his side. The water was stained pink from a cut on Hamra's head. Maashi clicked at him. The other didn't respond and made feeble attempts to free his legs.

"*Wait*," Maashi said, sending a simple telepathic message, "*I'll move the boulder. When I give the signal, push your legs out.*"

Maashi used all his strength to move the heavy boulder. It moved an inch. Not enough to free him.

"*Let me try again.*" This time, Maashi ignored his right hip and pushed with all his might.

The boulder moved a few inches, and this was enough for Hamra. He pushed hard with his upper extremities and freed himself. Using only his arms, he rose to the surface, where he took a big breath of air. Maashi swam upward and joined him. He grabbed him by the arm and said, "*Can you swim?*"

Hamra tilted his head sideways. "*I can't feel my legs. I can't move them.*"

Before Maashi could answer, the current carried them down the second waterfall. Maashi held on to him and they both went down fast. It was all he could do to maneuver and make sure they avoided the rocks at the bottom, but at last, they were out of danger. The water here was deeper and the current much slower. Maashi spotted a couple of Chamranlinas on the banks of the pool. He called out. "I need help. Hamra is injured."

Several Sawishas including a red Sawisha and three guards rushed over and dove in the pool to help Maashi and his injured opponent. The Chamis crowded the side of the pool, and a few yelled, "What happened? Why is the Sheffrou holding Hamra?"

The red Sawisha lifted Hamra out of the water carefully. Hamra's face was pale, and he spoke with effort. "I can't move my legs."

"He needs urgent attention," said Maashi who limped out of the pool, aided by a guard.

Benshimu came to his side and helped him walk to a healing station set up for the event. "Are you hurt?" said Benshimu, his brow thickening with concern.

"It's a superficial cut. I'm all right," said Maashi.

"What happened to Hamra?"

"He slammed into a boulder," said Maashi, "and wedged his legs between the rocks. I pulled him and kept him safe until the run was over. He can't move his legs."

Benshimu nodded. "I will inform the Elders."

The attending physician cleaned his wound and applied a clear dressing. "The formal hearing will start soon," he said. "Do you think you can attend?"

"Yes," said Maashi, "I'm feeling well enough."

Benshimu nodded. He called out to the guards. "Take him to his post." He turned and addressed the crowd. "Everyone, take your positions. The formal hearing will start soon."

Chapter 30

Tamara, with Chopa and Rahma at her side, followed the Chamis along the slippery tunnels to the cave where the run would end. They saw the first part of the dive on the giant virtual screen, but then everything got blurry. The water swirled and rushed downward, creating myriad trails of bubbles, and they lost track of the swimmers. Tamara fought to control her thumping heart. *Where was Maashi? Was he okay?* She couldn't wait to see him. Her hands shook as she trekked on the uneven path down to the cave where the run would end.

A large crowd of at least a hundred Chamis had gathered in the smaller cave at the bottom of the second set of falls. This cave was unlike any other Tamara had seen. Carved in beige-colored sandstone by centuries of relentless current, the smooth walls, a palette of tans and browns, rounded the main area and formed alcoves many of which remained hidden in shadows. Clusters of long stalactites hung here and there from the ceiling, creating an out worldly look. Sconces on the walls sent diffuse light across the cave and the golden skin of the Chamis glistened in contrast with the browns hues of the cave.

Sawishas and their entourage, including the barrel-chested green, Benshimu Hellowina, the venerable Shonava Shitan Garavella, and another Sawisha wearing a wide crimson sash, stood in front of the crowd of a hundred Chamis. The gaunt figure of Master Kokin Cronobutin, Maashi's former mentor with his characteristic floor-length purple sash had already taken a prominent place beside them.

The two accusers, Sheffrou Tomisho Sannalachan and Chari Varian, stood on an elevated platform apart from the crowd. Six Silver Guards circled Tomisho who, with a darkened brow and a stiff posture, clenched and unclenched his hands as he focused on Master Kokin. Chari Varian stayed impassive in his tight black outfit with a multicolored belt instead of a sash.

Tamara scanned the cave. The run had been completed. Opposite where she was, two Black Guards stood at Maashi's side. The Sheffrou's eyes were colorless, and his face was pale as alabaster, a sign he was in pain. He wore a simple khaki shirt and pants. She couldn't see any obvious injury, but she noticed he had transferred his weight to his left leg. She couldn't see his opponent Hamra.

"Chopa," she said in a low voice, "I think Maashi's hurt."

Rahma was the one who answered. "I agree. I don't think it is serious otherwise they would have taken him away."

"Where is the other swimmer?" Tamara said. "I can't see him."

Chopa bent down and whispered in her ear. "A guard told me he was injured, and they sent him to be treated."

"Does this mean Maashi is the winner?"

"The decision will be announced by the Elders," Chopa said. "We are waiting for their arrival."

As soon as he finished his sentence, a group of six Silver Guards entered the cave through a side tunnel. Three Elders, wearing knee-length silver coats with lapels embroidered in gold and olive-green shirts with a wide silver sash, appeared behind the guards. Tamara examined them. The three noble Elders looked quite old. Their white hair was laced with gray, and their faces showed wrinkles on the foreheads and cheeks. One Elder was bigger than the two others but, apart from that slight difference, she couldn't tell them apart. Rare wooden high-back chairs carved with intricate designs had been brought for them and they sat down one by one.

The stocky Elder sitting in the middle chair rose, and the crowd settled. He scanned the throng for a moment, then spoke in the Chami language. Chopa translated for Tamara.

The Elder declared the trial was completed and had been conducted according to the rules. He said he and his two colleagues agreed that Sheffrou Maashi was the winner. He praised Maashi's courage and the altruism he showed towards his opponent. Without his timely intervention, Hamra would have suffered life-threatening injuries. A murmur ran through the crowd. A few Chamis clicked and stomped their feet in approval. The Elder folded his arms across his chest and waited for silence. He resumed his speech in a forceful tone. He declared that troubling accusations and new evidence had been presented to the Council of Elders in the hours preceding the trial. He motioned to Chari Varian to address the crowd.

Hearing this, many younger Chamis clicked. A few hissed in disapproval. The Elder raised his arm, and the hissing dwindled to a low hum. He signaled Chari to come forth and speak. Chari stepped forward and faced the Chamis. His copper skin and raven hair glowed under the pale light of the cave.

To follow Maashi's wish and because most understood that language, Chari spoke in English. "A few weeks ago, I received an unexpected visitor in my sector," he said, "Sheffrou Maashi Torrenadanga."

The crowd went silent. The only sound in the cave was the sound of water lapping the banks of the pool.

"The Sheffrou came to the Burned Zone searching for answers. He seemed obsessed because three simultaneous attacks by the enemy occurred on the night of the Great Eclipse. He thought a Chamranlina was involved with the enemy to coordinate the multiple attacks which caused the death of his long-time friend, Sheffrou Shoban, the kidnapping of his best friend, Sheffrou Tomisho and of a pupil, Sheffrou Ashani. A long-time friend of his, Sheffrou Dasho Fontina, a respected physician, was seriously injured."

A loud rumble came from the crowd. Chari waited until it died and resumed. "His sorrow consumed him so much that he disregarded his own safety in his quest for answers and traveled through the tunnels without guards or Chowlis." Chari paused and then stared in the eyes of the Sawisha. "I was shocked by his visit and remember thinking at the time he was just another foolish Sheffrou trying to impress the Council of Elders."

Someone close to Master Kokin sneered. Kokin raised his head up high and glared at Maashi.

"I explained to him that the attacks on the night of the Great Eclipse," Chari said, "although serious, were a minor problem compared to the other huge and potentially catastrophic crisis we Chamranlinas are facing."

The Chamis stirred. A few stomped the ground, drowning the soft sounds of the lapping water. Tamara knew that the general population had been kept in the dark about the plague. Most Chamis were unaware of the unspeakable loss of the young offspring. She observed the three Elders. With solemn expressions, they sat motionless in their chairs. The one sitting in the middle who had spoken before rose. He put his hands together, gathered himself, and said, "It is my sad duty to inform you that in the last four months, we have experienced the biggest challenge we have ever faced as a species since our arrival on Chitina."

A wave of surprise and disbelief rolled among the Chamis, and they clicked and hissed in unison.

Shonava Benshimu stepped forward, raised his arms, and demanded in a loud voice, "Elder, what are you speaking of? And if this challenge is so serious, why haven't we been informed months ago?"

The Elder answered in a slow and deliberate manner. "This matter is so grave we chose not to inform the colony at large. Only specific Chamranlinas involved in the search for solutions were notified to avoid a large-scale panic. We realize now this was an error."

Exclamations of suspicion and disparagement resonated in the cave.

The Elder consulted briefly with the two other Elders and then lifted both arms up high. "We were trying to protect the fertile Pure Colors including the Sheffrous from information we considered detrimental to their well-being. We kept them in the dark about the situation without knowing they were part of the solution."

With these words, all the ones present clicked, hissed, and stomped, producing a loud clamor which echoed all over. Chopa and Rahma glanced at each other, lowered their heads as if in silent prayer.

Tamara's heart sank at the thought of the distraught Fanellas who had waited in vain for months for help for their little ones. She remembered how desperate Ileana had been and how she said she stayed awake night and day for a sign from Maashi without knowing he was fighting for his own life. How sad and isolated she must've felt. Tears filled Tamara's eyes at the thought of the horrible loss of life. She understood her pain. She also had felt isolated and consumed with worry not knowing at first where Maashi was when he was first reported missing. Then, when they found him poisoned by the methane gas and she worried if he would ever regain his health.

When the sounds from the crowd died down at last, Chari faced the assembly and spoke in a firm voice. "What the Elder is trying to say," he bowed ever so slightly to the Elder who acknowledged him by a simple nod, "is that we are facing a plague. A catastrophe we have never faced before."

Again, the Chamis stomped and hissed. One guard, standing in the back, yelled, "What are you talking about, Ghouli Ghouli? How do you know of this and why do you know of it when we don't?"

Chari took a step forward and raised his voice. "Listen, all of you. The Elders could not treat the disease."

A loud murmur traveled across the cave as each Chami reacted and commented on that revelation.

Chari waited until the sound died down. "They secretly sent emissaries to meet and work with scientists all over the colony, including the Burned Zone." He glanced at the crowd and said, "Sadly, we were unable to help them."

Clicks and shouts were heard. A tall Chami in the back wearing a multicolor red sash cried out. "Unable or unwilling? Some of us remember the Rebellion fifty-eight sequences ago."

A few Chamis hissed. Two Sawishas stomped their feet.

"Quiet," Shonava Benshimu said in a thunderous voice. "Let us listen to him now so we can find out what's going on."

Chari continued. "I told Sheffrou Maashi that day that a strange wasting disease had appeared in the Fanella Compound, the one next to the Central Compound. The disease affects the most vulnerable among us: the one and two-sequence old."

A bleak silence spread in the cave.

"It is with great sorrow," said the Elder, "that I inform you today that all seven one-sequence old have died and there is only one two-sequence old still alive as we speak."

In shock, the onlookers stood as still as a row of granite boulders.

Chari crossed the width of the cave to stand directly in front of the Sawishas. "I had been sworn to secrecy by the Council of Elders, but I decided it was best to inform Sheffrou Maashi of a more pressing and grave problem than the traitor involved in the attacks. I admit I violated my oath, but I didn't know at the time that all the offspring who were afflicted by the disease were Sheffrou Maashi's offspring." He glanced in Maashi's direction on the other side of the cave. His eyes softened for a moment. The guards were helping a pale Maashi settle in a chair. "Shaken by my revelation, and in total shock and disbelief, Sheffrou Maashi unlawfully entered the Fanella compound to see for himself if his offspring were safe." Chari paused for maximum effect. "Only one remained, weak but alive. The Sheffrou held her and wrapped her in his clothing. Her condition improved. But too soon, the Gray Feeders were alerted. To save his life, he escaped to the surface and hid in the Goolalong Fields." Chari ran his black hand through his unruly hair and stood under the light with an expression of disgust.

A rumble went through the crowd. Several Chamis hugged together. Some wailed. The Silver Guards hissed and kicked the ground.

"Sheffrou Maashi's Chowlis, Chopa and Rahma, and I searched for days until we found him, close to death from methane poisoning and grief. Since then, he has been recovering under the care of Tousanou Chendor Aramashan."

Hearing Chendor's name, Shonava Shitan turned and whispered something in Shonava Benshimu's ear.

"I will now let Chopa," said Chari, "Sheffrou Maashi's Chowli, enlighten you about the most recent developments."

Tamara let go of Chopa's hand she had grasped without noticing. Distressed by the recounting of Maashi's perilous journey, she knew the worse had yet to be revealed. Her chest felt tight. She closed her eyes and took some deep breaths. Chopa clicked something to Rahma who lifted her in his arms and a guard brought her a container of water. After a few sips, she felt better.

Chopa adjusted his shirt, tightened his sash, and stepped forward in front of the crowd. He said in a clear voice devoid of emotion, "No one will want to hear what I have to say."

A black guard in the back yelled, "Get on with it Chowli. We are wasting time."

Tamara slipped out of Rahma's arms, went silently across the cave, and climbed on Maashi's lap. He hugged her, kissed her forehead, and held her close.

Chopa straightened his shoulders and said, "When Sheffrou Maashi went to the Fanella compound, he suffered a small cut to his left side and developed an abscess caused by a thorn. Tamara Walsh, Sheffrou Maashi's Chimitanga, removed the thorn, which I analyzed with the help of a colleague. The thorn comes from a variant of the cookra plant that produces chorila nuts."

Master Kokin interrupted Chopa in his dry, raspy voice. "We all know you are well versed in botany, but we do not need a basic lesson on plants today. Get to the point Chowli."

Chopa's eyes became small, black slits. He fisted his hands and continued. "As you know, the edible chorila nuts are speckled, whereas the plain ones may contain worms. Neither of the two varieties grows with thorns. This new variety possesses thorns on the main stalk of the plant, produces also lightly speckled nuts, and contains zanil, a strong poison." He stopped and took a long breath in. "If ingested daily, zanil causes weakness, loss of appetite, and apathy with significant neurological changes. These side effects are mild in adults, but the nuts are deadly in young offspring. We confirmed the presence of these plants growing side by side with the original variety in the Fanella compound." Chopa looked around the cave, expecting questions. When there were none, he went back to his place beside Rahma.

"So," Sawisha Shitan Garavella declared, "the enigma of the plague is solved. We must destroy all the chorila plants with thorns and all the nuts. It is extremely sad that it took so long to find the cause of the sickness. We have suffered the unimaginable loss of all the one and almost all the two-sequence old. We will address this issue with the Council." He eyed the Elders with a harsh expression. "We need more transparency. An earlier intervention might have saved lives. However, one question remains. Where did this variety originate from? All plants and their genomes are controlled by the official botanists. How could this happen?"

"We have found the answer to your question, Shonava," said Chari in a somber tone.

A few impatient Chamis stomped in unison.

Shonava Benshimu cried out, "Pray tell us of your findings. We aren't pleased with the news you bring and wish to end this horrible tale."

"Of course," said Chari. "I will dive in the subject." Instead of speaking right away, he paced in front of the Sawishas. "The plants and the nuts were a gift from Master Kokin to the Fanellas for their youngest offspring. He claimed the nuts were highly nutritious ---"

"What?" Said Kokin, his voice harsh. "You despicable liar. Yes, I provided nuts to the Fanellas, but they weren't poisonous. I would never have made a mistake of this magnitude."

One Silver Guard eased himself close to Kokin. Another one did the same and said, "Silence, or you will be removed."

Kokin hissed under his breath.

"As you know," said Chari, "Master Kokin is a renowned botanist with years of experience in genetic manipulation of plants. We have evidence Kokin's assistant, Noolin, developed this specific variety and sent seedlings and nuts to the Fanellas. He stressed the fact that the nuts were an excellent source of protein, and the young ones would benefit from their consumption during the winter months."

Master Kokin's brow blackened. He hissed so loud it echoed in the cave. "This is all a fabrication. I never developed the variant. I never sent these nuts. How dare you say such a thing?"

Sawisha Shitan Garavella asked Chari, "What proof do you have of this?"

Without hesitation, Chari said, "Our sources are without reproach, and have all been disclosed to the Council. We obtained the information directly from the computers of Master Kokin's assistant who is present here today. The side effects of

this plant were noted in the records. There were several genera-
tions of those plants produced to increase the concentration of
poison in the nuts."

Loud hissing clamored and echoed throughout the cave.
The Silver Guards surrounded Kokin and his young assistant.

"Noolin," said Master Kokin in a voice that roared across
the cave, "explain yourself. What is the meaning of all this?"

The young purple stared at his master with a cunning smile.
Without hesitation, he said, "Master, don't you understand? I
was only carrying out your wishes. For years, you have harbored
a hatred for Sheffrous and searched for ways to destroy them.
I pursued your goal one step further, and did my utmost to
destroy their offspring, starting with Sheffrou Maashi, the one
you despise the most."

No one expected that response. All the Chamis held their
breath in total shock.

Maashi pushed Tamara gently aside and sprang off his chair,
eyes wild and fiery.

Kokin shrieked and slapped Noolin with such force blood
poured from his nose. "You! My first assistant! The one I trusted
with my research. How could you carry out this horrible deed?"
He caught his breath and continued. "What you did, killing
these innocent Fanellas without my knowledge or approval, is
beyond comprehension. It's appalling." His chest heaved, and
with his raspy voice, he yelled at the top of his lungs. "I disown
you Noolin. You are less than the dirt beneath my feet. I ---".

Maashi crossed the cave in long strides.

Chari's brow blackened. His eyes glowed as he said, "I accuse Master Kokin Cronobutin and his assistant Noolin of poisoning the youngest and most vulnerable among us: Sheffrou
Maashi's offspring."

The enraged Kokin screamed and tore his shirt. He turned to face the crowd, then the Elders and spoke. "I admit I hate Sheffrous. I have despised them for the longest time. They are the ones who prevented us Sawishas from being chosen for mating. Maashi, my pupil, produced seven offspring two sequences in a row like the famous Shanadou did sixty sequences ago." Kokin stopped and spat thick foul saliva on the ground. "But I have never been a part of this awful deed of poisoning innocent Fanellas."

Maashi slid between the guards and Chari. His eyes were wild as he approached Kokin step after calculated step. "It was you," he said. "You were the one who plotted with the enemy. I can see it in your mind clear as bright stars against the black of night. You. You gave the coordinates to the Krakoran."

Kokin took a step back and searched for his words. "Someone, guards, hold him back. It is obvious Maashi has lost his mind. Don't you see?"

"You planned the whole thing," Maashi spoke with conviction. "You had access to the coordinates of all the parties since you were involved with the Council of Elders. It was easy to transmit them without anyone ever suspecting your horrible plan." Maashi grabbed his old master by the throat. "Admit your sins or I will destroy your mind."

Rahma went to Maashi's side and tried to pull him away. "Sir, you must release him."

He glanced at Chari who signaled Rahma to step away.

Benshimu came close to Maashi and Kokin. "Tell us the truth Kokin. No more lies."

Maashi released his hold just enough so Kokin could speak.

"Tell everyone what I see in your wretched mind," said Maashi.

With eyes boiling with anger, Kokin said, "I admit plotting with the enemy. I gave them the coordinates of the tunnels so they could plan their attacks on the night of the Great Eclipse Celebration." Kokin stopped then spoke with a voice filled with venom, "I intervened sixty sequences ago to annihilate Shanadou and intervened a second time with Maashi."

Hissing surged from all parts of the cave. Loud whispers filled the air.

Master Kokin coughed and then with all the hatred he could muster said, "I am glad you suffered Maashi. I despise you and wish the Krakoran had destroyed you. I orchestrated the attack on your group last sequence, and I was the one who sent you the sculpture of a little worker hoping you would die from fright."

Taking a step closer, Chari said, "And I smashed the awful thing way far on the surface. No one will ever see it again."

With an unexpected burst of energy, Maashi roared and punched Kokin with such force the purple crumpled to the ground. He yanked Kokin's purple sash and stomped on it. With a voice filled with hatred, he said, "I will make sure all your privileges are revoked and your life will be utter misery from now on. May the souls of your ancestors have pity on you because no one on Chitina will." He spit in Kokin's face.

While all eyes were on Maashi and Kokin, Noolin leaped and grabbed Tamara who had followed Maashi and was looking on with horror. With an arm tight under her neck, he held her off the ground and dangled her in front of everyone. At first Tamara struggled, but soon she stilled, and made only feeble gurgling sounds.

Maashi lunged towards Noolin who strengthened his hold and snarled. "My plan was to kill all the ones you love, Sheffrou. This one too. One step closer and she dies."

Maashi snapped backwards. In a strained voice, he said, "Let her go Noolin. She isn't part of this. Put her down."

With an evil rictus, Noolin grunted and said, "You will lose this one as well."

Tamara uttered low moans. Her face became gray and, eyes wide with fear, she gasped for air.

Out from the shadows of the nearest alcove, a huge Chami stepped in the light. He wore a dove gray overcoat with ornate gold symbols on the shoulders and chest and a long midnight blue sash. All Chamis turned and stared. A large scar ran across the stranger's face, highlighting his dignified features without making it hideous. He said to Noolin in a powerful voice, "Release her now. She is not yours to take."

Noolin spat on the ground. "Don't come closer or she dies."

"Release her now."

"She will die."

Chendor locked eyes on Noolin and raised his right hand and pointed his fingers at Noolin's throat. "I command you to release her."

Noolin's face changed. He tried to inhale but couldn't. His hands went for his throat. He made choking sounds and dropped the barely conscious Tamara to the ground. His face turned gray, and he collapsed.

Maashi rushed over and picked Tamara up. He applied his lips on hers and breathed in a long breath. She coughed and made a small whining sound. Maashi held her close against his chest and rested her head on his shoulder. "You're safe, Chumpi," he whispered.

Two Silver Guards grabbed Noolin and held him.

Chendor walked over to Maashi's side and placed a soothing hand on the nape of his neck. Maashi nodded sideways and said, "Thank you."

"Thank you, Shonava," said Chendor. His face softened, and his scar lost all ugliness. "I am the one who must thank you. You taught me to face my fears and to put my trust in others. You instilled courage in me. You have freed me from the gilded prison I had built."

Maashi's face regained its warmth. His amber eyes glowed with Chendor's words. His whole frame relaxed as he kissed Chendor's neck in a sign of respect.

"All of you," Chari said in a proud voice, "I would like to introduce Tousanou Chendor Aramashan. He is a Sheffrou 6 formerly known as Shanadou Aramashan. Please welcome him among you. He is the one who healed Sheffrou Maashi after his rescue from the Goolalong Fields."

A cry of joy echoed around the cave as Shonava Shitan Garavella charged ahead, pushing Chamis aside and making his way to Chendor. He took his face in his hands and said in a tremulous voice, "Is it really you, my friend? Alive and well after all these sequences?"

Chendor smiled, and his violet eyes filled with tears. Although the smile was crooked, Shitan couldn't contain his delight. "By the bones of my ancestors, in a day filled with horrendous news, I am thrilled to see you and hold you." Shitan, overcome with emotion, hugged his old friend and showered him with kisses.

Tamara put her arms around Maashi's neck and pressed her face against his cheek. Her throat too sore for words, she let Maashi kiss her for a long moment. She glimpsed at Kokin as he boiled over with rage when he recognized Shanadou, the Sheffrou he thought he had obliterated over sixty sequences ago.

Maashi set Tamara down by Chopa and Rahma who both smiled and kissed his shoulder. Maashi turned and in two strides was at Tomisho's side. The tall Sheffrou hesitated, but Maashi grinned at him. They kissed and hugged each other for a long moment.

The three Elders rose. The middle Elder raised his arms, and the crowd settled down. He said in a soft-spoken tone, "I commend you all for listening and following this tragic narrative to the end. We have conferred with all the members of the Council and came to this final decision. From this day forward, Kokin Cronobutin will be forever known as 'the traitor'. Both Kokin and Noolin will be escorted and transferred to the Northern Compound to work in the mines until their last days. It is a fitting sentence for the ones who have wrought so much pain and destroyed so many lives."

The Silver Guards jumped into action and seized Kokin. They held the crumpled and stone-faced Noolin who stared at the crowd in hateful contempt. The two were escorted out, accompanied by hissing and stomping by the Chamis. The thunderous sound resonated high and far in the cave.

The Elder scrutinized the crowd and added, "This sequence will be a time of healing. We encourage you to join and connect with old and new alike. For the ones among you who have fathered offspring, we are pleased to announce these new rules with you: unlimited visits with your offspring under supervision by the Gray Feeders."

The news took everyone by surprise. The Sawishas were elated. They emitted a loud chorus of clicks and shouts. They held on to their Chowlis with glee and shed tears of joy.

"On behalf of the members of the Council of Elders, to all who have suffered, we share your deep sorrow," said the Elder. "We will endeavor to do everything in our power to ensure the safety of the colony from this day forward. The Council, after much deliberation, has decided that individuals among the general population including Sawishas, Multicolors, Ghouli Ghouli, and Fanellas will be chosen for their sense of duty and righteousness and will join our assemblies to become active participants in the decision-making processes. We leave you now to rejoin and reflect with long-lost friends."

The other two Elders rose.

"Let me now finish by saying we are pleased to take this opportunity to convey our heartfelt gratitude to the ones involved in solving the plague. Some of you have risked their lives and others have faced enormous challenges with unrelenting fortitude and your names will be remembered forever."

"On behalf of the three of us, I want to offer to Sheffrou Maashi Torrenadanga our heartfelt condolences for the loss of his offspring and congratulations for winning the trial. I would also like to express my most sincere gratitude to Sheffrou Maashi and Tousanou Chendor Aramashan and their Chowlis, Chari Varian, commander of the Burned Zone, and Chimitanga Tamara Walsh for her precious collaboration." The Elder paused and pressed his hands together. "May the spirits of our ancestors look down favorably upon you always. Until we meet again, we salute you."

The three Elders bowed to the crowd and left, accompanied by the Silver Guards.

The other Sawishas present came one by one to greet and embrace Chendor. His Chowlis, who had spent the last few weeks in close contact with Maashi and then with Tomisho appeared in the cave, and came to kiss and greet the two Sheffrous. Chari approached Chendor and said something, which made the big Sheffrou roar with laughter. Chendor pulled him close, tousled Chari's unruly raven hair, and they kissed.

Tamara, shaken but alive, had remained a few feet away from the group and observed the scene with joy mixed with sadness. Rahma had sauntered off to greet a young purple with a scar above his left eye. Tamara recognized him as being one of Rahma's six close friends who had been instrumental in retrieving critical data from Noolin's computer.

Although Chopa stayed close to her, Tamara felt disconnected with the Chamis world. Maashi remained a popular figure among the Pure Colors. She could see how he beamed with happiness as the Sawishas came one after the other to greet and offer him comfort. The tall Tomisho was like a shadow at his side. When all the Chamis had offered their condolences, he whispered something in Maashi's ear, then embraced him in a big bear hug.

"Sheffrou Tomisho is back," said Chopa.

"Yes, he is." Tamara pursed her lips. She loved Maashi but knew she would have to share him with his three Chowlis, Rahma, Chopa, and Chari, and now also Tomisho.

Chopa said in a detached tone, "The two aliens from Earth are leaving in one day. Their ship has been repaired and they are anxious to go. They have requested to see you. They want you to go with them. Do you want me to set up a visit?"

Tamara looked up at Chopa. Her chest felt tight. She didn't say a word but nodded.

Chapter 31

L ater that afternoon, Tamara went back to her old quarters. She smiled at the sight of her elegant yet simple receiving room with its sky-blue ceiling and cream-colored walls and carpet and settled on her favorite couch. She grabbed her tablet, the one Maashi had given her when she first arrived on Chitina.

The incredible attack by that sleazy Noolin had left her bruised and shaken. She inhaled deeply and shuddered. What would've happened if Chendor had not suddenly shown up and saved her life? She wanted to remember every moment of this memorable day, even that moment of terror, so she wrote a long note to her daughter. Writing things down helped her to focus and see things more clearly when her mind struggled with critical decisions. The humans were leaving tomorrow. She was waiting for Chopa to bring her to see the humans once more.

A moment later, he was at the door.

Chopa bowed and said, "Ready?"

"Yes."

"I suggest we keep the conversation to a minimum. The Humans are suspicious and becoming more aggressive every day. No need to rouse their anger."

"Why are they angry?"

"They have been confined to their quarters for security reasons and this is something unacceptable to them. We refused to let them communicate with their main ship for the same reasons. Also, the food is not to their liking. Although they have not complained, their private conversations revolve around this subject."

Tamara understood how all this could offend the two men. Humans wanted to be free and in control. The Chamis limited their movements for their own safety, but she was sure the humans didn't agree.

She followed Chopa and a guard down the hall and through a long tunnel.

She entered with Chopa at her side, and the door on the opposite wall slid open. The two men walked in. They both had grown a rough beard since she saw them last. Their long limbs flailed when they saw her.

"Good day to you. I hope you are well," she said.

Lieutenant Yoon stared at her and used his translator to respond. "Are you a'right? We were concerned about your welfare. The aliens have promised to let us leave tomorrow. We ave no choice but to trust them."

"Yes, that's correct. They will be true to their word." Tamara fisted her hands and bit her lower lip. "I understand you have enough space on your ship for a passenger."

"We will not leave without you. It would be against regulations. Our ship can transport six passengers, so one more aboard is a'right."

"Where will we go?"

"We will reach the Innovation, our main ship, then you will be sent to the colony to rejoin your fellow colonists."

Tamara decided it was best not to press the matter of where she came from. She would have ample opportunity to explain herself later.

Lieutenant Yoon asked her, "Do you know how the aliens will transport us aboard the ship?"

Tamara turned to Chopa. "How will this work?"

Chopa tilted his head to one side. "One of our ships will attain an orbit right by the Humans' ship. Our transporter will send your particles through space, and you will materialize on their ship. It is the safest way."

Tamara stood there with her mouth open, then she nodded. "Is this how you usually do it?"

"Yes, Tamara," said Chopa.

The lieutenant grunted and his arms moved like a puppet's arms. "This is highly irregular. We use a tunnel to connect between ships and it is safe and efficient."

Annoyed by the lieutenant's comment, Chopa adjusted his shirt and said, "Our ships do not have these types of portals. They are cumbersome and add too much weight to the overall load. The transport will be completed within a few minutes without problems."

"Beware, alien. Any malfunction during transport will be viewed as an act of aggression by our commander."

Tamara could see how his bland face had suddenly turned red and large veins bulged in his neck.

"Sir," said Patel who had remained silent, "we must communicate with the Innovation before our departure."

Chopa said, "I will convey your request to the appropriate authorities. This can be arranged before you leave tomorrow. Have a good day."

As Tamara turned to leave, the lieutenant bent down and stared at her neck. "What 'ave they done to you? Did they urt you?"

She had forgotten about her near-death experience with Noolin. The bruises on her neck were unmistakable signs of violence. She should've thought about hiding them with a scarf. Too late now. She struggled to find an appropriate answer.

Chopa saved the situation. "Tamara is prone to accidents, and she fell in the hands of a dangerous creature. Fortunately, she was saved and suffered no long-term harm."

"Is this true?" Lieutenant Yoon's suspicions wouldn't be easily quelled.

"Yes," she said, "some of these caves have dangerous creatures and I was lucky to be accompanied by Chopa and a guard."

"We are leaving tomorrow." He eyed Chopa and said, "Keep her away from harm until then."

Tamara pulled her lips into a nervous smile. She followed Chopa out.

"That was close." She looked up at the Chowli. "Thanks for the quick thinking."

Chopa said in a soft voice, "You are welcome."

Tamara let out a long-held breath. "So, how is it going to work tomorrow? When are we leaving?"

"It will be early morning. You may pack a small bag with a change of clothing and your pad. The three of you will board one of our ships and within the hour you will be in the Human's ship."

"That simple. Okay then."

Chopa bowed. "I'll see you in the morning."

Chapter 32

That evening, Maashi invited Tamara to his quarters. She longed to spend time with him but hesitated to go see him because she thought he would be overwhelmed by numerous Chamis, and she would have to answer the inevitable questions about her future.

A guard accompanied her to Maashi's quarters. He opened the door for her with a simple signal from his wristband, and she stepped into Maashi's receiving room. The familiar polished granite walls the color of warm sunsets and the rectangular couches filled with huge cushions in shades of blue, green, and gold were soothing after the glow of Chendor's domain. She grinned when she glanced at the encounter room against the back wall. A room filled with memories. Close to it, a pedestal displayed an impressive three-foot tall Shoshan sculpture, the same amber color as Maashi's eyes.

Wearing wide cobalt blue pants and a dove gray shirt, Maashi sat alone on a couch surrounded by cushions. He looked like the Maashi she knew before the Great Eclipse Celebration, the night when everything and everyone went awry. He opened his arms and said, "Come, Chumpi."

Tamara hastened her pace and approached him. She studied the new addition in the room.

"The sculpture is a gift from Chendor," said Maashi.

"It's gorgeous. It's a stallion, isn't it?" The proud stance, the pointed ears, and the flared nostrils conveyed power and grace.

"Yes, it is." Maashi smiled. "Chendor told me the thing he missed the most while living so deep underground was riding these beautiful creatures." He tilted his head to the side. "One day, I was upset and irritated. I insulted him because he had never left his section. That's when he told me to go back to my compound and we parted ways, both of us displeased with each other. But the day of the trial, he conquered his crushing fear of tunnels and came to support me. His decision saved you from that evil Noolin." Maashi stopped, his voice failing him. His breathing came in brief spurts. He inhaled a long breath and continued. "Of course, he has gained so much weight he will never ride again, but he says it will be a pleasure to see others ride."

"I'm glad for him. He's an exceptional individual. He took great care of you. And he saved my life."

She sat beside him. With shining eyes, he extended his arms, lifted her, and sat her on his lap. "How are you, little one?" Without waiting for an answer, he hugged her close. She inhaled his fragrant holoma.

He said, his voice a mere whisper, "Thank you for everything you've done. Your help has been invaluable. Chari told me how impressed he is with you. It would have been incredibly difficult to understand the clues, to solve the puzzle of the betrayal of our people, and to find the one responsible for the deadly plague without you."

"I wish we could've found the traitor sooner. We've lived through such a sad series of events." With light fingers, she traced the curved designs of his quatay on his chest.

Maashi took her hand and pressed his lips on the tips of each finger and on her palm. "Yes, I wish that also," he sighed a long deep sigh, "but it wasn't meant to be."

"Have you heard about Shalina? Is she doing well?"

"She is healing, a little stronger every day. We will call her by her name and not mention the fact that she is the last offspring. She is young and will forget the sisters who shared her first two years. The young pregnant females impregnated this sequence will deliver soon and a new generation of little Fanellas will grow with her. When she is much older, we can explain what happened."

"Isn't there one you mated with pregnant with twins? How is she?"

"She is healthy. Her pregnancy is progressing well. She should deliver in three months."

Tamara smiled. "Four months. Such short pregnancies compared to ours."

Maashi lowered his head and kissed her neck. "I missed you, Tamara." He rose and held her in his arms. "Come swim in the pool with me," he said. He raised her chin with one finger and gazed into her eyes. "I lowered the lights to ensure our privacy."

Tamara shook her head and smiled. "You and your plans. I hope you're not expecting anyone."

He grinned and his blue tongue flashed. "I have left strict instructions." His amber eyes mocked her. "I know how much you hate to be disturbed when we're together."

He set her down and ambled over to the turquoise pool next to his quarters, the one Tamara called the Blue Lagoon. He turned, and said, "Let me help you with those clothes." He opened her shirt, held her breasts, and kissed them with soft, warm lips.

A chill of excitement and desire shook her body.

He quickly removed her pants and underwear and dropped his own clothes on the floor, keeping only his chemcha,

"Isn't being naked much better?" he said. "I never enjoyed wearing clothes. I am Sheffrou and must dress according to my rank when in public, but in my own quarters, I have the freedom to wear clothes or only a chemcha."

"You're sharing secrets today. My question is, why wear a chemcha at all?"

Still holding her, Maashi stepped into the pool and kneeled in front of her. "Little Chimitanga," he said with a mocking smile, "it has been my experience that wearing a chemcha is best. Fanellas are more delicate than Sawishas. They..."

A mocking smile crossed her lips. "I think the word you're looking for is," she poked at his chest and giggled, "they freak out when they see you naked."

His eyes grew bigger. With a low chuckle, he took her head in his hands and gave her a long, soft kiss. She welcomed his luscious tongue and let pleasure fill her mind. He slid in the water and set her on top of his chest. Without any effort at all, he glided in the cool water, and they rested in each other's arms. They circled the pool twice.

"Mm, this is so nice and refreshing. I missed swimming with you." She caressed his chest.

Maashi swam towards the side of the pool, held her up, and sat her on the edge. He dipped his fingers in a white mousse from a small container on the wall. He spread it generously on her body, her neck, and her breasts until she purred with contentment.

"Ooh," she said, "this makes my skin tingle."

Reaching controls hidden on the floor, he summoned a thick mattress, eased himself out of the water and settled on it. Tamara scooted close to him. He lay on his side and kissed her with abandon.

A warm feeling of contentment spread through her. Her arms circled his neck, and she tousled his hair with her fingers. "I've been wanting to do that for the longest time."

Tamara let his tongue reach inside her mouth and tasted his sweet saliva. She kissed him back, then rubbed her cheeks against his. His whiskerless face felt luscious and soft. "Caress me, Maashi," she whispered. "Touch me. I want you inside me."

He clicked soft, soothing sounds. His slender fingers glided over her back and massaged her buttocks. Touching in between her legs, he slid a finger deep inside her. He withdrew and licked it. His body arched back, and she heard him groan with pleasure.

He bent down and pulled her to him. His tongue reached between her legs. Tamara opened them wide, rocked, and moaned. "Maashi, Maashi." She grabbed his hair and held on. She closed her eyes and savored the heavenly feel of his mouth on her. Soon she cried out, engulfed in exquisite pleasure, and dropped limp on the mattress. He turned over on his back and his golden skin color changed to a deep blue, which spread all over his body.

Tamara watched in mild alarm when he stopped breathing. A powerful aroma of warm caramel emanated from him and saturated the air in the room.

"Maashi, are you all right?"

Laying still on his back, he reached for her hand and squeezed it. After a few minutes, he opened his eyes.

Drawing her close, he whispered. "I will miss you, Chumpi."

She blinked her tears and turned her head away.

Maashi took a strand of her hair and rolled it between his fingers. "I will always remember how your hair shines under the light, how you taste when you reach your climax, and the glow of your skin when you feel pleasure." He paused. She locked her gaze on his and saw tears in his now colorless eyes.

She cleared her throat and said in a low voice, "You know about my decision to leave."

"Yes, Tamara," he said in a voice so soft she strained to hear. "It's the logical choice. You have one chance to rejoin your own species. You must go with them." He gently lapped her tears and hugged her. "I will miss you and you will miss me, but it is what is meant to be." He gently pressed his lips on her forehead. "You are Sheffrou. You are stronger than you know."

Tamara blinked. "That doesn't mean it's going to be easy."

"Nothing in life that is worthwhile is easy."

He stood, picked her up, wrapped her in a fuzzy towel, and patted her dry. He warmed his skin and for a short instant he stood in a cloud of water vapor. He strolled back in his receiving room and set her on a couch where a new set of clothes including a turquoise sash with a blue wave awaited. Tamara slipped the clothes on.

"There is something else," he said as he sat by her side.

Tamara raised her head. "What?"

"I did a thorough physical exam while you were sleeping last night. My suspicions were confirmed."

Tamara wasn't surprised. He could be as stealthy as a ghost. "What do you mean?"

"The constant exposure to the mold and algae in the tunnels is affecting you. The problem started months ago when you were living underground, but my proximity counteracted that effect." Maashi tilted his head. "You developed more symptoms in Chendor's sector because the environment is more humid, and the mold is omnipresent. Also, my absence put you at increased risk and the infection progressed."

So, it was true. *She wasn't imagining things.* To Maashi, she said, "The infection? What are you talking about?"

"There is increasing fibrosis in your lungs caused by the mold. Your body is fighting it and actually making things worse."

Tamara looked away. She had suspected all this coughing and wheezing was unusual. "Like some type of autoimmune reaction?"

"Yes," said Maashi. "Because of your strong immune system, you're producing antibodies in large quantities, and these are accumulating in your bronchia and also in your large joints."

Tamara straightened. "Is the damage serious?"

"It is mild now and its only consequence is to increase your risk of falling but with time, I suspect it would cause considerable joint pain. The good thing is that leaving this environment will stop the inflammation and you will heal completely."

Tamara was crestfallen. "That explains my symptoms, the continuous cough and clumsiness." Her eyes filled with tears again. She blinked them away.

Maashi took her face in his hands and kissed her forehead.

She whispered, "I guess it's time to go to my quarters and get ready."

He nodded. "Yes."

"Will you come and see me go?"

"No."

She frowned. "No?"

"You will need to be focused and listen to instructions and directives. I would only distract you," he lowered his head and spread his fingers on his knees, "and Chendor said my emotional state isn't stable enough to withstand that kind of stress." He looked deep in her eyes. "It's not acceptable for Sheffrous to cry in public. Everybody gets upset."

She cleared her throat. "I understand." Putting on a brave face, she rose and walked to the door. "Thank you, for everything."

He rose and bowed to her. "Until we meet again, gentle Ishkibu."

Tamara nodded, turned, and left with a sorrowful heart but filled with hope for a new future.

Chapter 33

Minutes later, Tomisho strolled in Maashi's quarters. He had recovered his characteristic swagger and beaming smile. Maashi was sitting on his couch, bent over with his head in his hands.

"Did Tamara leave?"

Maashi raised his head ever so slightly and said, "Yes." He inhaled a long breath and let the air out slowly.

Tomisho sat beside Maashi and caressed the nape of his neck. Maashi straightened and turned towards his friend. Tomisho, a good head taller, bent low and showered Maashi with kisses. They hugged for the longest time.

Maashi pulled back and said, "I missed you. I don't want you to leave, ever again. I don't like it when the ones I love go away...." His brow darkened. His eyes searched in his friends' eyes.

Tomisho took Maashi's face in his hands. "No need to worry, Shapinka. Ever since I came back, I can't take a step forward or backward without stomping on a Silver Guard. Believe me, I will never leave you." He added with a more serious expression. "And you shouldn't be talking about leaving. When I saw you dive into the Gorganna gorge with that idiot Hamra, I wanted to dive behind you to make sure you were safe. I was so scared I almost threw up and I had to keep reminding myself to play the role of accuser. That's a role I never want to repeat." He grunted. "Forgive me for making you doubt my loyalty."

"I never really doubted you. I was angry and confused, convinced someone was manipulating you." Shaking his head, Maashi added, "I thank the spirits of my ancestors for helping us get through this time of great sorrow."

Tomisho put his arms around him and clicked soothing clicks. He hugged him tight and said, "When I found out about the other attacks that occurred the night of the celebration, my heart went out to all who suffered and especially to Sheffrou Shoban and the guards who lost their lives. I heard Dasho is making progress: his injuries are severe, but he's a strong and resilient individual. I'm sure he will make a complete recovery. As for Ashani, Chendor told me we are still looking for him. No one knows where he is."

Maashi nodded. "May the souls of our ancestors protect him."

"I...I don't know how to tell you how deeply sorry I am for the loss of your little offspring. I still can't believe this tragedy happened."

"Between the methane poisoning and the death of the little ones, I almost lost my mind." Maashi took Tomisho's hands in his. "Chari found me in the Goolalong Fields and Chendor fought to bring my mind back from darkness. Without Tamara's help and the help of everyone else, I wouldn't be here today."

"We came so close to losing each other," said Tomisho, his voice soft and sad.

Maashi kissed the other's neck. A chime rang, a sign someone was waiting at the door.

"Who is it?" asked Tomisho.

Maashi tilted his head sideways. "I am scheduled in the next few minutes to visit the Fanella compound and see Shalina, my daughter."

"Right now?"

"Yes."

"You don't look pleased."

"I am but was hoping to spend more time alone with you." Maashi hugged Tomisho and gave him a long kiss. He sensed the other back away ever so slightly. "What's wrong Tom Tom?"

Tomisho looked away, then back at Maashi with a sheepish look. "I understand why you were so hesitant to engage in deep contact months ago." He cleared his voice and added, "After my experience with the Krakoran and having lived through their particular way of torturing Sheffrous, you know, when they force you to share your pleasure, I have developed an aversion for deep kisses."

"I see." Maashi squeezed Tomisho's arm and said, "I can assure you it's something that will dissipate with time."

"I hope so."

Maashi encircled his friend's waist and said, "Why don't you come with me to the Fanella compound? I could use a familiar presence. My last visit was quite unpleasant."

"Me?" Tomisho's eyes widened. "Will the Gray Feeders let me in?"

"Of course. You're Sheffrou and if you accompany me, it's acceptable. Tamara told me once that on Earth, other adults called uncles can play an important role in raising offspring. So, you'll be the uncle."

"Uncle, hey? I like it." Tomisho's face shone with sudden excitement. "Will there be Fanellas? Can I see them?"

"Yes. You will see them, and they will see you. It's all part of the new plan."

"What new plan? I didn't know about all this part. Nobody said I could accompany you."

"You just got back and you're already complaining?" Maashi chuckled. "The Elder mentioned it after the trial. Don't you remember?"

Tomisho looked down and with an apologizing expression, said, "I was so out of it at that point. With what happened to Tamara, and you being so upset, I missed most of what the Elder said. I was just relieved to see that both of you were safe."

"Something I never believed would happen, did." Maashi shook his head. "The Council of Elders came to an agreement which is going to change most significantly the lives of the offspring, the Fanellas, and of course, our lives."

Tomisho tilted his head sideways. "What?"

"All Sawishas and Sheffrous may visit their offspring regularly as long as they are under supervision of the Gray Feeders. The Fanellas, young and old, will become comfortable with the Sawishas and the Sheffrous' presence and everyone hopes that this will improve mating success. The Sawishas have approved the project with enthusiasm because this also means they may regain the right to mate if conditions improve."

"Sounds like a beautiful project. Too good to be true," said Tomisho.

"It's so simple and elegant. It's a wonder we haven't thought about it sooner." Maashi's face shone with joy.

A second chime rang. They both rose and streamed out of Maashi's quarters. Chopa, Rahma, and soon Chari joined the two Sheffrous flanked by two Silver Guards. The Chowlis glanced at each other when they noticed Tomisho's wide grin.

Chopa tilted his head. He glanced at Rahma and Chari, smiled, and said, "Don't ask."

<The End of Book 2>

If you enjoyed **Sheffrou Betrayed** please post a review and stay tuned for the epic ending to The Sheffrou Trilogy in ***The Sheffrou's Gambit***.

Glossary

Ara and Kori: names of Chitina's two moons.

Chamtali: original world of the Chamranlinas.

Chamranlinas: name the aliens call themselves.

Charissa: "joie de vivre", a feeling of well-being.

Chemcha: protective underwear worn by Sheffrous and Sawishas.

Chimitanga: Sheffrou's little friend.

Chitina: planet where the Chamranlinas live.

Choma: shower.

Choun: breastmilk.

Chowli: close companion to a Sheffrou or a Sawisha.

Chuckie: colored candy containing psychotropic drugs.

Chumpi: sweet one.

Cookra: plant with or without thorns which gives nuts called chorila.

Draharma trials: three trials all Sheffrous and Sawishas must complete to gain the right to mate.

Encounter room: small oval room designed for intimate meetings and sexual encounters.

Fanella: female, much smaller and slender than the male.

Ghouli Ghouli Chamranlinas: a race of Chamranlina characterized by copper color skin and black hands and feet.

Googlian: fungus found in deep caves, glows in the dark.

Goolalong Fields: a region containing pockets of methane gas trapped under the surface. Some of the toxic gas is released in the air.

Holoma: fragrant aroma produced by mature Sheffrous when they feel pleasure.

Ishkibu: a special kind of Sheffrou who can travel through wormholes.

Kego plant: fragrant plant which has numerous twigs.

Krakoran: also called Untouchables, aliens, enemies of the Chamranlinas.

Loola: delicacy, edible green jelly usually presented as a mold.

Multicolors: also called multi, refers to Chamranlinas with multiple colors on their tongues. Apart from a few exceptions, they are infertile.

Nateet: a sweater with a hood.

Pure Colors: Chamranlinas with a tongue with only one color. They are fertile and part of the elite.

Quatay: characteristic erogenous markings on the chest of Sawishas and Sheffrous.

Rashandamora cave: immense cave where the Great Eclipse Celebration is held.

Rue Kish: intense sexual desire.

Runshama: recurrence of suppressed memories.

Saweya: life energy.

Sawisha: part of the elite group of Pure Color Chamranlinas, their tongue is unicolor.

Schloppies: testicles.

Sequence: one year on Chitina or 712 Earth days. The sequence is divided in 17 months; 16 months of 42 days and 1 month of 40 days. One week is 10 days and one day is 26 Earth hours.

Shapinka: precious one.

Sheffrou: third gender, may be male or female. Sheffrous are Pure colors, their tongue is blue.

Shonava: lord.

Shoshans: large antelope-like quadrupeds.

Shoulans: male Chamranlinas between 20 and 40 sequences old.

Tellisha flowers: plant indigenous to Chitina with rapid growth and which produces lavender flowers with a yellow center.

Tinqua plant: leaves are used to add flavor to drinks.

Toughi: fruit which tastes and looks like a blend of pear and apple.

Tousanou: title given to a therapist.

Vizinem: aliens allies of the Chamranlinas.

Acknowledgements

I would like to thank my family, my friends, and my fellow writers of the Surfside Chapter of the South Carolina Writers' Association, especially Trilby Plants and Richard Lutman, for their continued help and support.

Meet the Author

As a child, I dreamed of becoming an astronaut and traveling to faraway worlds.

Born in Montreal, I currently live in South Carolina and enjoy reading, traveling, and I'm still fascinated by stories about alien worlds. After a successful career as an obstetrician-gynecologist and four children, I divide my time between my family and creating my own science-fiction stories. When not busy writing, I ride my tricycle around the neighborhood or work in my bee and butterfly friendly garden.

I would be delighted if, after reading *Sheffrou Betrayed*, you would consider leaving a review on Amazon and Goodreads or any website of your choice.

Book 3, *The Sheffrou's Gambit,* will be published in 2024.

Good Readings to all!

Cami Michaels

Website: CamiMichaels.com

Email: CamiMichaelsscifiauthor@gmail.com

Facebook: Cami Michaels Sci-fi Author

www.ingramcontent.com/pod-product-compliance
Lightning Source LLC
Chambersburg PA
CBHW022105310726
48972CB00007B/1889